A.B. Funkhauser

Heuer

Lost And Found

Cover Art:
Michelle Crocker

http://mlcdesigns4you.weebly.com/

Publisher's Note:

This is a work of fiction. All names, characters, places, and events are the work of the author's imagination.

Any resemblance to real persons, places, or events is coincidental.

Solstice Publishing - www.solsticepublishing.com

For Jenny with a "y"
So glad it's you!!
xo

Heuer Lost and Found

A.B. Funkhauser

Best A.B. Funkhauser
July 2015

3

Dedication

For M

Chapter One

"Heuer," as in "lawyer": Heuer, the lawyer.

The year 2010

Monday, 9:00 A.M.

Enid Krause crashed through the back door, falling three steps down onto the floor below. It was another morning after the night before, where she and Aaron had sworn to quit after the second drink and hadn't.

"Is that you, dear?"

That might have been her conscience, or the Lord Almighty speaking to her in reassuring tones, but not so. It was Charles Emerson Forsythe, bon vivant and human being extraordinaire. Flesh, blood, and deeply flawed, he was the managing director of Weibigand Brothers, the funeral establishment where they both worked.

"Yes, Charlie. It's me."

That took every ounce of wit she could muster. Charlie was something of a guru in matters of the human condition and no amount of hyperbole confounded him.

"Did you fall over your feet again?"

Enid was a gifted bullshitter, but in matters physical, terribly clumsy. Charlie, on the other hand, quite simply was not, and she relied on his tact and good manners to bypass the need for a real explanation. He was her litmus test and moral laboratory, and it would kill her to lie to him, especially when he saw everything.

"'Fraid so."

It was happening more and more—the missteps and unexpected tumbles. She could blame it on the man shoes she wore with unbridled pride, for as much as she had fought and won the right to wear them over strenuous objections from management, they did on occasion betray her. Or she could blame the time of year—May had given over to June with its outdoor patios and brain blasting surround sound systems—zesty realities that didn't always mesh with work. Or she could blame Aaron, her husband and willing accomplice in the pursuit of quality life experiences. Or—

Mr. Forsythe, ensconced in his office at the end of the hall, swiveled round in his big, creaky Thinking Chair to get a better look. "I'm waiting, dear."

Her stomach balled up into what her furtive imagination could only compare to owl pellets or feline fur clumps. Perhaps she'd tell him the truth after all? Not a chance. She and Aaron had been partying the night before, for no reason other than it was a full moon and they were alive to see it. They were on their feet, pulling the house down as Neil Diamond's *Hot August Night* blasted loud and unselfconsciously in complete disregard for the neighbors that had to work the next day. Their fifteen-year-old son, Evan, demanded they cut it by several decibels, and they complied, laughingly.

In their forties, they liked to think they had "evolved" beyond the typical old farts that lived on their street. By all appearances, they had. They celebrated each other's accomplishments, were never competitive, and congratulated themselves for not being jealous. Together for twenty years, they might have shouted six times. Even when they were actually annoyed with each other, they would voice it in a way that was logical and controlled. Friends marveled at their matrimonial congruity.

"We should never listen to The Neil on work nights," Enid complained when the five a.m. alarm sounded: Two drinks led to six; four songs led to two hours later; and four hours sleep led to a catastrophic hangover. Neil Diamond was like New Year's: designated driver required.

Enid wiped her slavering forehead as she prepared to

lie to Charlie, the beats in her temples gaining speed with each add on: she slept in, there was traffic, her youngest had a bad night.

I must stop drinking.

Inside her head, the synapses played. Praying with all urgency to The Unseen Thing, she half believed *It* was there. But Enid Estelle Krause wasn't fooling anyone. Not really. She had taken a chance on a Sunday night and came up short first thing Monday morning.

She screwed her eyes tight in a physically conscious effort to focus. The production board, a crummy green chalkboard that hung opposite the prep room door, had a fresh name on it.

"Who's dead?" she yelled out, effecting a casual 'oh I'm just fine' with a sweep of her great coat, now dust covered from the dirty floor.

Peering from behind decade's old granny glasses, Charlie smiled at her, as only Charlie could. From the crinkles of soft flesh gathering around his nominally cloudy old eyes, she knew *he knew* she was still hammered from the night before. Even as she stumbled the long walk down the hall, past the prep room with its stainless steel tables—waiting—the casket selection room with the boxes her daughter called 'dead people beds' and the nefarious Quiet Room with its gurgling pond and ancient furniture, she couldn't travel far or fast enough.

"Good save the Queen," Charlie offered, pushing coffee into her hands getting her ready to go out again.

"Charlie, you know I'm a Portside, Michigan, Republican."

Charlie cocked an eyebrow. "All's the more reason to pick yourself up sister."

Enid grunted. What choice had she? Heuer was dead and his body needed attention.

***

8:07 A.M.

The call came first thing in the morning and it was taken by Carla Moretto Salinger Blue, a licensed funeral director and work colleague of Enid Krause. Part Irish, part Italian, Carla Blue, on surface, was everything Enid was not. Dark, brooding, and incapable of subtlety, she was lethal when crossed, but generous to the point of ruin when loved.

Carla struggled daily to balance hope and doubt; most of the time, she won. This Monday marked the start of her morning shift and it was her responsibility to unlock the house, check the fax and email, and respond appropriately in the event a death had occurred overnight. Sometimes the early morning routine—which she quite liked—was rudely interrupted by an actual phone call. The Death Call, as it was known in the business, was the first link in a chain of events that could last for days, weeks or even months, depending on the complexities of the funeral, the size of the estate left behind, and the cast of characters involved in the decision-making process. Some files dragged on for years and those were the ones she really hated, likening them to a calamity raging exponentially out of control. Weibigand's once faced legal action over taking direction from a spouse who actually turned out to be an ex. They would have cremated the deceased were it not for a very dramatic late day appearance from the legal wife who ordered the body transferred to another service provider that arranged a burial instead. It didn't end with the court settlement that arrived five years after the fact. The dead man's family— wanting more—went on to complain to the Board of Mortuary Science, charging incompetence and malfeasance. For a brief, frightening time, Carla faced suspension.

Why hadn't the Profs at mortuary school warned her about days like that? The answer belonged more in nostalgia than present day reality. The bereaved, too grief stricken to cope, required empathy not sympathy from the funeral director, along with attention to detail and excellent organizational skills. For their dedication, directors received ample reward in the knowledge that their altruism did some good. But experience, along with generous anecdotes from old timers, like Forsythe, painted a different picture; that of survivors at odds over the bones and residue that death always leaves; the wives, ex-husbands, life partners, and lovers as they wrung out their hands over the departed. Many were genuinely broken and in need of assistance, but others, not so much. They cried reptile tears because the stakes were too high, and the booty was out of reach. These were the Pirate Bereaved who, in cases of cremation, promised to collect the ashes after they had come to grips with the death. Only they never did. The question of what to do with the cremated remains was ignored, or forgotten after the estate was settled and the lawyers were paid. Weibigand's basement quickly filled up with little boxes of unclaimed human remains. These wound up in common ground and that was a shame.

When the phone rang at 8:07 a.m., Carla was prepared for the worst.

"What are you wearing beautiful?"

"Carter? What the hell?"

Carter Bilsson was one of four rotating city morgue attendants whose shift coincided with hers.

"It's an answer at least," Carter laughed. "What are you wearing?"

She rolled her eyes. Carter made a point of flirting with all the funeral women, but he claimed her as a particular favorite. Her filthy potty mouth notwithstanding, she had a reputation for being *flagrante delicto* owing to multiple marriages and a preponderance of water cooler gossip that followed her wherever she went.

"Rubber boots and a smock," she answered, keeping

things light.

"Anything else?" Bilsson was never satisfied.

"A meat cleaver." She was growing flinty.

"That's hot. When are you going to leave your husband?"

Carla grew cold. She and Danny were in the dumper again, and although Carter had no way of knowing this, his remark rankled.

"Who's dead Carter?"

Sometimes it was better to cut the idle patter and get to it.

"Young guy."

"Cause?"

Carla needed to know this if she was to pack appropriately for the trip downtown.

"Heart implosion, most likely. Madman splatter. Didn't know what hit him. Took a header into the carpet."

"Nice," she said, ignoring the crassness of his commentary. She'd been at this too long to feign offense. "How long's he been gone?"

"'Bout a week, maybe more," Carter replied easily. "Double bag, eh. House was hot."

"Just what I need. Thanks for nothing. Kisses."

"Listen, his kin's gonna call you first thing. They're kinda weird."

Carla imagined an estranged wife-pregnant girlfriend scenario, a veritable smorgasbord of regret and revenge, and her spirits lifted at the possibility of a good fight. "Blondes or redheads?"

"Naw, nothing like that Bumble Bee. It's the parents, older than shit, and they're prickly too."

Carla cringed. The law was pretty clear on the pecking order for decision-making when it came to funeral planning. Parents could only mean that sonny boy lacked significant others to mourn his loss and that could make for a pretty dull funeral. Still, parents nosing around the coroner's office did not necessarily cancel out the possibility of a love child as yet unknown. The promise of a large cash remuneration after probate usually flushed a couple of them out, often just days before the service. But Carla was getting ahead of herself.

"How old's this kid?"

"Fifty. Hasn't been a kid for a while."

At fifty-two, Carla had to agree. She thanked Carter for the heads up. It wasn't a real death call in that it came from a buddy who'd overheard a conversation. The mom and dad were ancient, and while they spoke in a language her friend did not know, "Weibigand's" rang out loud and clear. Carter's call was a promise of future business on a sunny summer morning, and she was grateful that she could, at least, get in that first cup of coffee and maybe a crossword before the real work began.

***

6:00 A.M.

From where Charlie Forsythe stood, this Monday was no different from any other. He rose at the appointed hour, switched on CLASSICAL Radio One, caught the morning news, and consumed the light breakfast of a poached egg and grapefruit that had been placed on the settee by his faithful steward Bernard.

He took the morning meal in his boudoir; as always a place of calm, studied elegance. It was, he thought, worlds removed from the hideousness and brutality of the street below. In actuality, it afforded him the tactile calm one needed to make a living off other people's misery. And the room was positioned beautifully, facing east to catch the rising sun.

The condominium he called home was well placed at the centre of his city, with tony shops and fine dining mere steps away. Secured with gates that covered off locked doors, and a concierge to keep out those he cared not to meet, it was a testament to a life of hard work and the rewards it reaps. His success was his own, and he achieved it boldly and unapologetically.

His manner of dress was dictated by personal choice, buttressed by confidence gained through years of slips and falls. Charlie, without question, was above critique. It was, for example, going to be a hot day, yet this did not dissuade him from choosing the winter weight Savile Row in charcoal. To that, he paired a Nautica button down shirt in grandee pink, and a Milano silk tie with tumbling cascades of diagonal bars in strawberry and slate. He did not wear the Italian cufflinks, newly acquired through the broker. In a conservative business like his, these were too rude, too over the top; a gross advertisement that hinted at poor taste.

"There are the poorer elements to think of," he laughed, addressing the oil portrait of Her Majesty, Victoria, who rested stately above the large marble fireplace. A closet monarchist committed to the belief that the Revolution was a mistake, Charlie regarded her as so much more than a portrait; more a source of pride characterized by her location: this fireplace was the only one of its kind in the building because Charlie had the penthouse suite.

Fit for a Queen.

What was not fit, however, was the current state of affairs at the funeral home. Years of fat bought lives of ease for those that owned the place. When paired with an over-exaggerated sense of entitlement belying the bottom line, disasters naturally followed.

Profits were down and the Weibigand brothers, to Charlie's extreme irritation, refused to recognize this, spending as if it were 1967—a great year for what was a large, established, family run funeral parlor. Not the case in 2010, where even the most creative accounting maneuvers could not cover up the fact that they were bleeding.

Weibigand's depended as much on reputation as it

did on demographics to literally bring the bodies in. Normally, when things slowed down, the business went out into the community to jog the collective memory. Sponsoring sports teams, funding high school yearbook runs, and providing grub for a church tambola or two was usually enough to get the hearse rolling. But things changed in the second decade of the twenty-first century; numbers were down, not because Weibigand's lacked in the corporate citizenship department, but because the babies that were supposed to be born in the 1930's weren't. Economic depression had intervened, so what never lived couldn't die either. This hit the bottom line too.

"I cannot go out and shoot people," Charlie would say in his own defense, after a thorough dressing down from management over less than satisfying production figures. "I can only be present and available when things pick up."

Things always picked up.

Charlie came from a long line of pig farmers steeled in Bible verse and the *Farmer's Almanac,* so he was uniquely equipped to handle whatever pox or curse came his way. These could include anything from low speed multi-car collisions in a funeral procession, to unopened graves on service day, to intoxicated clergy that no-showed or, worse, *did.* There were funeral directors that revolved through the place en route to other careers in nursing, pathology, hotel management. He didn't mind that they didn't stay: they were just trying it on. What irked him were the drama queens who, while there, turned the workday into a trial by nausea. These were the ones who took the work home when they should have left it at the back door. Spiritless types, that took solace in the bottle, they were sleepless with intractable emotions, sometimes unfit to carry out their duties. He'd lost a few: one to the gun; the other to the rope; others to love affairs gone badly wrong. To these he was especially severe. Hubris floored him, but self-destruction was contemptible.

Pulling into the funeral home parking lot just after eight-thirty, he was struck by the shabbiness of the place. Three storied, stone-faced, with jagged courses of irregular shaped brick, she was more sea anemone than siren, prickly and unlovely. Where she had once stood apart from her ramshackle neighbors, the reverse was now true. The facade was flaking, the surfaces cracked. It was worse inside. She was falling farther and farther behind and C.E. Forsythe was at a loss as to how to help her.

"It's amazing what you can get used to," she seemed to say.

Even irrelevance?

Charlie willed the individual perspiration pellets welling beneath his skin to stay in their pores. It was a fantastic thought, but he believed himself capable of such tricks. Self-delusion, after all, played a huge part in the life he had chosen and he credited it for his career longevity.

The aged Weibigand brothers, likewise, had been fooling themselves for years, believing that their brand would endure simply because the building stayed up. Like so many sons and daughters born into a way of life, they fell back luxuriously on something ready-made, giving no thought to future plans. The clientele that paid for the cottage and the mistresses and the waterfront condos would die off, but their kin would continue to come. Right?

We're so fucked, Charlie thought.

He took deliberate steps to the back door like he always did, never knowing what he'd find on the other side. This was the essence of funeral service: no two days were ever alike, no two families ever the same. No matter what was thrown at you, you survived on wits and the zealot's belief that what you were doing was right.

Charlie reached for the mottled brass doorknob. Finding a strange proteinaceous material on its surface, he recoiled. It was sticky and did not belong. Wrapping a silk handkerchief—the new one from Sak's—around the offensive knob, he tried the door again, only to find that it resisted.

Damn that Carla! She was supposed to unlock all of the doors all of the time.

It would have been un-Christian like to condemn so hastily on a Monday morning before coffee and obits, but something had to be done about that girl. He banged on the back door.

"Carla! Carla!"

He was the manager for the love of God. He didn't have a key. He didn't need one. He had staff.

The sweat broke through the Nautica button down, reminding him that he was losing it and should probably get a grip before the others saw him. The parking lot might have been empty, but it didn't mean that the brothers weren't there, up on the third floor, watching bemused from their closed circuit television monitors.

He turned on his heel, taking care not to trip on the concrete shards loosed from the previous winter. This was undoubtedly Carla's fault too, given her penchant for salt over ice melt. At least the fleet was intact, parked safely to his right along the east wall. The hearse, the utility van, the two lead cars, sat silent, undisturbed. He gave thanks. They'd lost one last year; drove clean off the lot in the middle of the night.

Stomping the length of the parking lot to the front doors he reminded himself that the Cadillac had never been recovered, and he decided to blame Carla for that too. He pushed open the heavy oak doors and walked into the lobby with its ceiling vault and leaky skylight. Six steps up and straight ahead was the darkened hallway that led to the four visitation suites – Rose, Begonia, Wisteria and Astilbe – so named after the floral favorites of the late Mrs. Irmtraut Weibigand Sr. The oak paneled chapel, with its mock Drexel inlays, stained glass and chartreuse tapestries, lay to the right of the main stair which concealed rather cleverly, the cloak room and floor length double wide mirror which opened up to the ramp that led to the prep room below.

The front office was located next to the chapel with a large picture window fronting the street and it was to this space that an increasingly vexed Charlie Forsythe strode. The desk phone flickered in protest; line one was ringing and Carla was not answering.

"Weibigand Brothers, Charles Forsythe speaking."

An elderly gentleman at the other end spoke, his voice carrying the undeniable timbre of an olde tymy Deutscher who'd forgotten to repent.

"This is Werner Heuer, Herr Forsythe. My wife and I have need of your services today. My son is dead."

Forty years of service and a prescient need to make payroll that month set the old fox into action. "Please do accept my condolences, Herr Heuer," Charlie responded with a Tyrolean lilt that made him sound more Austrian than German. "I remember your family well. You will, of course, be wanting the same as last time?"

In addition to the faux accent, Charlie could also mimic German-English speech pattern; a unique blend of passive-aggressive Oxfordian singsong that sounded almost sinister, especially when spoken by the genuine article; someone like Werner Heuer.

"Of course," the old man replied, his voice betraying nothing of the emotion he had to be feeling.

Charlie, calculating profit after disbursements, felt better already.

***

One floor below, in the garage she called second home, Carla Blue vomited into the organic waste pail. She was in a raw state. And while the genesis of her behavior could easily be guessed at, Charlie, entering the garage at the moment of her expulsion *plus fort,* decided not to call her out.

"Anything new, sister?"

Carla raised her head, a generous goober of stomach bile co-mixed with pink goo swaying to and fro from her lower lip. This, she casually flicked against the wall with a toss of her head, the spittle crisscrossing nicely with the others, placed over time, affirming the strange altercation inside her biology.

He smiled at her: Of course there was something new, and she was well aware of it, because of her habit of eavesdropping on conversations through the building's ancient ventilation system.

"Your call aside, I took one from downtown," she beamed through travertine teeth. "If Carter heard right, we got a live one coming."

By this, he presumed, she meant a casket over an urn. Charlie felt the rush; they hadn't had a real funeral in weeks, and if what she said panned out, it would mean a second death call in less than an hour and a good week for anyone expecting a paycheck. Of course, both directors, keen to get busy did not allow for the possibility that they were talking about the one and only Heuer; and as it was, it would not matter—just having him near would set off a chain of events (not to mention a rush of bodies)—that would chart a new course and force Weibigand's into the modern age.

"Praise the Lord and wipe your mouth. And ring your boyfriend back. Go get that call."

She bowed her head, all black sweaty locks standing on end without a single trace of grey to betray her age. Charlie wondered if she colored it, in spite of her insistence that she didn't. Her constitution was supernatural, she claimed, not unlike the grin that spread across her face.

Charlie beamed right back at her; she needed action as much as he did.

Chapter Two

Two Weeks Ago

The house, like the man who lived in it, was remarkable: a 1950s clapboard-brick number with a metal garage door that needed serious painting. Likewise, the windows, which had been replaced once in the Seventies under some home improvement program, then never again. They were wooden and they were cracked, allowing wasps and other insects inside.

This was of little consequence to him.

The neighbors, whom Heuer prodigiously ignored, would stare at the place. Greek, Italian, and house proud, they found the man's disdain for his own home objectionable. He could see it on their faces when he looked out at them through dirty windows.

To hell with them.

If the neighbors disapproved of the moss green roof with its tar shingles that habitually blew off, then let them replace it. Money didn't fall from the sky and if it did, he wouldn't spend it on improvements to please strangers.

They were insects.

And yet there were times when Jürgen Heuer was forced to compromise. Money, he learned, could solve just about anything. But not where the willful and the pernicious were concerned. These, once singled out, required special attention.

Alfons Vermiglia, the Genovese neighbor next door, had taken great offense to his acacia tree, a towering twenty-five foot behemoth that had grown from a cutting given to him by a lodge brother. The acacia was esteemed in Masonic lore appearing often in ritual, rendering it so much more than just mere tree. In practical terms, it provided relief, offering shade on hot days to the little things beneath it. And it bloomed semi-annually, whimsically releasing a preponderance of white petals that carried on the wind mystical scent—the same found in sacred incense and parfums.

What horseshit.

It was a dirty son of a bitch of a tree that dropped its leaves continuously from spring to fall, shedding tiny branches from its diffident margins. These were covered in nasty little thorns that damaged vinyl pool liners and soft feet alike. They also did a pretty amazing job of clogging Alfons' pool filter, turning his twenty-five hundred gallon toy pool green overnight.

This chemistry compromised the neighbor's pleasure and it heightened his passions, blinding Alfons to the true nature of his enemy. He crossed over onto Heuer's property and drove copper nails into the root system. It was an old trick, Byzantine in its treachery; the copper would kill the tree slowly over time leading no one to suspect foul play.

But Heuer was cagey and suspicious by nature, so when the tree displayed signs of failure, he knew where to look.

The acacia recovered and Alfons said nothing. Heuer planted aralia—the "Devil's Walking Stick"—along the fence line and this served as an even thornier reminder that *he knew.* And if there was any doubt at all, he went further by coating his neighbor's corkscrew hazel with a generous dose of Wipe Out.

Intrusive neighbors and their misplaced curiosities were, by turns, annoying and amusing and their interest, though unwanted, did not go unappreciated. The Greeks on the other side of him weren't combative in the least and they offered gardening advice whenever they caught him out of doors. The man, Panos, talked politics and cars, and expressed interest in the vehicle that sat shrouded and silent on Heuer's driveway. He spoke long and colorfully about the glory days of Detroit muscle cars and how it all got bungled and bargained away.

"They sacrificed an industry to please a bunch of big mouths in Hollywood," Panos would rant in complete disregard for history: Al Gore and Global Warming didn't kill the GTO; the OPEC oil crisis did. But there was no point in telling him that.

Panos was an armchair car guy and incurable conspiracy theorist. He also kept to his side of the fence, unlike his wife, Stavroula, who was driven by natural instinct. Not content to leave an unmarried man alone, she routinely crossed Heuer's weedy lawn, banging on the door with offers of food and a good housecleaning.

Heuer had no trouble accepting her cooking. But he declined her brush and broom. Was it kindness, or was she trying to see inside? He suspected the latter.

No one was ever seen entering Heuer's house and while this piqued public interest, he never gave in, not even to those who were kind to him. He liked Panos and Stavroula and he regretted poisoning their cat.

But not enough to let them in to his home.

Others on the street had less contact with him. Canvassers at election time would disturb him, in spite of the lawn sign warning the solicitous away. That this didn't apply to neighbor kids brave enough to pedal cookies and magazine subscriptions in spite of the sign, was a testament, perhaps, to some residual soft spot in his heart that endured.

Even so, he knew that people talked about him and, frankly, he had trouble accounting for their fascination. Short, curt, bespectacled, he courted an ethos that favored enforced detachment. When people got close enough to hear him speak, they detected a trace of an accent. Now faded after years of U.S. residency, his speech still bore the unmistakable patterns of someone undeniably foreign. Elaborate, overwrought and heavy on the adverbs, he spoke very much like his neighbors. Yet the distance between them was incalculable…

***

Day 1: Post Mortem

Heuer shook his head, finding it especially odd that he would think of such things at this particular moment. The circumstances, after all, were beyond peculiar. Coming out of thick, dense fog, standing upright, looking wildly around, and having difficulty comprehending, the last thing that should trouble him was human relations.

The man on the floor would have agreed, had he not lacked the resources to speak.

Heuer canvassed his surroundings. The room, still dark, the shades drawn, and the plants Stavroula forced on him, wilted and dry, bespoke of an unqualified sadness. His computer, left on and unattended, buzzed pointlessly in the corner, its screen saver, a multi-colored Spirograph montage, interspersed with translucent images of faceless Bond girls, twisting ad infinitum for an audience of none.

What happened here?

The bottle of Johnnie Black lay open and empty on the bedroom floor, along with a pack of Marlboro's, gifts from an old friend. The desk chair lay on its side, toppled, in keeping with the rest of the room. His bed sheets were twisted, the pillows on the floor, and there were stains on the walls; strange residues deposited over time representing neglect and a desire to tell.

He looked down at his hands. They kept changing; the veins, wavy, rose and fell like pots of worms.

Trippy.

There was no evidence of eating, however, and this was really weird, for it was in this room that Heuer lived. Flat screens, mounted on the ceiling and on the desktop, kept him in line with the world outside in ways that papers could not. Screens blasted twenty-four and seven with their talking heads and CNN, whereas papers were flat and dirty, suitable only for the bottoms of bird cages. He cancelled the dailies first and then the weeklies, seeing no value whatever in printed words.

Pictures were another matter. Several in paint and charcoal and sepia covered the walls and floors. He loved them all, and he stared at them for hours when he pondered. His beer fridge, humidor, and model rocket collection completed him; housing the things he loved, all within perfect reach.

His senses, though dulled, honed in on a scent, distant yet familiar, coming from inside the room. It was bog-like-foul like a place he'd visited long ago, buried under wood ash. He frowned.

What was the last thing he ate? Did he cook or go for takeout? He wanted to go down to the kitchen to check, but found, to his astonishment, that he could not get past the doorframe into the outer hall.

Nein, das kann nicht sein!—Now this is not right!—he fumed, switching to German. He would do this whenever he encountered static. The spit and sharp of it forced people back because they could not understand what he meant.

Unballing his fists he felt his chest, registering the sensation of "feel"—he could *feel* "touch," but he could not locate the beating heart. Consciously knitting his brows, he considered other bodily wants, his legal mind checking and balancing the laws of nature against the laws of the impossible. He could not, for example, feel "hunger" and he wasn't dying for a drink either.

Was this a mark of passage into the nether? The man on the floor had no comment.

He thought about his bowels and if they needed attention, but that, to his great relief, no longer appeared to matter. Regularity, in recent years, wasn't all it was cracked up to be. When he was young, he reveled in a good clean out after the morning coffee because it reset his clock and established the tone for the rest of the day. Not so latterly.

His prostate had kept its promise, letting him down, enlarging, pressing where it ought naught. Awake most nights, he lost sleep and dreams.

With this in mind, he bounced up and down on the soles of his expensive shoes in an effort to confirm if he was awake or not. Perhaps he was sleepwalking, or heading off to the can for another urinary evacuation that wouldn't come?

The man on the floor ruled out these options.

He tried the door again, and again, to his dismay, he could not leave.

What to do? What to do?

'I think, therefore I am,' went the popular saying, but what good was 'being' when one was confined to a bedroom like a rat in a cage?

He struggled to remain calm, just as he became aware of that heavy oppressive feeling one gets before receiving bad news. Pacing back and forth across the ancient floorboards in the house he was born into, he checked for the kinds of incriminating evidence the court of public opinion would hold against him once found. Pornography, loaded handguns, too many candy wrappers all had to be dispatched before someone inevitably broke the door down.

As light turned to dark and day gave over into night, Heuer's thoughts came faster and faster, in different languages, interspersed with corrugated images, accompanied by generous doses of Seventies rock; a fitting sound track for the old life, now ended.

He fell to his knees. Somewhere in this mélange was something to be grateful for and with time, he was sure, he would figure out what that single, great, thing might be. For now, all he could really do was take comfort in the fact that his death had been perfect.

***

It came on fast with a flash of brain-blasting pain—a red hot poker to the left side beneath the rib cage that meant either extreme heart burn or a breaking heart. Heuer's mouth went dry. The moist, squamous cells that lined his tar-stained interior turned to Velcro in milliseconds. His tongue ballooned to block his airway. He rose from his seat, a fantastic double-stitched leather beauty he'd craftily liberated from the third floor office when no one was looking. The chair hit the floor, hard. Heuer did the spin, lurching three hundred and sixty degrees aft in a *danse macabre* that had him grasping his thorax in a final act of self-love. He threw his head back in an effort to keep up with his eyes, which were rolling up and behind into the back of his head. He remembered seeing the brown discoloration on the ceiling, a parting gift, he supposed, from the accursed raccoon that put the hole in the roof that let the rain in. Panos' cat was an innocent caught in a poison plot meant to take this cretin out.

Touché.

The entire scene took seconds to enact. This was myocardial infarction—heart death by trans-fat in coronary arteries, choking off blood supply. It took years to make these blockages, but only moments to blacken a heart and make it quit.

Day 2: Post Mortem

Looking at the man on the floor, Heuer could not help but delight in his own good fortune. This was the man he used to be—the mortal coil—and he had escaped what others, left behind, had to look forward to: diapers, nursing homes, dementia, and dribble cups. The massive coronary had spared him all of that, and at just fifty years of age, his new self—what would he call it?—the preternatural residue?—had the rest of eternity to look forward to.

Heuer spun on his heel; arms extended, fingers drumming the stale air. What to do next? Wait to be found? Check messages? A quick glance at the cell phone confirmed that there weren't any. The light was not flashing. This didn't surprise him—entirely. Stressed out, overworked, he booked off two weeks and was not expected back until after Independence Day.

He shrugged, unfettered. Perhaps a little soul-cleansing, axe grinding was in order. Stepping over his body, he mulled the events of the last several months in search of a fitting tale to console him. There were several, but none worthy enough to do justice to the exceptional quality of his situation. A snarky comment or sexual rebuff tossed at him in the other life had little efficacy: he was extraordinary now. What he needed was a penultimate retrospective to make him feel *celestial*.

He looked over at the toppled chair; so beautiful, even in repose, and at that, he smiled broadly for the right story had presented itself:

The Termination of Roger the Idiot
or
—as others in the office called it behind his back—
The Revenge of the Evil Elf
By Jürgen Heuer

Roger Wilkinson, a well-liked junior attorney, joined corporate early the previous year under a banner that screamed "talent" and "going places." Handsome, clever, and fast with a turn of phrase, he could very well have gone to the top. But his boss and nemesis Jürgen Heuer could not stand him—disliked him on sight in fact—and resolved, quite early on, to do away with him.

Whereas Roger was popular and out-going, Heuer was dispossessed and withdrawn, hiding behind freaky rimless glasses and expensive suits. It was said that his standoffish behavior was deliberate, as if scripted in a play, and he did nothing to dissuade this contention; he was a lawyer, and lawyers are always deliberate.

The decision to ruin a young man half his age was taken lightly and on purpose, as if giving weight to the decision conferred unjust power on the youth. To Heuer, it was personal, but also a test to see if he could actually do it. In his new position as VP Legal, success in the matter would demonstrate how much power he actually had.

Watching Roger silently from a distance, the older man marked time, logging every misstep to ensure that reports made to the human resource director weren't dismissed out of hand for lack of foundation.

Roger Wilkinson did the rest. As talented as he was, he also partied like a veteran, boozing and serial dating his way through the second and third quarter, referring to the senior VP by first name, as if his superhero mantle conferred protections not available to the lesser folk that surrounded him.

But late morning starts combined with the obvious hangovers, and a crucial file gone missing thanks to Heuer's crafty intervention, was all that was needed to terminate someone who had everything to live for.

"You evil little elf," Roger hissed on receipt of his notice. A big guy, he rose up to his full six foot two inches, dwarfing his boss, who studied him owl-like, from behind his spectacles.

The older man sighed: It strained credulity that this oaf, this gargoyle of a human being, failed to comprehend the meaning behind successive warnings from HR. The hubris, amazing, cancelled any doubts that Heuer might have entertained in a moment of weakness.

Holding Roger's gaze, he blinked purposefully to appear calculating; he wanted his performance to appear premeditated, just like the scenes played out in the movies he'd seen with similar scenarios.

The young man, moving off into the south corner of what was no longer his office, looked down morosely at all the employed people on the street below.

"At last, you appreciate the gravity of the situation," Heuer offered, seating himself behind Roger's desk. "I like this," he said, fingering the two-tone black and red leather desk chair. I'll have it for myself after you are gone." Swinging his legs a top the desk, he made sure the younger man saw the crests burned on to the bottoms of his soles. The shoes, Italian, and recently acquired from David's, Toronto, were Harris wingtips in two-tone black and ox blood, and at $1,500 plus, they paid for themselves now.

He eyed the kid's shoes, low rent and deplorable: "I see you're wearing brogues with toe caps. They were on sale last week—Walmart, I believe. Love sales, don't you?"

Roger's assistant, Samantha, strode in. Tall heels and red hair, her figure perceptible through the gauzy fairy wing fabric of a retro-patterned mini, she was ready for savoring. Heuer rubbed his hands together. They made a *swish swish* sound like a knife on a sharpening stone. "Miss Samantha, you have arranged for the boxes?"

"Yes, Mr. Heuer."

"And the escort?"

"Just outside." The woman shifted uncomfortably on her Eduardo Montevideo blue-bottomed heels—they cost more than Harris, making Sam as expensive as she was scintillating.

He smiled. She looked away. His gaze made her uncomfortable—he knew—so he focused again on Roger to give her a break.

"Security will see you out. We'll see that you get packed up." Heuer smiled brightly.

"Aren't you forgetting something?" Roger asked evenly.

Heuer took his feet off the desk. His eyes were on the door now. "No. I think not."

"I saw you. That was you, the other night. I was there too."

Heuer brushed past Samantha, inhaling her as he moved out into the hallway. Roger the Idiot, former legal counsel, TRAVAT Ion, was no more.

"I never forget anything, darling," Heuer muttered coolly, obliterating, that moment, all thoughts of the young man and his fabulous chair. His work done, he would go home and enjoy an expensive bottle of single malt scotch.

The End
***

Night thickened and his cage, oppressive at any time, grew more so. *I saw you. I was there too.* What had the kid meant? Heuer, perplexed, did not care for uncertainty. This was his story to write any way he liked, yet reality intruded.

The day after he fired Roger, Heuer called in sick. Then he booked vacation time, citing the Indonesian mess and a need to foment core strategic plans in isolation as the primary reason behind the hasty leave-take.

Head office was not convinced. TRAVAT Ion was a large biochemical engineering firm based in Houston, and it had recently acquired its equally large competitor Covalent MITSEA. Heuer and crew from CMITSEA were absorbed with the takeover and for the first time ever, he accepted, under great pressure, a promotion.

He moved into the seventeenth floor corner office of the VP Legal Services. His motivation in accepting was greed, pure and simple. But the memos and tattling and political correctness that came with the new administration killed the joy. In six months he'd been warned twice about his tongue tic, advised to "dress it down a bit" where his suits were concerned and even re-think his beard. TRAVAT men were God fearing and clean-shaven, and it was unseemly to click one's tongue the way Heuer often did, "'specially 'round the ladies."

Heuer reminded Texas Bob, TRAVAT's corporate

chair, of a spruce grouse on the make. "Foul smelling bird and hard on the pallet too," Bob said at the first warning meeting. Their unmistakable clicking sound was meant to attract a mate, but it also brought hunters with shotguns more than willing to blast the suckers out of their evergreen perches.

The real reason behind the no-facial hair policy, Heuer later learned, came from Bob's intrinsic beliefs over what made a man, a man. Beards were bad, but Heuer's goatee was worse. "Goats" reminded Bob of something inherently female, which, by extension, attracted him to men who wore them.

And that was just too weird.

In knowing this, Heuer removed his, quickly.

The clothes were another matter. These came from Europe and he'd be damned if he'd exchange them for dungarees and Boulet cow boots...

* * * *

What did it matter now? He was waiting like a schmuck for an eye opening revelation that wasn't coming. He resumed the pace, covering off the four corners of his room, which, he suspected, was growing hotter. The man on the floor was changing, his complex carbohydrates breaking down into simpler compounds along with his protein. Mother Nature, the ever-efficient recycler, was turning his body's own enzymes against him. The amylase and protease meant to digest food were consuming him, and he, Jürgen Heuer, was forced to watch.

"Jesus Christ," he mouthed, breaking his first sweat since hitting the floor. "If there's a hell on earth, it's here and I'm standing right in the middle of it."

The man's face was blue and his arms, uncovered when he rolled up his sleeves for the last time, were breaking out in road maps; dark lines made by a vascular system falling apart. He had spoiled his suit too and the smell of it was getting to him.

Chapter Three

9:15 A.M.

*W*hy now, after twenty years?
No fan of sentiment, Enid Krause wanted to spit the words out but didn't. Her crusty side would be bested by thoughts of duty. There could be no other way.

"Heuer? What kind of a name is that?"

She willed her thoughts away as she made ready for her trip to the Office of the Chief Coroner: dangerous thoughts, sublimated to a code of ethics and a book of laws that forbade her to cry. Professionals do not cry.

"I'm German, like you."

In the prep room,[1] she assembled her props, fumbling for gloves, dis spray[2] and a fresh pouch[3] in case he needed one over and above what the coroner provided. "He's been dead awhile," Carla warned from her web in the doorway. "So get your head out of your ass. He's gonna be leaky."

Carla didn't know that she knew him and she wasn't going to tell.

"We must keep this between us, mein Schön, and if you are good..."

"I got it covered. See to yourself."

Day 3: Post Mortem

Nostalgia took Heuer to some very strange places, chief among them, The Wreck Room on Church Street. Large, subterranean, sprawling over four thousand square

---

[1] In the industry, prep room, embalming suite, O.R., and mortuary are used interchangeably to connote the same space.
[2] The disinfectant blue spray that careful FD's use on the guerney before and after each run to the morgue.
[3] Body bag, in layman's terms.

feet, the space was once owned by Spiro, a local hero idolized by every high school kid who cut class to play billiards. Heuer, at sixteen, was one of his biggest fans.

Spiro sponsored midget hockey and girls soccer teams, supported three high school yearbooks with generous two page advertisements, and provided support and encouragement to local street youth.

His billiard room was an impressive thing, with twelve snooker tables, a wet bar and arcade machines that yielded impressive takes after the shady figures that leased them took their percentage. Overseen by Spiro's sons Demetri and Georgios, the room was Heuer's classroom growing up. Spiro's tables had deep pockets, and through these, the boys conducted their fledgling drug business in direct contravention of their father's "Don't do your business in my business" policy.

From the sons, Heuer learned how to survive on a cash only basis, never filing taxes and never drawing attention to his activities. In addition to narcotics, he augmented his income as a frequent player, distinguishing himself for his reliability and tact on a hustle. He knew when to win and when to lose, cutting his sponsor in on the take. When the waiters from near-by restaurants came to play after their shifts, Spiro would call Heuer, knowing the kid could keep them playing for hours.

Young Heuer was good at other things too, connecting seamlessly with the affluent teenage girls who took the enriched French and English courses that he also favored. The jerks in the tech hall might have drawn other conclusions about him, but he was unfazed. In taking highbrow classes, he not only rubbed shoulders with some of the hottest pussy in school, but he made money, selling drugs to them too.

That was years ago in high school where, many a poet has argued, the best years of one's life occurs. Trapped in a room with a rotting corpse, Heuer scoured the photos littering the floor for evidence to prove just that. He looked down at the images in black and white, sepia and full color—most taken by him on a Pentax given him on his twelfth birthday. Smiling, drinking, playing games, they gazed back at him. Faces he knew well, others mere acquaintances, they reminded him of a life lived and lost, and this made his silent heart ache.

But reminiscences were not exclusive to dead men. He'd been dwelling on the past a lot in the days leading up to his passing, and it was, during one such session, that he decided to check out the old pool hall.

Hastened by another dispiriting class action suit—a nasty bit of business arising from Texas Bob's reckless commitment to outsourcing in the third world—the need for peace and a little comfort took Heuer out onto the street for an afterhours stroll through the downtown core. It was a perfect night, hot and sultry, coaxing his mind to wander in lockstep with his feet. The bars, the drunks, the people for sale, transported him far, far back to other times, when he traveled alone or with friends. The smell of spice wafting off a patio tickled his senses, and for a moment, he was on a barstool on Bourbon Street dreaming of the bayou.

That got him thinking, the cellular cultures used in the manufacture of Hexacort™, TRAVAT's latest foray into safe pesticide use in countries that didn't matter, were suspect in the deaths of hundreds. With the numbers climbing, damaged parties wanted Bob's ass on the next plane. Extradition was out of the question of course, but the time and effort required, and the materials, staff, and money needed to restore a reputation sullied by carelessness would be gargantuan. TRAVAT's disaster was nothing compared to Union Carbide's Bhopal Crisis, but it would take years to resolve nevertheless. And Heuer was sick and tired of crawling through the dirt holes of the world.

"They can kiss my ass," he said derisively, as he

rounded the corner onto Church Street. He'd pull up stakes, sell up, sell out, and once he was cashed up, he'd head south like he always wanted to.

The door to the old pool hall was painted black and the grocery store next to it was gone. He remembered Nicos the Stoner stealing steaks out of there and stashing them at Spiro's for pick up. Years later, Nicos was seen running through an all-night Winn Dixie in the west end with a gunman on his heels.

Heuer chuckled. He was a good guy, Nicos.

As were the guys at the bottom of the stairs, no doubt. Pushing the heavy door open, he descended familiar rungs now illuminated by tiny multi-colored rainbow lights. Music pulsing at a shattering decibel level was his first clue that this was not a pool hall anymore. The space opened up before him; an electric wonderland of blue lights and cigarette smoke that filled every corner, in spite of the by-law prohibiting the practice.

Totschkes like the rule of law didn't faze the proprietor, obviously, for The Wreck Room was a private club that permitted a lot of things. Men dressed in leather, studded thongs, pirate gear and flowing robes, neatly draped and gathered at the shoulders with delicate filigreed brooches, gallivanted about the place with a 'fuck you and your mother' attitude that he couldn't help but admire.

"Still," he sighed, not finishing the sentence, it was no longer the place where he came of age and to that, he registered a growing heaviness beneath his ribcage that announced the death of another sacred cow. Damn.

To the back of the hall, almost opaque in the din, a tallish man waved him a welcome. Young, drunk and framed by a pair of comely blokes who had just emerged from behind a curtained portico, he was offensive in his brute familiarity. "Come on over boss," he yelled, rising to his feet with a bob and weave that preceded a hip grind, incredibly disturbing for its well-honed execution: a perfect ten. Heuer moved along. He had no interest whatever in engaging in any kind of intercourse with Roger the Idiot. The following week, he would fire him.

Poor Spiro, Heuer thought. He'd roll over in his grave if he saw this. Or maybe not. Spiro had a Greek saying for just about anything, enabling him to rationalize away all things bad. He saw tremendous potential in young Heuer, for example, and encouraged him to reach beyond the billiard hall. Years later, when he told Spiro that he'd been accepted to law school, Heuer was surprised by his reaction. "You break my heart, boy. They will cripple your back and prostitute your spirit. And then you'll be an asshole like the rest of them."

Law was a natural choice for Heuer. He'd sold drugs in high schools, conned warlords in pool rooms, and always paid for sex. He called some of the strangest creatures, friends, and he never, ever felt dirty.

The sun was up again—he could perceive it bleeding through the horizontal blind that covered the bedroom window—and he tried in vain to see out onto the street. Though his hands passed over it, the blind remained fixed. He panicked a little. Over the last twenty-four hours, his senses had returned and sharpened. With them came his mind with all its nimble subtleties and exaggerations.

Spiro. Pah! And to hell with him for judging. In law, crime paid, and it paid handsomely.

"They will pay me to talk and they will have to listen to me too," Heuer said, mouthing the words to the immobile blind, just as he had to Spiro twenty-five years before.

"Damn it," he muttered, the past failing to comfort him. Spiro had sheltered him when he was out of doors; he'd even attended Heuer's high school graduation ceremony. And Heuer repaid him with scorn. The old man was so sure he knew the kid better than the kid himself. The old Greek could, after all, philosophize away the prostitutes, whom he fed coffee to free of charge in winter; the fags who could play as long as they stayed away from his sons; and the sons with their dope as long as they went to university and got their degrees. What he couldn't bear, he told Heuer that day, was insincerity.

Law school wouldn't change him, Heuer promised. He'd changed already. Not wanting to forget this, he made an event of it by never speaking to Spiro again.

Shadows cornered him, demanding explanation. He was in no mood. He surveyed his surroundings, taking in the detritus like a curator in a museum. What was left of him littered the floor; his possessions, his garbage: trophies of a life. And yet there was no comfort in them.

He hung his head before the window blind; the sound of children playing on the other side reminding him that life was there and he was no longer a part of it.

"I'm sorry," he cried. "I'm so sorry."

***

Day 4: Post Mortem

Another day passed and he was not found. And like the rusty car that sat alone and unattended on the driveway, his body continued to give in to the elements. He had not planned on dying so soon, yet he'd not taken steps to avoid it either. Fancying himself an iconoclast, he eschewed everything society deemed critically important: Recycling, green salads, cardio workouts. Heuer was a man living alone on his terms. With men's magazines as his moral governors, he favored landfills, deep fryers, and longer hunting seasons. Vegetables were silly and the people who wanted him to stop smoking were too ridiculous to think about.

Cars were better than women; they never talked back, and they loved unconditionally. The beast in the driveway, for example, had been in storage for years and would have remained so, had it not been for the sale of the building that housed her. He had sixty days to get her out of there, and it cost him plenty since her guts had seized and a flatbed was needed. With no time to find better accommodations, he had her delivered to his front door where she remained silent under her tarp. His Schön.

Seeing her again rekindled a long-buried desire to rescue her from a fate he was responsible for. Her rocker arms and wheel wells were rotten, as was her floor. But everything else was intact. The shattered grill was easily replaced and the emblems, long gone, could be found anywhere; vintage or reproduction, it wouldn't matter. The rockers and rear panels were out there somewhere in a barn in Saskatchewan, or Texas, or a wrecker's graveyard in Arizona or Australia. And, if the worst came to the worst, he could always pull something off a Ventura or a Nova. The purists on the car blog would bark, but at least he'd have her back.

I love your car.

Heuer scratched his head. She couldn't say it enough. Odd, the things he remembered.

His mobile, sitting on its charger, buzzed and, forgetting himself, he moved to answer it, sprinting towards the stately bureau from which it protested. Littered with receipts and coins and empty cigarette packs, the antique seemed absurd with its pricey Art Deco mirror he'd picked up real cheap at auction. Beautiful, but cluttered, the bureau said more about him than the pictures on the floor. It was a museum piece that needed care so that it could be preserved forever.

He sucked in the dusty air. The phone, with its flashing red light, was the only thing between him and being found. Sure as he was that someone was looking for him, the icons on the tiny screen said otherwise. It wasn't a phone call, just a no reply text from the "Parts Wanted" thread he'd posted on the classic car website days before he died. The guys on it were out there looking for the car's rocker arms and wheel wells. They would find mint condition 1968 parts, he was sure, because they were historians as much as they were mechanics and they could not stomach imitation. Only he was going to miss out.

Damn it all to hell again—times two.

***

Prevented from communicating his thoughts on social networks, barred from calling for help, and with no one to talk to, Heuer was forced to confront some truths and he didn't like it one bit. There was the business of the suit he was wearing, a nasty bit of haute couture forced, fitted, stream-lined, with no ass to speak of—in black with a mauve and Verdoro green striped lining that he'd overpaid for at Monsieur André. He'd bought it on a whim in a moment of weakness because the little man who'd sold it to him needed the commission "real bad." Now he was stuck with it for all eternity.

The next item that troubled him was the matter of this strange afterlife. While his hands were no longer moving and waving out their own acid freak show, he was still unable to manipulate objects like so many poltergeists did in the movies, cancelling out everything he believed a ghost should be. The reality of his new life was less than ideal, yet he was in no position to quibble because he did not know who controlled the scene. Logically, something had to give. He just had to sit back in his awful suit and wait for it.

And then the bugs came with their sick buzz song under the cracked sill he'd meant to caulk earlier that summer and never did. Their music was the only audible sound inside the room beyond his own voice, the timbre of which was changing along with his face: One minute he was twenty, next forty and then thirty years of age. And that's when he yelled, "Stop. This is me. This is how I want to be."

As a young man, he was a Super Sport—an "SS"—

like the car in the driveway, with a four on the floor and a thousand explosions under the hood.

Tilting his head back, he closed his eyes and remembered *her:*

Grasping the wheel,
Grasping her hair,
Dropping the hammer,
Moving fast,
Laying rubber,
To complete surrender amid smoke and screams.
And then over.
In seconds.

Touching his face, he was comforted. A fool in life, a poet in death, he was remarkable: blond again, the ridiculous rimless glasses that exaggerated his eyes to make him look like an anime character out of a cheap cartoon were gone; his skin, smooth and flawless, his jaw angular, and, best of all, his teeth—they were back, all of them.

Was sein wird, wird sein und was hineinschaut, schaut auch wieder raus—What will be, will be, and what looks in, looks out.

"I am beautiful."

Chapter Four

Day 5: Post Mortem

> ***HEUER, Jürgen M.****:*
> *Conformist, actor-provocateur, unconscionable ingrate, died suddenly and unexpectedly on a date not yet determined.*

H euer, piss-bored, had taken to reciting aloud an obituary of his own design.

> *Contributing large sums to causes he did not believe in, Mr. Heuer reveled in the gratitude conferred upon him by the sniveling recipients at the awards ceremonies he wore his tuxedo to. Part film expert and jazz aficionado jeu-jeu, he manufactured a life of details and activities, both real and imagined. His life, by all accounts, was immensely successful and hardly lonely. And he was happy.*

"Where is everybody??!" he screamed, from a vantage perch atop an ecru ottoman he never liked. "It's been five days!!!!" He'd left the world and the city continued to buzz outside his window.

But perhaps not as much as he.

Heuer had become a hummer—a body that goes undiscovered long enough to attract the blue bottle blowflies that came in under the sill. They buzzed and hummed, depositing their eggs on his mottling surface, their constant activity literally reanimating him. "Get off!" The insidious beasties responded to his paranormal hand flapping, but he was not sure if they could see him. They might have been reacting to the air currents he was generating.

Or maybe the sharp knock on the bay window that fronted the street?

Startled, he crossed the room, hoping his growing preternatural abilities with the blowflies would have a similar effect on the blinds. He attempted to throw them back to no avail. The slats shifted by inches, not feet. Yet this was enough to frighten Mr. Panos, the neighbor, who had climbed Heuer's catalpa tree for a look inside.

Peering through the filthy window, Panos might have had enough time to perceive the shape of a man in repose on a litter-strewn floor. Or maybe he saw Heuer, twenty years younger, standing upright and staring back at him through the space his hands just made.

Heuer would never find out.

Stavroula, shouting from her stoop that her husband should be careful, doubtless contributed to the unfolding drama. Heuer, staring intently at the man who he almost called friend, placed a hand on the window just inches from Panos' face. "What are you doing here? Did she put you up to this?"

Panos, steadying himself on the branch that held him, had just enough time to place his hand on the window directly opposite Heuer's own, before losing his footing and dropping onto the hood of the 68 Chevelle below.

Stavroula's frantic screams moved him as much as the sick *schlump thunk* sound of her husband splattering across the old car's hood. Heuer pushed again, and this time, the blinds gave way.

"Panayiotis! Panayiotis!" she shouted, darting out from the safety of her porch.

Heuer sighed. A religious woman, Stavroula was attuned to the signs of God and never ignored them when they appeared. There were many times over the years, when she'd point to a neighbor's house and whisper conspiratorially: "Sometheeng eez not right, Meester Heuer."

The large gathering of insects outside his window must have been her first clue.

She vaulted over the fence that divided their properties, arms outstretched. "Baby mou, baby mou." she yelled desperately as Panos' eyes pooled blood at their centers.

He needed an ambulance, or an undertaker, but Heuer could not call for either one. Alfons Vermiglia, the Genovese tree-hater, appeared from his side of the lawn, his cell phone pressed to his ear.

"He sees something," Stavroula babbled, pointing to the offending spirit lingering at the window above. Her eyes wild and wet with moisture, she insisted that someone was up there. "The blinds. See? They move." She gestured frantically, her red fingernails flashing, her body draping her husband's.

Panos had rolled off the hood after impact and onto the ground leaving a stream of bright red oxygenated blood on the Chevelle's tarp, which he pulled free with a grasping hand before his heart stopped.

What a piece of shit, Heuer thought on seeing the rusted out hulk of the old Chevelle, which had further deteriorated after eight years of wintering on the driveway. Alfons, ever the arbiter of good taste in the neighborhood, shook his head, as if expecting something better from his incredibly secretive neighbor.

The little party beneath Heuer's window quickly

grew: Alfons' nosey wife Gina, Quan from Beijing, who lived across the street, and bland Mrs. Wilson, the Anglo who could not forgive him for World War II and the damage the evil Germans had done, descended on Stavroula, along with her adult children, who joined her in rapid succession; they just living mere streets away. Together, they enveloped Mr. and Mrs. Panos, like protective bubble wrap, offering what comfort they could while they waited for the response team. It was a remarkable show of solidarity in tragedy.

Heuer didn't know a great deal about response times or crime scenes, but he knew from years of network television that *his* body, once found, would be poked and chalked, unlike Panos' whose cause of death was dismally straightforward. He shuddered, as thoughts of The Wreck Room and Roger the Idiot overtook him. Conclusions would be drawn, and without a voice with which to defend his position, it would all be bad.

Grousing and fuming, he eyed the annoying corpse on the floor then walked off the room at a lawyer's pace, circling his quarry with eagle precision, ready to swoop, vivisect and consume. The blue bottles, unrelenting in their buzzy pursuit, augmented the temerity of his situation.

"At least he'll have an open lid," Heuer complained to the body on the floor. "You, mate, won't be so lucky."

Panos would probably go to the big Greek funeral home north of the city; that's where all the Greeks went. There, the mourners would sit quietly in neat little rows, saying nothing as per custom; their silence a show of respect for a man who was infinitely lovable.

"What about me? What will everyone say if anyone comes at all?"

Such were the things that preoccupied Heuer's thoughts, so much so, that he was unaware of the footfalls on his stairs and the foul oaths that accompanied them. It was not until the door to his room gave way that his full attention was redrawn to the real-time situation playing out before his eyes. The man stood calmly in the doorframe, silhouetted improbably by ethereal beams of light and shadow cast courtesy of the late day sun. *Of course it would be him*, Heuer thought, loving the irony.

"Yes. I called a moment ago," Alfons said into his cell phone. "We need another ambulance. Or something. Our neighbor—the other one—is also dead.

Chapter Five

Day 5: Post Mortem

How many friends had he won and lost and how many of these associations really mattered? These were but two of the pressing questions that nagged Heuer. There were other concerns too, like his ever-sharpening senses, which were growing by the quarter hour. These, more so than the missing friends that lacked the decency to find him, bothered him most. With vampire precision, he could now cross his room without thought or effort. This, he decided, was the essence of "being" which was pretty cool. But when sight and smell and the ability to perceive the sweat and heat of others were added—well—that was madness. Why taste if he couldn't eat?

Panos' adventure in snooping restored Heuer's ability to move things, but only in specific instances. Natural laws—gravity in particular—applied in the supernatural world, which meant that he could take part physically—but only when his emotions were provoked. That was torture. He could do without food; suffer without booze; hell, he could even forgo smokes. What he could not do without was the human touch—being touched—and that's what finally brought him to tears.

The James Bond girls on his screen saver continued to dance soundlessly in the evening light; their bodies freaked out helixes, counter spinning. Heuer, wanting to join them, expanded, the preternatural residue filling the room. His molecules burst apart, then regrouped, a Frankenstein of atomic rings gone ballistic. And then he was back, reassembled, young and beautiful again, but no closer to the physical pleasures he so craved.

He resumed pouting, wondering if he was being punished for offenses unknown.

"What if I am?" he demanded, drying his tears on his

44

sleeve. What was out there beyond the living world? The undiscovered country? And if that were the case, would he have to fall to his knees, contrite and pleading, to get there?

Screw that. He'd rather stay here.

Heuer leaned forward into the window blind and blew softly upon it. The slats surrendered, fluttering a near perfect sensual response. He felt the soft breeze and it was Divine for it was, surely, an artful segue that would bring him closer to the gates of heaven. It was a blessing that Stavroula couldn't leave well enough alone. Panos' funeral would probably fall on the same day as his, and this would do much to eliminate some of the nastier talk that funerals always brought on. The neighbors would be too busy with Panos to care about anything Heuer's survivors could cook up.

Red lights flashed outside beyond the slats, which he brushed aside with ease. He felt the fear now. They were getting closer. Heuer had spent a great deal of time wondering about people's reactions once they learned of his passing, and he delighted in the mock scenarios he conjured. What he did not consider were the circumstances of his discovery and as his front door gave way for the second time, he found himself rapidly coming to terms with it. He felt uneasy about what was coming, worrying as any secretive person would, about what they would find.

I'd pray, he thought, but he never really believed in God, and St. Peter had failed to email an invitation. The white light that shone into his clear blue eyes was not God the Father, Son, and Holy So and So, but flashlights from the uniformed officers who pushed their way in through the darkness. They recoiled at the stench and he was hurt. It was dark again and the halogen beams brought to light the gossamer spider silk that hung from the ceiling fan and cornices that supported dust bunnies, suspended mid-flight, without a place to go. His collection of Second World War propaganda posters, barely visible in the din, went unnoticed.

"Here!" a female voice called out. Dr. Veronika Schaufuss, investigative coroner on duty for the southwest quadrant, had tagged along in an effort to make time with the much younger Detective she soon hoped to bang, or so it appeared to Heuer who read her thoughts. She stood over the body, directing the flat foots to turn it gently, so that she could shine a pencil thin beam into its cloudy eyes.

Someone turned a light on. Heuer leaned in close so as to speak to the poor withered carcass on the floor:

Never let anyone know what you have, and never let them in on what you've taken from them.

He overheard the coroner's discussion with Dispatch and was more than a little put out when she jovially referred to him as a hermit. "House's a mess," she declared, "and no one I spoke to seems to really know him."

Dr. Schaufuss was pretty hot for a snoop and he felt his nonexistent pulse race as he considered her clothing and what might lie beneath. He licked his lips wondering if he could lean into her without detection. She talked to his neighbors, announcing his death, setting tongues a wagging over the strange man who had lived in their midst.

She went through his drawers and, finding his pills, decided to bag them so that she could confirm the toxicology, later, once his tissue samples had stewed through. She was looking at all of his things offering no comment other than the occasional "Hmmmmmm" and "What tha—?"

He buried his face in her hair, giving it a good sniff, perceiving—he thought—the slightest trace of pomegranate. He imagined her lithe and willing and he noticed, with unbridled pleasure, what felt like a hint of a stiffy as he ran his hands over her fabulous ass.

Things were getting better: He was getting everything he needed, consequence free, and she was completely unaware of what he was doing to her.

That excited him even more. How many times had he suffered the fake protests with limp threats of retributive action? And the half-hearted face slaps amid the sweat and desperation that came with the wanting?

She went into his closet and was immediately taken by the incredible richness of his wardrobe. She'd been talking to the Dispatcher the entire time on her buzzy device about what she was seeing, including references to the idiot savant she wasted her time on the previous night on a lousy date and then she said, "Wait a minute." She examined the labels, the fabrics and the linings. She looked down at his shoes, shined and neatly stacked on shelves he had custom made himself, his jewelry—the watches, so many watches—and she caught her breath, realizing that she was looking at a quarter mill right there in his closet.

She called out with a child's enthusiasm; as if she had just seen something she ought not to have and could not wait to let the rest of the school yard know: "Hell-Ohhhh Kitt-EEE! You should see the clothes this guy has." They were all looking into his closet, nodding, chuckling; some were even rolling their eyes.

"He's definitely queer, possibly left for dead. We'll find him out after we post him."

The city was getting ready for Pride Week and the rainbow flags were popping up everywhere so she made the great leap. Her lapse in logic made him want to throttle her, but at this point, he could only move flies and horizontal window blinds. He would have to practice, and once he'd mastered the art of large object manipulation, he would pay her a visit.

Heuer looked at the doorframe. All he had to do was leave.

Chapter Six

*T*he *funeral home, like so many family-owned businesses, had a long and storied history in the community. Founded in 1937, it made its debut thanks to chaos and uncertainty. The First War had ended, but not the social unrest that underpinned it. Fascism had been creeping its way across Europe for the better part of a decade, beginning famously in the Twenties with Il Duce in Rome and Franco in Madrid.*

But it was Hitler's ascent to the Chancellery that really got people's attention. German-Americans listened with awe and concern, adjusting their short waves as the rhetoric spewed out from the Sportzpalast in Berlin. Der Führer and his mouthpiece Goebbels were stoking the flames of nationalism in conjunction with Churchill's edgy warnings of impending war.

Many Germans on both sides of the ocean paid attention. Those arrived on a safer shore struggled with conflicting allegiances and fears for the safety of the loved ones they might have to shoot at later on.

Karl Heinz Weibigand Sr. was one such German. He was a Leichenbestatter, a mortician, who'd served his Kaiser bravely in the Great War, where craft was learned on the battlefield under heavy gunfire and in the dark. Untrained, he stepped into the breach, tending the wounded and then the dead. He was good at it, and he thanked the war for it.

But WWI did more than enable him to cut his teeth in a business he would go on to love: It accorded him the good sense to know when to get the hell out of Europe before the Zeitgeist[4] got him a second time.

"Why build on ruins when we can start with nothing?" he said famously to his wife Irmtraut as they

---

[4] German. "Spirit of the times."

packed their bags for Ellis Island. This quotation was one of the Old Man's favorites, and it often made its way into conversation, usually when sales were down.

The Weibigand's immigrated to the United States and it wasn't long before they found a kindred spirit sympathetic to their cause. Hartmut Fläche was a mortician and transplant from the old country, eager to assist a fellow Landsmann[5] who'd work for cheap. Fläche owned Seltenheit and Son's, the neighborhood funeral parlor that, by virtue of its geographic location, catered almost exclusively to Germans.[6]

Although employed and so, by definition, "on his way,"[7] Karl Heinz still struggled with the transition from old world to new. Surveying their tiny apartment on a ramshackle street in Lower Portside, he dismissed it with more than a little hubris: "If I had a match, I would burn this place to the ground."

Irmtraut, cowed, did not share the majority opinion. "Our people killed their people. This country let us in. Be quiet, and be grateful." Great advice to be sure. Karl Heinz had talent and language, while Irmtraut had a strong back and a provençal's gratitude that shone whenever she scrubbed Fläche's toilets.

The apprenticeship bore fruit. Fläche had employed a man of integrity, which was something of a marvel given the boss's own spotty reputation. Long rumored to cut corners—Seltenheit's allegedly re-used caskets—Weibigand was credited with halting the practice. He also provided services in kind, going out of pocket, when necessary, to put on a decent funeral for the poorest in his

---

[5] German. "Countryman."

[6] People of like background settled around the churches in the new world. There, they found like-minded's, financiers, matchmakers, and undertakers.

[7] These were different times. Without benefit of a welfare state, a man with a job was seen to be a man with a future.

community. For this, he was loved, earning the enmity of the man who helped him get his start.

The opportunity was ripe for an ethical alternative, and by the summer of '36, Karl Heinz had gathered up enough financial support to go out on his own. By the spring of '37, Weibigand's was open and thriving, giving Fläche his first real competition.

Hartmut reacted badly. Drinking and ranting, he was at first dumbfounded—then he felt betrayed. He had invested time and money in a middle-aged immigrant looking for a fresh start and was repaid with a slap to the face. Swearing revenge, Fläche committed to a course where personal animosity was passed from one generation to the next...

***

Enid winced, her stomach churning against last night's scotch and her own raging hormones. She raised and lowered her arms in rapid, flapping motion, dislodging the sticky fabric of her soaked dress shirt from the moistness of her steaming armpits.

"Bloody menopause," she cursed, hating above all else, those things she could not control.

***

Charlie Forsythe's intercom buzzed at the precise moment it should not have. The funeral home was coming alive with phone calls and faxes and emails from faraway places. Word of the new death was traveling fast. People were calling for service times and the family hadn't even picked out a casket. Slowly, he picked up the handset. The last thing he needed was a frivolous request from the old sonofabitch upstairs.

"Hell-Ohhhh," Charlie mouthed, drawing out the last syllable, as was his custom when speaking to the boss.

"Who is this guy?" Carla yelled, interrupting Charlie. Emails of condolence were coming in from Ohio, Cape Town, Montevideo. Montevideo?

50

Charlie made a fist at her.

"Shut the hell up, why dontcha," said Fat Dougie, the funeral director's assistant (FDA) seated next to her in the lower office adjacent Charlie's. Sandy-haired, porcine and squinty-eyed, Dougie was the foil to Carla's fall guy. Sometimes, the things he said actually made sense. "The dead guy's a rich lawyer asshole. You can bet the old bastards are all wet over it."

They looked at Charlie, bobbing and weaving in the threadbare Thinking Chair. "Yessss, yessss," he intoned, nodding into the receiver. "Noooo, noooo."

"How does he do that?" Dougie wondered. "Talk to them without saying anything."

The Weibigand Brothers—Karl and Ziggy—came into their own after the war. Too young to drive cars, they were just old enough to work for their father. By the time Charlie joined the firm in 1967, the old man was dead and the sons were well established.

"Wives, kids, church deacons. The whole shebang," Carla explained. "Charlie signed on so they could run off and play."

Dougie reached for the old, stale doughnut parked conveniently at arm's-length on Carla's blotter. She slapped his hand away. "Not for you, asshole."

The FDA withdrew his hand, the sweetie not worth losing a finger over. "I hear the old boys were real players back in the day." He inclined his head, eyes to the ceiling.

Carla snorted. "Are ya new?"

"I've been here six years," Dougie interjected, hurt infusing his squidgy voice.

"Sure, sure," she said dismissively. Messing with Dougie was more fun than setting fire to grasshoppers. "Karl and Ziggy screwed around a lot, which was understandable when you looked at the wives. Real livestock, ya know? And their old man was no better...or so I've been told."

She caught Charlie's eye; he was positively radiating his I-don't-have-time-for-this-shit-right-now look.

"Yessss, yessss, Ziggy," he purred. "I'll see to it."

Carla chuckled. Of course, it was Ziggy on the other end. Who else could it be? They saw Karl-Heinz Jr. so seldom that it was comfortable to believe he was no longer alive, but stuffed and in his rocker on the third floor, Psycho style.

She leaned in to Dougie, dropping her voice an octave: "He says nothing to avoid getting caught. I don't think the old cuckers hear half of what he says."

They were, after all, very, very old.

"Carla Blue!" Charlie demanded, his voice admonishing.

"Yes, dear?" She swung around.

Charlie's face cracked open; a playful grin revealing evenly matched pairs of gold teeth. He hit the speaker button so that all could hear.

"Mister Forsythe," Ziggy creaked, his voice, paper-like, transcending modernity. "The floral study in Astilbe has been moved and I will not tolerate alterations without prior consent. You will address this and quickly. *She* knows better."

Carla and Dougie exchanged knowing glances. The "She" of course was Jocasta Binns, Ziggy's half-sister. An old sack, drunkenly conceived in the Forties between funerals (her mother, Mrs. Loom, played the organ), she was illegitimate and a pretender to the Weibigand name. As such, she had embarrassing delusions about her power position at the funeral home and the staff had to endure it.

The floral study Ziggy referred to was a hideous still life painting accepted in trade from a long time repeater family that could not pay their recent account. Large and over the top, the painting featured feathery blossoms of unintelligible origin. Rendered in unlikely pinks and puce, the blooms had pomegranate centers that split evenly down the centre, dividing petals sensuously into twin folds. It was a painting that even the most tolerant found disturbing—a green sea of colossal floating sex organs—and Jocasta had gone well beyond her mandate by removing it, most likely, to the basement.

"I'll find it," Enid Krause offered, stumbling into the room. Visibly impaired, she snapped to at the sharp incline of Carla's head, which gestured towards Charlie's empty coffee cup.

"Refill," Carla commanded, swallowing her bile. "I thought you'd left already?"

Enid shrugged. Her eyes vacant.

"Whatever," Carla huffed. The intake at the coroner's office would have to wait until the ugly poony picture was found.

"I'll take care of it Ziggy," Charlie said, eyeing Enid from beneath his wire rimmed glasses. "Good-byeeee."

He took the cup, replenished with two hour old brew as black as soy sauce. "Well go on, dear." He shooed Enid away. "We have one now, three by lunch."

Carla beamed. Deaths happened in three's; the hummer at the coroner's office was only the first in a series.

***

Enid walked with purpose. She had an *objet d'art* to recover and if doing this could roast some tail fat off the Jocastrator, so much the better.

In addition to being a Weibigand *de facto,* Jocasta was also the pre-need arrangement counselor. Charged with the task of drumming up business before it happened, she preyed on the weakened defenses of the bereaved who, still raw, bought into her claptrap about how imperative it was to pre-arrange one's own funeral. As their loved ones lay in wistful repose, Jocasta would approach the mourners, expounding the virtues attached to "being ready."

"Just think about what you've been through with

mother and no arrangements in place. Do you want your children to go through the same thing?" was her favorite opening volley. Enid, on the sidelines mucking with the cumbersome funeral florals that people still sent in great volumes, would shake her spiky hair every time she overheard the wretched beast recite her lines. Emotional up-selling, coupled with heavy doses of guilt, worked every time, and as much as she was loathe to credit the office nemesis with anything positive, Enid had to admit that Jocasta's prowess at making a sale also made her an artiste.

Unlike the rest of Weibigand's worker bees, Jocasta was not licensed to embalm or take out funerals. As such, she was not bound by the same laws or ethical codes that governed the licensees. This, in many ways, empowered her more than the strong resemblance she bore to the company founder, whose portrait, prominently displayed in the main lobby, never failed to remind everyone who she was. Nor did an absence of licensure prevent her from wearing the same costume as they did. Donning stripes[8] and making a pretense at being a real undertaker was more galling to staff than her lofty insults, which she spewed whenever possible. Yet there was nothing they could do.

"Leave it alone," Charlie would say whenever Jocasta's coworkers dared to complain. "History dictates her path. And history cannot be undone."

Maybe so, Enid observed ruefully, *but no one said it couldn't be undermined.*

Smoothing her ratty hair, she took the twelve steps up to the main level, conquering the creaky treaders by two's. She crossed the main hall, catching the breeze that crept in through the mighty oak doors that fronted the street; the weather stripping, cracked and eroded, invited all manner of air current inside. "Gonna be a scorcher today," she said,

---

[8] The funeral director's costume, largely abandoned by modern firms, consisted of black jacket, vest, tie and black and grey striped pants; hence: stripes.

nodding to the portrait of old Weibigand, who, in his silence, hastened her on.

Down the north corridor past the illegal smoking room, set up in violation of Michigan state law, Enid crossed into the visually offensive pink and pickled pine arrangement office, complete with its Finn Juhl by Niels Vodder chesterfield in wool and teak. This piece had its day in 1941. Seventy years later, it was still here.

Enid sighed. Behind the gawd awful couch, an ancient door opened out into a darkened stairway that led to the not often seen second basement. She descended without a torch, anticipation guiding her steps. Breathing in the fetid air, she beamed with satisfaction: This part of the building was her favorite.

Soaked in mythology advanced by Charlie's stories, and embellished by the re-imaginings of Eldon Wheeler, Weibigand's most senior director under the manager, the basement was living history incarnate. Pushing spider silk out of her face, she walked the darkened hallways, her hand grazing crystal knobs that opened doors to the past. The old lounge piled high with boxes, its art deco furniture dirty, but intact; the old box toilet with the brass pull cord, and the old embalming room that, in the late Thirties, also doubled as a *Schlachterei*, a place where pork was readied and then forced into sausage casings. Old Weibigand rationalized that directors needed things to do during the down times and pushing pork through a bratwurst press, quite frankly, made good sense to him.

Enid lingered in the doorway of this room, surveying the porcelain tables with their little openings at the foot ends that drained into steel buckets that still hung on their hooks, corroded. This space fell into disuse when the new state of the art prep room was built in the Fifties. Over time, the old O.R. accumulated equipment deemed too antiquated or barbaric for modern times—the gravity perks, bulb syringes and pneumonic collars—took their place here, along with braided strapping, locking rings and cast iron positioning hooks. Other pieces, acquired for cheap at garage sales from other family-runs gone belly up were kept here too. Like trophies.

She shivered, remembering her time at Seltenheit's in the Eighties: Eduard Fläche and his coterie of ghouls; many of their things were here as well. Running cool fingers across a black box leather case, its surface embossed with the old Seltenheit logo, she listened for hints of old voices long-silenced. Nothing. Thank God. She touched it again. She knew this box—a baby box used to transfer from the place of death—and while she'd never used it, she remembered seeing Fläche with it. It was enough for her to find her feet and leave the room; nothing good came from staying too long.

She tried to focus on the task at hand, but time scattered her: "Be fast," Eldon Wheeler would bark whenever he sent her down here, usually to seek out an old file some ancestry hound needed to unlock a misplaced heritage. "Irmtraut Weibigand never approved of lady undertakers, so if you smell perfume, it's her."

There'd never been a sighting, but staff heard plenty of bangs in the night, and if the old cow could provide an assist—help her find the painting—then maybe Enid would make it to the coroner's and back before Charlie's eleven a.m. appointment with the dead guy's family.

"Where is it Irmtraut?" Enid called out, peering behind every dusty box and moldy stick of furniture big enough to conceal the painted fright. It wasn't anywhere to be found, and Enid, filthy with her effort grew vexed. "What the hell has she done with it?" she scowled. Ziggy would rampage if it wasn't located. That was what happened when the silk floral arrangements styled personally by Ziggy's late wife Louisa found their way into the old lounge. Next to go were the brushed metal torchieres with the mahogany waists and griffin's feet, and the upright pewter ashtrays, liberated from the Seltenheit fire sale, with the attractive indigo blue lined bowls. No longer politically correct, but damn pretty nonetheless, their beauty was lost on Jocasta Binns, who saw fit to remove these too.

Moving anything in the building without the expressed permission of the brothers was forbidden, yet Binns, with her unique heritage, was nonplussed by the obsessive-compulsive behavior engendered in her half-brother whenever she did just that.

"Come on Irmtraut," Enid implored. "You know how Ziggy is. If we don't find it, he'll clamp down—we'll never get to the bathroom without permission."

Her mind whirred with the pressure: Jocasta didn't hate the painting because it was dirty; she hated it because its brush strokes were garish, its color pallet *louche*. She hated potted palms, too, as well as the *Fleur De Lys* chandeliers hand forged in wrought iron that her father picked up second hand at auction. Most of all she loathed the thick red French velvet curtains that hung aloft in the chapel above the solid oak church pews with their fake Drexel inlays. They were old and dated—too eccentric to be believed—and they embarrassed her. She ranted at the staff about everything that was wrong with Weibigand's and how a 'steady hand backed by a mind with vision' could put everything to rights. Not so secretly, she dreamt of inheriting large, but there were issues with the legitimate heirs and they weren't dead yet.

Enid clasped her hands together in prayer. "Show me. Show me where it is. She is not your daughter, but she'll have this place if she can."

She didn't like taunting the dead, but if invoking past indignities would show her the way, then why not? Enid retraced her steps back to the old crapper, its door warped and resistant to her touch. Applying shoulder to surface after a half-hearted run up, she dislodged the obstruction, which gave way with a nails-on-chalkboard screech.

There. There it is.

Clothed in a blanket of dust bunnies, she pulled at the pocket door shoehorned in behind the toilet box where Irmtraut liked to hide her liquor bottles back in the day. Neither an educated guess built on logical assumptions, nor an intuitive sense fostered with help from the grave was responsible for Enid's success. It was pure fluke.

"Thank you," Enid said, bowing in homage to the Weibigand matriarch. The painting was there, intact, in its original Voom Linquvist frame.

10:00 A.M.

In the time it took Enid to reclaim and re-hang the weird picture, Weibigand Brother's had three more death calls. The influx of business—four files in two hours—was greeted with equal amounts of relief and *Dieu merci.*

"It's a German family too," Charlie gushed to Eldon Wheeler, newly returned from the monthly round of blood work that kept his autoimmune disorder in check. "You know how long it's been since we've had a real one?"

Eldon, examining his fingers, buffed and polished, huffed in haughty disdain. "I know it's been long enough. And now that the gates are open, we'll be struggling to keep up." He cast a withering glance at Enid, dust covered and effecting invisibility behind one of three flat screen monitors used by staff.

"I've got some Ipecac[9] stashed in the prep room if you need some, honey," he offered, caustically.

In addition to being elegant and charming, Eldon had a tendency to be vicious; a character affectation he never tried to hide.

Ignoring him, Charlie zoned out, running a hand

---

[9] A purgative used in the treatment of alcoholism.

across the crumbling west wall in his office, its moisture soaked surface coated with a soft green fuzz connoting yet another breach in the foundation. Karl and Ziggy approved the application of stucco over the old brick years before, one of a series of rapid changes made after their father's death. Time had undone their good efforts.

"We'll crack five figures for sure," Charlie muttered, fighting off waves of nostalgia. "It's an old tymy Hitler family."

He recalled the excitement and optimism that took hold of the place back in '67. Under the young owners, Weibigand's appeal extended beyond the Western Europeans that made up the bulk of their clientele. Anglos, Pollacks, Philippinos and Greeks—Americans of all stripes—were moving into the neighborhood and the Weibigand's took care of all of them. This made Karl and Ziggy indecently rich.

"We haven't had a Nazi in years," Enid offered offhandedly.

"And what would you know about that, eh?" Eldon jumped in. "We put guys in boxes in full uniform before you were born."

This was quite true, though not widely known: Just how these families brought whole uniforms—boots too—out of Europe while evading the war crimes tribunal always piqued Charlie's curiosity.

"Enough, children," he interceded, zeroing in on poor Enid, who's pallid complexion had finally come around to a piteous pink. "Find Carla, and get moving. Doug's taking care of the intake at City General, and you," he turned to Eldon, "You're going to Exeter with Toole and Soames[10] to get the other one. I want to see four in the prep room by one p.m."

---

[10] A funeral service provider catering only to funeral homes, supplying embalmings, transfers, vehicles and extra staff as needed.

Charlie's intercom buzzed for the third time that morning. "Yessss?"

"Ziggy," Eldon huffed.

Ziggy, indeed—Charlie flashed them a mercurial stare. The toilet seats were up when they should be down; the china cups in the upper lounge weren't arranged right and the Caps Lock feature on the keyboard in Arrangement Office Two were left in the ON position.

"Yessss, Ziggy," he breathed wearily. "I'll check on that too."

Enid smiled at Eldon. "I love this job. Love it. Love it. Love it."

Chapter Seven

10:15 A.M.

The ride was uneventful save for the usual bullshit with construction pylons and lane reductions.

"You could drive a little faster, sister," Carla huffed.

Enid didn't dare. Dying on the road to the Coroner's Office held no special appeal.

"One day, we'll meet again in a good place."

She doubted that.

"You listening to me?"

Fuck, no. I'm trying to keep my shit together.

She turned to Carla. "Yah, yah, Sure, sure."

And then I took that dress off and I never saw him again.

"Look at that stupid bastard," Carla sputtered, spying the foot cop behind the thicket with the radar gun. "What's he gonna do? Run after us?"

This was classic Carla, bitchy and scratchy, no matter what the hour. "He'll run the plate and show up at the parlor," Enid warned, reaching for her coworker's crumpled pack of smokes. "Then Ziggy'll have a fit and take it out of my pay. You know how cheap he is."

Carla scowled. Over policing was a bone of contention with her, and she never missed an opportunity to tell Enid so. "They should get the hell out of the bushes and back into their Interceptors. It's a matter of fair play for cryin' out loud!" She shook her head and shoulders to break up the rage.

"Have a smoke," Enid offered, changing lanes expertly while striking a heady sulfur match; one of several found stashed away in the old basement.

"Where in hell did you get matches?" Carla asked, grabbing the smoke greedily out of her companion's mouth.

Enid beamed; her crusty friend was making nice for a change. "The old basement; I was sent down there on a mission. Remember?"

Carla shivered; her disdain for the place was about as well-known as her intolerance for cops. "I don't know how you go down there. It gives me the freakin' creeps."

"Basement's full of history," she replied, shifting uncomfortably on her glutes. The greasy food from the night before, sliding back and forth between the pyloric sphincter of her stomach and the sausage casing of her small intestine, only added to her discomfort.

"It's full of junk," Carla countered. "There's enough crap down there to fill six dumpsters."

Enid chuckled, waving off thick clouds of cigarette smoke that filled the cabin of their body van. "So that's what history means to you—garbage?"

"Yep. Ain't nothin' in yesterday worth holdin' onto today. That's what I say, sista."

Enid checked her watch: 10:20. Not much farther now.

They made the left onto the street they were heading to and Carla, on the cusp of saying something more, clammed up. Making another left into a winding driveway, Enid maneuvered the van down a long ramp around the Mercedes and Bimmers parked in irregular clusters in the tiny underground lot that serviced the Office of the Chief Coroner.

Suddenly, Carla's mood transformed.

"Hey, slinky. How's your head?"

Carla, patting her stomach, didn't know what he was yelling about.

Carter Bilsson, pop can in hand, advanced toward her van without waiting for it to come to a full stop. Typical for Carter, who knew relatively few boundaries, he attempted a lutz onto their hood, missing the mark and coming to rest by the front passenger side tire.

"Your head cold," he said, bouncing back to take position next to the vehicle, now parked. "You said you weren't feeling well."

"Oh, yeah, that's right," she said, not remembering any of it and cursing the brain fart that she held responsible for the lapse.

Carter Bilsson looked back at her with incorrigible green eyes that complimented a massive thatch of unruly ginger hair. She grinned stupidly at him as the thing in her stomach, waking, lurched to life.

"Yeah, it's getting better," she drawled, eyeing the Celtic tattoos that laced his arms, their story growing more compelling with every visit. They locked eyes, as Enid, audibly uncomfortable in the driver's seat, suppressed a dry heave. They stared at her and she returned the favor with patent leather eyes. Carter pulled back.

"Whoa. She looks like shit."

Carla laughed, a mixture of amusement and vexation: their moment was gone. "She needs to clean up her act. You got a hummer in there and she needs to be sharp."

Carter agreed. Although not a director himself, he was well aware of the power The State Board had over the likes of Enid and the likes of her. In fact, the Board didn't tolerate any show of human frailty in the funeral directors they monitored, for like all energetic consumer advocates, it placed public interest above everything else. Boozing, merry making, fornicating, heroic lapses in judgment and questionable tastes had no place in the profession.

They continued to eye Enid, who replied with a lame

ass: "I'm good. I'm good."

"Of course she is," Carter offered, good-naturedly. Throwing open the back hatch, he helped himself to the gurney with its brandy-colored velveteen zip body bag. He turned to Carla. "You, on the other hand, haven't exactly been yourself."

She shrugged, not wanting to say more.

"The witch, again?" Carter prodded, abandoning the gurney in favor of helping her out of the van.

"You know it, kid."

Jocasta Binns had been doing a hell of a lot more than moving pictures around the place. She'd been riding Carla too, and hard, with her "pick up the trash" and "bleach out the toilet" decrees. But it was her "kill that filthy rat" command that completely rankled her sensibilities. Everybody knew about the rat that lived in the funeral home garage and his special relationship with her, and the Jocastrator knew it too. Her insistence that he be killed, and by Carla, of all people, was just plain mean.

"I could kick her down the stairs," Enid, moving at last from the driver's seat, volunteered. "Shoot her up with a strong fluid."

Carla couldn't dispute it. "It would be an improvement."

"Bag her in burlap. Shove her in the attic. No one would ever find her."

Carla, grabbing the smoke from Carter's loquacious mouth, took a deep draw. "Sooner or later, that bitch'll get what's comin' to her. Meantime, we can only wait—"

"—for her uterus to dry up and drop out?" Enid Krause was waking up.

"Exactly."

Enid circled the van coveting Carter's smoke—a Raleigh—her brand, before quitting.

Poor dear, Carla thought, the hunger on her coworker's face was obvious. Just one hit would straighten her right out, and she'd be fine for the rest of the day.

Carter seemed to know it too. "I got a real juicy one for you, kiddo," he teased. "A real embalming challenge." He looked back at Carla. "What's his name again?"

Carla fumbled through her jacket pockets for the release slip that bore the deceased's name. Male, fifty, lawyer, five days autolysis at scene, and five more days parked at the coroner's. She frowned. "Ten days gone and you can't remember his name Carter?"

Of course it was an unfair question: Club Med for the Dead played host to hundreds. Some, whole or in pieces, lay unclaimed for years. Carter shrugged, missing the opportunity to point out the obvious. "Been up for days. Been awake since four a.m. Can't remember my mother's name." He waved his pass card across the scanner opening large glass double doors. A waft of sodden earth and sour vomit greeted them.

Enid recoiled. The house was full.

"It's foreign," Carter said absently, waving them inside. "The name. The letters don't make sense when I sound them out."

"Phonics only works when it's your language, precious," Carla chided. "This dude's a Kraut. Remember his folks? Real winners."

"Yeah," Carter said, a smile more suited to a lottery winner breaking out over his gorgeous face. "Real old— you could smell the pee."

Carla rolled her eyes, for as much as Carter's hard edges were appealing; his cardinal insensitivity at times undid everything in a shot. Locating the crumpled piece of paper, she narrowed her eyes, which, in the absence of her trusty bifocals, had to be willed into focus. Carter was right; the letters didn't make sense at all: "Hoo-Er. Jer-Gin Hoo-Er. Something like that."

***

When she was young—very young in fact—Enid knew

a boy who taught her to smoke. He wasn't tall, but he had a really great car...

"There's no 'ooer' in German," Enid sputtered amidst a rush of heat from the furnace that was her changing body. Somewhere in her endocrine system, testosterone was overtaking her girl hormones, awaking the inner man that had no patience for incompetence. *Hooer, JerGin.* Christ Almighty. Her colleague's Irish-Italian roots had butchered the phonics, but not enough to confound her. "There has to be an umlaut in there somewhere." The funny little dots that appear all over German words probably hadn't made it onto the sheet, and even if they had, Carla wouldn't know what to do with them.

"I don't see any dots, sweetie," Carla shrugged.

"Something to make it "awyer," like lawyer. Let me see." She grabbed the paper with a little too much force because she knew who it was.

"Breathe. Breathe it in," he said, gripping the steering wheel. "Then blow."

Enid winced. There were a few things in this life that freaked her out: chainsaws, bad comedy, taking orders from idiots. But there were worse things: home invasions, getting caught on the sauce...

"Mächen. Mächen.[11] You are too young to be drinking..."

And then there were the unwelcomed visits from those no better than strangers. Enid, looking hard at the crumpled sheet in her hands, took a deep breath and then exhaled. "It's Heuer," she said matter-of-factly. "As in lawyer; Heuer the lawyer."

---

[11] German – little girl.

Chapter Eight

*E*nid *liked to roll things over in her head, never wanting to forget. She would do this whenever she couldn't believe her good fortune or her shit luck. She was sixteen years old, on her back, on her bed, staring up at the ceiling fan, conjuring with the entire force of her brain and heart, images of him...*

"Hey, Spaz!" Carla stuck her face in hers, forcing her back to earth. "You just zoned out."

Enid glared at her erstwhile concomitant. *It can't be him. It just can't.* She should have puked all over her shoes. She should have spewed all over Carla too, but she didn't. Instead of repeating, her guts steadied to a workable calm, just like they always did in the face of a threat. It washed over her: incredible calm, interminable resolve; the result of a nervous system switching off everything not necessary for the task at hand.

She looked intently at her colleague and her tattooed love interest. "It's Jürgen Heuer. I used to know him."

"Come with me then, and I will show you worlds you can't imagine..."

Of course, she knew him. How many guys in the city had a name like that? Mr. Heuer: A silly name—silly now; silly thirty years ago. She couldn't conceive of it ever being hers, even when she was young.

"You all right there, kiddo?" Carter asked. Granted, his one year of pre-med put him on par with her, maybe even bumped him up a notch, but his superior looks—and the way he used them—reminded her of someone else she used to know. Was it even possible that right now, for once, he was not occupying the centre of the universe?

"Gimme that," Enid replied, pulling the cigarette from his mouth. The glass doors snapped shut with a *clack*, sealing off the deplorable stink inside.

"I used to know him," she said again, puffing on the

tasty Carolina cigarette. God, how she missed them—the butts.

Mike wasn't home and mom's Catalina was in the shop. That's why mom sent him to pick me up. It was raining...

Enid looked at Carla and Carter staring at her through a veil of smoke, judging.

I used to know him. I used to know him.

The thought, skipping like a vinyl record stuck in the groove, repeated over and over again; words—just words—pounding: they hurt her.

She ground out the smoke, the better to push past Carla. Back at the van, she searched for the second pair of gloves she'd need because he'd been dead a long time, and autopsied too.

Autopsied.

Bloody hell!

"Let's use the old stretcher," she yelled over her shoulder.

"Huh?" Carla plodded up behind her, the heavy man shoes she wore vibrating a clamorous echo in their subterranean vault.

"You heard me!" She grabbed hold of Old Gimpy, the rusty stretcher still covered in sawdust and tree sap; the former, coming from Eldon's saw when he cut plywood sheets to make cremation containers; the latter, from the trailer park, where she and Fat Dougie had carried out their last removal, a real bruiser jammed between the crapper and the vanity.

"But—" Carla interjected, her dark brows knitted together in a frown that preceded words intended to invade her privacy.

"But nothing. You wanna get shit all over the good one?" She tugged at Old Gimpy, which, for all its rust, resisted, as if it wanted nothing to do with him either.

"And if you are good, very good, there will be

more..."

She pulled harder at the old stretcher, and it gave way.

"Look, I know you're a little worse for wear today, but you're acting pretty weird," Carla intruded. "This Hooer guy mean something to you or what?"

Enid pushed Gimpy towards the glass doors, which Carter reopened with a *whoosh* of his uniquely coded I.D. card. The stretcher squeaked and skidded under worn tires; dated, heavy and sorely in need of repairs, it had all the makings of a classic ride.

"I love your car..."

"I've never put a finger on someone I know. It's a strange feeling. Okay?"

Carter acquiesced. "Good thing you weren't at the house then. A real freak show. Shit all over the walls. Dr. Schaufuss told me—"

Enid, pausing, wondered how a man could be so oblivious to events going on around him.

"That's enough, idiot boy," Carla glared. "Try being useful and fetch the papers."

"Oh, hell, right," he said, not missing a beat. "I don't even know what drawer he's in."

***

The body lockers, arranged with mathematical precision, rested row on row in large banks; there were ten of these. With five drawers running floor to ceiling, and twenty-five running lengthwise, a bank could accommodate one hundred and twenty five intakes *per side*. Heuer was in drawer 35, which made him one out of a potential 2,500 intakes in the space Enid now stood in. Some occupants had been there for years.

Her throat tightened. There was an unusually high number of "Blue Labels" behind some of those doors, and their odors had overtaken the space with a ferocity easily likened to a fish market on a hot August day. They were the unclaimed deceased, held in storage for months until family was located. Heuer was not a Blue Label, but something much worse. He had family, yet he died alone and had remained unfound for many days. That bothered her.

Patting the stretcher with a gloved hand, she hesitated. It was so wrong that he'd ride out of here on Old Gimpy. It was a lousy ride; he deserved better wheels.

"There you are," Carla said, rejoining her. "I had to spew. Think I have a bad oyster..." She pointed to her gut.

Was this an attempt at levity?

"Carter?"

"He's gone ahead. I have the DC."

The Death Certificate Carla referred to is issued by the examining coroner, and provided the kind of useful information every embalmer needs to perform an effective operation: time, place, cause of death, *unless* the cause was 'pending'. In hoping for a Pending, as they liked to call it, Enid confirmed her growing dread: she didn't want to know how he died, didn't want to invade his privacy.

She held out her hand. "Which one we get?"

A Pending merely gave an estimated date of death and known place of death and nothing more. Cause was left to autopsy and toxicology results, which could take weeks, and once those results were in, only the family would know.

"We must keep this to ourselves..."

"Pending," Carla said. "You'll be flying blind."[12]

Enid closed her eyes. "I used to know him."

"I know, I know," Carla said, her voice uncharacteristically soft. "You don't have to—"

"Don't have to what? Do my job? Are you insane?" Enid had said way too much already; the gossip back at the funeral parlor would be gawd awful.

---

[12] In the absence of a definitive cause of death, a key variable in determining solution strength for embalming, funeral directors use tissue condition as a guide.

"*Ich muss.*"[13]

"Ick what?"

Carla didn't speak German, and for all they knew back at HQ, neither did Enid.

"Never mind," she said, thinking of the bottle of Johnny Walker waiting for her back at home. "What drawer? I forget."

Heuer was in the last bank on the far side of the east wall up near the ceiling. Carter had already popped open the heavy stainless steel door with its ponderous latch, releasing a waft that made Carla wrinkle her nose.

"He's baaaad!!!!!" Carter bleated from atop the god perch that was the hydraulic body lifter he'd use to move Heuer from his temporary resting place.

Enid held her breath. The stainless steel tray upon which the body rested swayed to and fro in reaction to the pull of gravity beneath. "Big boy," Carter called out, his tattoos flexing against the dead weight. "205's my guess." He swung the door shut with an echoing bang, and threw the lever, bringing them to ground.

Enid recoiled as Carla moved Old Gimpy into position; Heuer's shroud was blood-soaked in spite of staff's best efforts to prevent such.

"Any jewelry?" she croaked.

"Already picked up. His folks..." Carter studied her intently. "There was a key, too."

They had to identify him by matching wrist band and toe tag to Carter's documents, which would remain on file; his death, like his birth, preserved by the state for all time. To do this, they would have to open him.

Carter reached for the zipper, but Carla stayed his hand.

"I used to know him," Enid whispered.

"We know," Carla said gently. "That's why you're

---

[13] Geman. "I must."

not going to see him now."

Chapter Nine

11:00 A.M.

Heuer wanted to get out of there, but knew he could not. After all, it had taken some finesse to escape the house, and this was accomplished only after much effort.

Perched on the frayed arm of a creaky Scandinavian chesterfield, he moaned. His current location was not what he was expecting and it irritated him that he could not teleport to locations of his own choosing. Had he a 'say' in decisions, he would have preferred a beach in Dominica, or, at least, a seat at a half decent bar anywhere in North America. Yet, this was not the case. Heuer had hoped to beam himself around at will, but discovered that he could only go to his home, his office and now, weirdly, his funeral parlor.

Clearly, a higher authority continued to work against him, curtailing his ambitions. If the law had taught him anything, there was a way to go round. All he had to do was figure it out.

"Werner, Hannelore." The well-dressed man who greeted his parents extended a hand of welcome. Clad in wool Savile Row and Prada monk strap loafers, he seemed familiar.

"Herr Forsythe," Werner Heuer replied stiffly, pulling Heuer's mother into a seat.

Heuer guffawed: "Pah!" If anyone bore witness to his surreal circumstances, they would call him unfortunate, or cursed. Flicking an oversized fur ball off the dusty windowsill, he hoped to gain their attention.

No one noticed.

The old undertaker cleared his throat as he took up his place behind a modern pickled pine desk. "Before we begin with the arrangements—"

"Same as before," Werner interrupted, wiping his bulbous nose on a wrinkled handkerchief. "We don't need to go through all of your business."

Heuer's cousin Christophe was buried out of Weibigand's, and. if memory served, his dad had to pony up the cash to cover cost over-runs generated by his aunt, a hysterical woman of Slavic origin.

Mr. Forsythe betrayed the slightest of smiles. "I merely wanted to confirm next of kin. Your son had no children?"

Heuer watched as Hannelore squirmed. Old, in her eighties, she did not display typical grief signs like those he'd observed at other funerals. Hand wringing, copious tears, heart-felt pronouncements signifying regret, were not present. Likewise, the old man, whose main concern, if he'd interpreted correctly, was that his body be dispatched as quickly as possible.

"No wife? Girlfriend?"

Heuer was beginning to like Charlie Forsythe, not just for his snappy dressing, but for pressing the old man's buttons.

Werner squared his shoulders. "No one." He cast a disparaging glance at his wife, whom he'd left decades before, but had not found the need to divorce. "Unless *you* are concealing something."

The old woman hung her head. Silent, she moved to the ratty chesterfield, stirring with her movements, a hint of something wrong.

Heuer sniffed the air; her tangs of violet commixing with scents of must, like the old place back home in Europe. He leaned into her: "Remember, *Mutter*[14]—the place by the lake with the belching sink and artesian well? And the soap you used—"

"It smelled like rain," Hannelore said suddenly.

---

[14] German – mother.

"Be still," Werner muttered.

Heuer scratched an itch, absolving himself of their welfare; they were going to be okay. Whatever misgivings or regrets they might have, they would not show it. They were Germans and Germans didn't do that.

Forsythe pulled out a calculator with oversized buttons: "And now, Herr Heuer—" he paused to nod to Hannelore, "Frau—now that we have determined that there are no others, that you are the only kin, we can proceed with the larger decisions."

Werner moved to cut him off again with a wave of his expansive paw, but Forsythe bulldozed him: "Did your son ever express a preference?"

The old man blanched. "Preference? What are you talking about?"

"Funerals. Did he ever discuss it; comment in passing on what he might have wanted?"

"No."

"Perhaps he mentioned something at Christophe's funeral?"

"NO!" Werner shouted, pushing his chair away from the absurd girly-pink desk.

Heuer fixated on the room: with its tattered furniture and peeling walls, it was sad, worn and an affront to everything he liked or considered fashionable. Sniffing the air, he detected for the second time, overpowering notes of must, the odor perhaps creeping out from the cold air returns, or was the stink coming up through the floor boards from somewhere down below? Fighting the desire to check, he choked on the pungent smell. Must. Must I?

The door opened and a woman walked in. Wearing a large black overcoat and a morning suit, much like the ones bridegrooms wear in England, she was a welcomed addition to the proceedings.

He moved closer for a better look. Tall, broad shouldered, she was strong; had to be, he thought, imagining sinews straining beneath her clothes: she was a body mover.

"I'm sorry for the interruption," she apologized, smiling kindly at the old people, while, at the same time, doing him the great honor of bearing her teeth, an alluring set, white and sharp, that had not diminished with the years.

Charlie Forsythe replaced the calculator in a large desk drawer that housed, among other things, saltine crackers, disposable lighters, several pens and this month's edition of *Car and Driver*. "This is Enid Krause, one of our best."

Enid fobbed an awkward bow. Mannish, it was charming.

"Our son—" Hannelore managed.

"Is here," Forsythe said, finishing her sentence seamlessly.

Heuer took his place next to Enid, who, appearing nervous, fumbled with a pair of black leather gloves that were much too heavy for the summer weather. He blew softly into her hair. Of course he knew she was at Weibigand's—knew all along. Her brother kept him informed.

"Mr. Forsythe. A word?" She touched the old man's shoulder with a leather hand, pushing loose strands of spiky blonde hair away from her face with the other.

"Of course, Mrs. Krause," Charlie Forsythe said, rising from his seat.

"It's Engler," Heuer corrected, remembering something from a long time ago. "Her name is Enid Engler."

***

Charlie held his arms out to her imploring. "For once we are busy, my darling, and you tell me that you can't?"

Enid met his twinkly eyes head on. He was happy, excited—the house was full of bodies—and now she was acting up like a rank amateur.

"I'm just saying...he's *bad.*"

"Don't mind her," Eldon interrupted, striding elegantly down the semi-darkened corridor outside the pukey pink arrangement office, where Jürgen Heuer's parents were duking it out in loud verbal fashion. "She hasn't even looked at him."

He cast a withering glance at Enid, and for once, she wanted to deck him, consequences be damned. But Wheeler was the senior guy, her mentor. Steering her through the drudgery of apprenticeship, he guided her hand until she got her eyes enabling her to find the vascular bundles with ease. Such was human anatomy—all anatomy for that matter—sneaky, the structures needed to do the job annoyingly similar in appearance, areolar connective tissue concealing ropes of arteries, veins, and nerves in one cleverly concealed package. Wheeler showed her how: there wasn't anything in her head about embalming that hadn't been put there by him.

"I'm just saying," she faltered, fidgeting with a black glove. "I haven't encountered—"

"My god," Eldon thundered. "It's Pride Week, and we're having our first Queen Attack!"

She focused on Charlie. "I haven't had a chance to speak with you. He's beyond restoration. You must push for a closed casket—"

"Or cremation, I suppose?" Eldon offered snidely. "It's about time we tell families what's best." He glared at Enid. "Decision-maker be damned."

Enid held her breath. Wheeler was just being an obstinate prick. Of course, it was the family's decision, but a director has a responsibility to lay out all the options, difficult as they may be. Sometimes one cannot have what one wants.

"Easy, children," Charlie soothed. He looked at

Eldon: "You are sounding a titch like a Board stooge[15]. I know what she's trying to say."

Enid exhaled. Did he really know? She shifted from one foot to the other, her trusty brogues expanding and contracting with the rise and fall of her middle-aged feet. Did he really know that all she wanted to do was get out of the embalming?

---

[15] Common speak for an inspector dispatched by the industry regulator who quotes the rules chapter and verse.

Chapter Ten

11:15 A.M.

"Her name is Enid Engler." He kept saying it, over and over again. Even after she left the room with her old boss in tow, he kept saying it, as if to make her hear, apparently to no avail.

This wasn't the first time she'd left him behind to thrash and fume, like a jerk caught with his dick in his hand.

"Summer '81," he said, a trace of irony tickling his upper register.

He'd come to her cottage with the sound of wildlife clanging in his ears. Bullfrogs, tweetie birds, a moronic loon cackling unremittingly in the bay: it was a miracle that he tolerated any of it. His surroundings teemed with living things: bumble bees and hockey puck-sized spiders—these bastards had fur—and moths, caught and sucked dry, in webs alongside legions of ants parading assiduously in logical columns up the wall next to his head. He considered the room with its aged broadloom and cracked furniture, the cheap faux paneling—so prominent in tri state cottages—and the dirty little window above his feet, shaded by equally dirty, but oddly pleasing, dime store curtains.

Flipping on his side, he noticed the pile of twisted bed sheets, dispatched without care in the heat of cannabis and beer. Beneath the filament that passed for lingerie, something dark and barely perceptible flitted, discovered, trying to hide from the grotesque daylight.

He was naked and she was gone. The optics, incredibly poor, left him gasping.

Anyone outside his rarified space would not understand: They would see crimes committed against a pastiche of really bad behavior and they would single him out and blame him. His lungs, fighting to process the humid air, chugged and heaved against his efforts to breathe and he bit back the fear. If the choice to be made was between light and dark, discovery and subterfuge, he would choose the latter, of course. There was a big lie to assemble and without a point of reference—what time was it? Where was her brother? Where had she got to?—he was operating perilously short of intelligence.

Yesterday, he'd smashed the car and spilled the shell casings from the Smith and Wesson all over the front seat, along with an open fifth of vodka. The Chevelle, still connected to a large tree stump on the neighbor's lawn, sported a shattered grille and passenger side panel. Bent all to hell, it sent Mike Engler into peels of hysterics, so much so that Heuer, enraged at the affront, left him behind to drink the night away over cards and dice with their associates.

Equally drunk and way more stoned, Heuer embarked on an odyssey in the swamp marked by despair, cuts and bruises, and hallucinations that included, but were not limited to, analogous goat-men darned with flappy, waifish ribbons. Lost—so damned lost—he wandered in search of answers until—at last—he happened upon young Enid, whom he took to bed and prodigiously rammed from behind until he was angry no more.

Oh, shit.

Heuer gave his head a shake. He was in a darker place now, having left the confines of the ugly pink office and his bickering parents for the relative peace and calm of the Weibigand basement. Stretching out his arms, he ran the length of the dusty hallway. Dank and moist, the old plaster, reeking with history, pulled deeper, keen to tell a story. That he was entering a subterranean world of ghosts was not lost on him: he'd read Marlowe and Dante, and had anticipated a descent into hell. Quite long, the corridor possessed many doors, each accentuated by a comely knob made of crystal. "Odd," he thought, trying the first one, which resisted his machinations like a woman with things to hide.

Enid's brother, his friend, was a six foot three lay-about with a sweet nature that went south whenever he was crossed. Heuer had violated his sister; worse still it had got out of hand.

He smirked, touching his cheek.

She slapped him hard, his face ballooning on contact. Were it not for the uncertainty, the not knowing about what would happen next, he would have stayed for more. Definitely more.

He stopped mid-step, his foot frozen absurdly above the floor. Enid Engler...Krause—it's Krause now, and he resisted the temptation to re imagine her wedding day, which he had surreptitiously not been invited to: candlesticks, crystal, a new feather bed, people dancing in circles with big hats on their heads. He put his foot down. Ludicrous.

"That bothers you?" A voice, clear and cutting like a lonesome prisoner's in an adjacent cellblock, echoed out from an indeterminate location.

He reeled, at first startled, and then pleased: someone or something was reaching out to him.

"She married a Jew," the voice, decidedly female, continued.

"No—yes—no." He moved slowly, not wanting to alarm the source. "No. It doesn't bother me," he repeated, grabbing hold of the nearest doorknob for support. "But, that I am hearing things does."

A flutter of dust and a light chuckle, gauged, no doubt, to reassure him that it was not sinister, had some effect, although his language became impossibly formal. "And how is it then, that you know my mind, and I, not yours?" More titters.

"You speak English like an immigrant. Then, too, I should know. I am one also."

Heuer wiped his forehead with a free sleeve—he was sweating; or was it condensation born of his warming skin in the fetid damp? "I repeat," he said, a little high on the curt side, "How is it that you can read me?"

"You think you can read the minds of others and I cannot?" came the reply. "You have been doing it since your waking. And what you think you hear, you are merely *perceiving*."

A weird oracle to be sure, it spoke in riddles, like every ethereal being he'd encountered in literature. And what was this talk of waking? He'd waked himself, or so he thought. Time to go on a limb:

"My Lord?" Heuer asked, half-serious.

"No."

Ragged lace curtains, fluttering from a distant window further down the corridor announced the onset of fresh air that filled the space like copious amounts of Amazon rain.

"Someone who knows," it continued.

Heuer hated gamesmanship; he'd play acted his entire life. Surely, this would stop in the Afterwards.

"I think you want to get out of here very badly," the voice continued, gently, "and it is within my means to provide you everything that you need to that end."

A tall lamp of ancient origin flickered in a large room ahead of him. Piled high with boxes and debris—a compendium of past lives—the space reminded him of a place he'd just come from and was not anxious to see again.

"You are correct in this," he said, eyeing the lamp that continued to flicker improbably, its cord frayed, the electrical plug, undisturbed and unconnected, lying dimly on the dirty floor. "I want to leave, but—" He cast eyes at the inanimate object before him; brass, wood, brushed metal: it might have been beautiful once, but not anymore.

"You were expecting a burning bush?" The voice sounded disappointed.

"No," he said quickly. "I've met far too many of those."

Chapter Eleven

A German wannabe, Werner Adolphus Heuer was a polymorphous cretin of Austrian origin. Small, both in mind and body, he had tremendous appetites, all of which skewed towards becoming more than what he actually was. More open-minded folk would have called his drive ambitious, others less charitable, ignominious. His tact, classic in its narcissism, embraced the moldy old ethos of ethnicity over geography, and, as such, he was first in line when Anschluss[16] came to Vienna.

For him, the rhythmic tapping of jackboots on pavement went beyond forced occupation; it was the end of the road after a long trek. His belief that he belonged to something bigger was made whole when Austria disappeared into the German Reich and this belief remained, outlasting any bon mots that western democracy could temp him with.

So committed was he to the idea of his Germanity that, years later, on receipt of his first American passport, he got into a protracted and embarrassing pissing match with Ingham County, insisting that his birthplace was Vienna, Greater Germany and not Austria—"a place of violins and homosexuals."

His request was politely declined on the grounds that, music and queers notwithstanding, Austria was very much Austria in 1920, and that fact was immutable no matter how looney the argument got.

11:45 A.M.

Heuer yawned. The arrangements were dragging, and while he rooted for Charlie Forsythe, he could not help but

---

[16] The annexation of Austria by Germany prior to the Second World War.

admire old Werner, whose obstinance in the face of skilled salesmanship outmatched the man in the snappy loafers.

At the mere suggestion of immediate cremation, he got his hackles up, demanding to know what the funeral director was trying to hide from him.

"My son was identified through finger prints, and on the strength of this I had to believe the authorities that it was him. Now you want to rush him off to the ovens. I'll have none of this."

Charlie looked aloft as if contemplating a deep thought. In fact he was. There were whispers of inconsistencies at the coroner's office where the death was concerned: An unlocked door where eight dead bolts had been installed—presumably, by the late Mr. Heuer himself—lights on in every room except for the bedroom, strange inclusions in the bed suggesting another person was present...

Heuer winced.

"Stop it," Hannelore interjected in Deutsch. "The war is over. Must you bring the Jews into everything?"

Charlie Forsythe swallowed hard, for while he was not fluent in German, he appeared to know what a *Juden* was. Were his parents equating the proposed cremation with the Holocaust, Heuer wondered? The undertaker jumped in before the old folks had a chance to pursue it further. "There is nothing being hidden here. My concern is a practical one. There is the question of appearance and the malodorant nature of..." He studied his hands. "I just thought—"

Heuer chuckled at the notion he stank. Given his obsession with appearances, his body state was just another in a series of comeuppances designed to bring him to heel. Yet it had the opposite effect; there was no desire on his part to be on display in a casket—he eschewed the spotlight now as ever before—and his stinkiness *de facto* would merely confirm what coworkers and fair-weather friends knew all along as far as his character was concerned.

Werner cut Charlie Forsythe off. *His* family always went with oak caskets and three days of visiting. That's how it was. "And that is how it will be now. *Verstehen Sie?*—understand?" the old man asserted. "We *will* have a casket. And I trust, Herr Forsythe that you will make this so and without mistakes."

Heuer rubbed his hands together. This was a very clear dig at Cousin Christophe's funeral, and the costs associated with it. Aunt Vilma pushed the boundaries when she ordered the full stationery package; but when she ordered two seven seater limousines—one for her and one for the rest (so that she wouldn't have to sit in the same cabin as Werner)—she went over the top.

"I never paid for those limousines," Werner reminded Charlie, "and I'm not going to start now." He looked at Hannelore, his eyes withering. "I've paid enough."

From his perch on the dusty Finn Juhl, Heuer assented. Like the old man, he had no time for chicanery; less time for careless expense. Charlie Forsythe looked down at the carpet, smiling at some secret knowledge not readily apparent to his customers. A little beast, four-legged, black and shiny, played with the buckles on his fine Prada shoes and the old man didn't seem to mind.

"A strange place," Heuer conceded, remembering his conversation with the lamp. "A strange place, indeed."

***

Enid hadn't seen Heuer in a very long time and thought it foolish to make more out of this than what it really was.

"You've been smoking," Fat Dougie said, accusatorially. Slouched and rumpled in the adjacent office chair, he was annoying on a good day. That she had to wrestle with questions both moral and ethical made his presence all the more vexatious.

"You're smelling Carla," she said, dismissively.

Dougie's porcine eyes disappeared in crinkles of dimpled pink flesh. "Whatever." He got up and walked over to the selection room where he switched on the light. "Come give me a hand."

Enid huffed. "With what? Charlie's talking them down to cremation. They don't need to see caskets." She surveyed the room, deciding that nothing in there was suitable for him anyway.

"Why are you hiding up here?" he asked. "Come down to the party."

"I can't," Enid replied, drawing the chenille comforter tightly around her body. "It's too hot out there."

Actually, it was too hot in her bedroom. Heuer looked over his shoulder at her as he locked the door...

Dougie moved from casket to casket, fluffing each cushion expertly. "That's not what I was told," he said, brushing a thick coat of dusk off the top of the oak rental with a sweep of his hand.

"What do you mean?" she countered, her voice commanding.

"Whoa!" Dougie looked at his watch. "Almost lunch. You gonna eat before you embalm?"

"I don't have permission to embalm," she countered, taking her place next to him where she fine-tuned his work. "There." She brushed off the last casket, a magnificent mahogany with a generous three-inch plank. "And besides, Charlie's talking them into a dump." She hated to use that term—dump—because it was disrespectful, intimating that Heuer was garbage. Yet the practice of cremating first and having a service at a later date had been reduced in the industry nomenclature to just that—a dump.

Dougie replaced the laminated price card with essential merchandise details on top of the mahogany. "Uh, uh. Eldon says they're going for oak, and that we're to call

Pastor Ubel for Saturday."

Enid froze. Saturday was five days away. She couldn't have Heuer under foot for five days—it would break her mind.

He meant the world to her. She already had the dress picked out.

"Eldon had to take off," Dougie continued. "Didn't say what for, but I'll betcha he's gone to do his laundry, lazy bastard."

Enid was still stuck on Saturday as well as the choice of clergy. "Ubel? Logan Ubel?? He's a creep."

Dougie inclined his big head, eyeing the over-sized air duct that spewed out musty air and dust on the newly cleaned caskets. "Don't let the Jocastrator hear that. She's devoted to Logan Ubel."

It figured. Jocasta pre-arranged the funerals and Ubel buried the bodies soon after—too soon many said. Enid wondered if they were in league, serving some darker purpose.

Dougie continued to rattle on about his food and the strange pastor, while Enid, moving on, hung her head in quiet contemplation.

Why is this happening to me?

In small towns, undertakers always embalmed people they knew. And in cases where family members were involved, an embalmer from a neighboring town was brought in. Heuer wasn't family, but he was no stranger either. At the same time, *too much* time had gone by, and she questioned her right to feel bad about his passing. Was this an excuse to abandon her duty?

"You want anything?" Dougie asked, heading for the door and outside, where a number of highly unhealthy, but very tasty, food choices awaited.

"Courage," she mumbled. "Lots and lots of courage."

Chapter Twelve

12:30 p.m.

■ ■ I would think very carefully before blundering around upstairs," the lamp cautioned, as Heuer resolved to see Enid again. They had, how could he put it, parted on the worst of terms, and he was especially curious to see how she was handling his presence.

"I'm surprised you ever gave her a second glance," the lamp offered somewhat snidely.

He stopped, one foot on the first treader leading to the upstairs and her.

"Your tastes were, shall we say, low rent?"

Back in 1994, when Heuer was in his thirties and should have known better, he disappointed a woman, who, in turn, threw him out of her apartment. "Thanks fer nothin'," she yelled, with a bitchiness that confirmed her place in society, along with a trucker belch to match. He had only himself to blame. He'd been slumming in a drecky bar not consciously looking, but hoping for something willing to come his way. It was late and it didn't take long for her to find him.

"You lonely?" Her teeth were gapped and grey. "I'm lonely."

It was a troll culled from a nightmare, and it was well-suited to his surroundings—cramped, pungent and marked by scents of perspiration and fish. Drunk and smoking, she pressed her big ass cheek into his side. Smells made acute by an ancient fryer in the back advanced across the room. Beer batter wafting with the aid of large ceiling fans co-mingled with human notes of urine and beer to complete the parfum excellence. She blew on him, her breath rank, her brazenness an homage to that old cliché that you get what you deserve.

He smiled. His skin was better than hers.

"There is a cure for that," he said. "Loneliness."
His accent, strange and unfamiliar, rolled across her and having the desired effect, she got to the point.

"There's wine and a fuck back at my place."

He leaned back inviting her to apply her hands, which she did with easy self-assured strokes. The heat crept across his abdomen tightening the hairs in their follicles, twisting. She was good; real good: the kind of good that many years of applied field work made possible.

"Well?" Her tone was commanding.

She was not tall and she was not pretty. But she had the je ne sais quoi that demanded a second look. Her grip on him tightened. Heuer narrowed his little eyes, stripping away her paint and her arts.

He was intrigued by her callousness—she was very crude—and by her certainty. She might have been forty or a really rough thirty-five—it was difficult to tell in the smoke and neon. If she was a door, her weather stripping would be cracked and peeling. He reached for her, rolling lengths of dry colored hair through smooth hands.

A pro to be certain, she was also a bleary old douche bag, deflated in spots, and her insistence forced the issue. He'd emerged after a lengthy dry spell broken by a disparate coffee shop girl who was morosely tight, sexually bereft and, lacking common decency, had not the wherewithal to fake it. This one at least looked like she would and she wouldn't cost a dime either.

Back at her place—her home where she washed dishes and slept off her excesses—he tried to remember her name but could not. This was because he hadn't bothered to ask. What he would remember—and this would rank as one of those great life moments—was her thick pink candy-colored lip gloss, which deposited thick tarry skids on his body as she worked him. Well worth the risk of catching fleas.

In hindsight, she deserved a reward—the pearl necklace she begged for through hastened gulps of forced air. But he didn't give it to her. He had too much to drink and with a trunk full of problems waiting in the parking lot, he allowed the facts to rule over him. In this, he made a colossal blunder.

"What's wrong with you?" she demanded, impatient. The accent, the inane foreignness that had so charmed her earlier was a source of irritation now, and she did not hold back. "You some kind of faggot?"

Heuer, unmoved, decided that the creature with her lined and tired face suited the deprecatory remark, and as she paused to extract a stray hair from her top teeth, he wondered what it would be like to hit her very hard.

"Who talks that way?" he said, vowels thickening. He rose as if to cash in poker chips at a Vegas table. "I thought you capable of better restraint."

She looked at him, features agog. Clearly, she was unaccustomed to such heady treatment. The Old Boy, hard, yet unmoved, could have very easily spit back into her sloe eyes, but that would have been a waste of precious natural resources. Instead, Heuer opted for an apology to his longest most enduring friend—for putting him at risk, for allowing him to go down her weather beaten old throat. This he said out loud when he could have just as easily kept it in. It was a cruel thing to do and she, not surprisingly, took offense, withdrawing all favors with a clipped 'get the fuck out.'

She called him a prick. She called him an asshole. Perhaps he was…

***

From Heuer's point of view, nothing could have been better. He was the audience and first principal in a very strange play, and as a nascent arts aficionado, he wasn't about to let this one go without savoring it to full effect.

Enid Krause nee Engler had made her way down to the embalming room where he lay waiting for her. She paused on her way to dither over some emails and, he noted with approval, to check out Kijiji for vintage GTO's. Next, she mucked about with the coffee maker, juicing up her brew with two bags of pre-packaged Columbian. This, he noted wryly, was not the wisest thing to do when one's hands were already shaky. It was apparent to him that she liked her booze as much as he did, and if she were to play around with sharp things, she stood a good chance of facing him sooner, rather than later.

"It is here that you must speak to her," the lamp intruded, muddling his thoughts and destroying his pleasure. He did not like this popping in and out at will inside his head. He hoped her powers were limited to audiences in the basement, but not so—she was a body trapped in a house she did not choose, yet her spirit travelled, permeating the mind at will. "If you want to move on, it must be so. Put things right, *mein Schön.*"[17]

He frowned at her use of '*Schön.*' It was his term of endearment, yet she took it for her own, as if her right to trample him escheated once he agreed to do her bidding.

Make amends. Sure. The Holy Moly Book of Hooey said so, but to which place would he go thereafter? The land of milk and honey, where everyone ran around in bed sheets? Or the other place, where no amount of sunscreen would help? "Neither," the lamp said confidently, her words ironic, because she was a lamp and obviously hadn't been anywhere. "To your purpose," she said, twisting him in the direction of Enid, who muttered under her breath as she fumbled with her earrings.

He grinned, longing to see what she would do next: Fraulein Engler was obviously struggling over his dramatic return, and for good reason. They had not parted on the best

---

[17] My beautiful.

of terms. She wept sentimentally in the coroner's suite—
woman's tears—much to her colleague's chagrin, and now
she was dragging her feet like a shotgun bride. Walking
alongside her, he thought about theatres and floorboards
and actors moving from mark to mark, their steps mapped
out strategically on the floor with sticky tape. "This is why
people spend so much time and money on make believe,
Mächen,"[18] he said. "It's so much better to watch."

Enid managed to get past the door that separated the
O.R. from Weibigand's outer hall, where she was greeted
by the buzz and hum of a big fan that would keep his stink
off of her. He concentrated on the noisy traffic that was her
brain: like car tires spinning, rubber burning, a lonely heart
hammering, and an incomprehensible fear. He was in
despicable shape and it would take every ounce of skill to
bring him to heel.

The prep room, variously known by Weibigand
employees as the morgue, mortuary, O.R., and Theatre of
the Arts, was unspectacular. No bigger than ten by thirteen
feet, it was tiled from floor to ceiling in that troublesome
mint green from the 1950s, which, much to Heuer's
irritation, had made an unwelcomed comeback at his
workplace. It insinuated itself on to walls and, more
preposterously, on to the boardroom table top by way of a
vintage Lalique insert that turned out to be fake. Give him
Augusta or Verdoro green on a Sixties era Catalina or 2+2
and he was golden. But ersatz green in a slaughterhouse?

"Ugh." It made him think of boogies.

Everything else in the room was either stainless steel
or glass block; the former for better sterilization, the latter
for conferring light while cleverly blocking out the view of
prying eyes from the street.

Discomfited, he watched as she ignored him, striding
past the prep table with its shrouded occupant to the far

---

[18] German. "Little girl."

wall, where her instruments and chemicals were stored in sensible metal cabinets. Every color and parts per million was represented in sixteen ounce plastic bottles that she now sorted through. It was all formaldehyde to him, but to her it was the stuff that would keep him around just long enough until everyone could finally say 'goodbye.'

He noted with interest, her running monologue as she pulled bottles from the shelves and emptied them into an innocuous looking machine. 'Portals of entry.' 'Tissue gas.' 'Crepitation.' Things he'd not heard of before. He was fascinated.

She stirred up a garish red solution that apparently would do the trick, although he wouldn't bet money on it. He was worsening by the hour and, in contradiction to everything he thought he knew about her, so was she. She was perspiring, depositing copious amounts of fluid on to her collar. But even more perturbing was the satisfying nod she loosed off as she snapped on her surgical gloves. They made a *crack, crack* sound that reminded him of ice breaking under tremendous pressure.

She took hold of the zipper and pulled, looking at him for the first time.

He'd been her brother's friend and a fixture in her house growing up.

Nothing more.

Heuer, standing behind her, spoke to her thoughts, a place where he always had the greatest impact when they were alive, young, vital. "He's nothing. Do your job."

Shadow crossed over to play with the messages in her cerebral cortex.

So the feeling grabbing hold of her guts was a human reaction to a fellow traveler's death?

"Yes," he replied, "Nothing more."

And you didn't come back here to punish me?

"You know I can't answer that."

***

Her mouth was warm and wet, and her teeth, still sharp with the newness of youth, tapped rhythmically together as she rattled on about some boring documentary she had seen. It was the only way she could catch her breath. "I love animal shows," she said into his ear, the scent of her carrying ethereally on the air. "The cheetah. The chase. The blood."

"Yes. Yes. I love them too," he agreed, silencing her mouth with his own. They met head on, tongues twisting, his hands beneath her clothes, grabbing. She let him do this. She did not mind.

1:00 P.M.

He drew closer for a better look: Her face, although aged, was still good and he delighted at her nearness, at once feeling the intimacy of the small room.

"Oh, Heuer. What the hell?"

This wasn't the first time he'd heard her speak that day, but it was the first time she'd addressed him directly and by name. Moreover, she spoke English, which was not her way when they were alone.

"*Einfach.*[19] Have you forgotten our language?" he said. "Have you forgotten so entirely?"

Apparently she had, her mind, cluttered with strange questions clearly meant for god or the unseen thing or whatever the hell it was she still believed in, smothered anything that passed for common sense. Still, the circumstances being what they were, he could concede a little softness.

"I have not forgotten," he whispered. "I haven't forgotten a thing."

Mike, of course, had kept him up to date on her whereabouts and the things she did, although he took care

---

[19] Take it easy; easy now.

not to ask too often, not wanting to alert her brother to anything other than a casual interest.

She bent over to adjust the table he lay on, a tinny thing with beveled sides and a drain hole that opened into a large sink that washed away all the human goop her ministrations would produce.

A surge of emotion overtook him.

"I loved that car," she said.

Heuer gripped his shoulders to shake off the chill. She was referring to the SS with the rally wheels that were so hard to find. She pretended to love that car because the car meant everything to him.

"Remember me," he said, feeling ridiculous—he was not Hamlet's father and this wasn't Shakespeare.

"Where have you been all these years?" she asked, wondering what type of behavior brought him into her care.

Had he read her correctly? It was a good question. Had he stuck around the coroner's office long enough, he might have found out. But years of careful, secretive drinking had almost convinced him that he didn't have a problem. Once faced with the hot coroner and her circular saw, he felt otherwise, tempering his curiosity by quitting the scene. He, quite simply, had no desire to see with his own eyes the true state of his liver.

Enid removed the heavy, polyethylene plastic bag that had been his cocoon for close to a week. What emerged was far from butterfly. Adjusting her mask, she condemned him for things he could not control, the rapid rate of decomposition being one of those.

His faced darkened, remembering their dance—not a physical one in a hall—but the obscure, effluvial one that stank, rotting in its insincerity. How long did he wait for her while she traipsed around without a compass to guide her?

He reached out for her, but she remained stiff and unresponsive, straining against the weight of his body, pushing him, arranging him "just so" on her ludicrous table with "positioning devices" meant to keep his hands in place.

This angered him and he wanted to shake her for not hearing, but she was too busy, examining him for punctures and abrasions over and above the mess left by the coroner's examination. She cut him top to bottom in an effort to confirm or deny foul play, and still, had not figured him out.

Enid's eyes burned incandescent, backlit by the light of the afternoon sun. It shone through the glass blocks, reflecting fluidly off the shiny tiles that surround them. She murmured something inaudible.

"Ah—" he said, combing amorphous fingers through her bleached, choppy hair. "You cut it. You cut your hair." Another disappointment in what should have been a heart-warming reunion. *Gemütlichkeit,*[20] it was not. "Why would you do such a thing?"

She let go of his hand and it hit the table hard. "I'm sorry."

Heuer stopped, hoping he'd gotten to her. The lamp warned him this might happen, and of the consequences if it did. He had been brutal to her, and if he could not make her soften, he could never leave.

She picked up his hand again, cracking each knuckle with the effort.

He strained to catch her thoughts, his supernatural abilities increasing exponentially with the weight of what he was seeing:

Be gentle. Tissue's poor. Cause of death unknown. Where the hell have you been?

He drew back, like a kid stumbling in on his parents after spying something he ought not to have.

"When was the last time I saw you?" she demanded,

---

[20] An atmosphere of good feeling.

97

her vertebrae cracking as she returned to her full height.

"*You* know," he accused. "*You'd* never forget a detail like that!"

She reached for a medieval-looking levered tool with a bolt-action spring slide. This, she turned over in her gloved hands, spinning the barrel with a *whoosh, whoosh* between thumb and forefinger. It was a needle injector; its application wince-inducing.

"What shall it be Herr Heuer? The barbs or the sutures?"

The needle injector was used to wire the jaws, a necessary atrocity to keep a dead man's mouth shut. She tugged at his lower lip, testing the integrity of the tissue. It gave way, separating from the bone. Enid scowled. He'd never been easy with her—at least, that's what she thought, as she rapidly re-wrote history before his eyes. "There's no way you'll take a stitch," she hissed, loading a tiny nail with a long brass wire attached on the flat end into the barrel of her lethal weapon.

Heuer shrugged, crestfallen. "Everything's my fault, eh? At least it won't hurt anymore."

She tilted her chin in agreement. Barbs would be "easier"—he'd need two; one above the top teeth and another under the bottom row—and if that didn't work—if the bones shattered because of osteoporosis—she could do something extreme with a big needle and a butcher cord.

1:30 P.M.

She adjusted her grip on the large blade. Fingers encircling the hilt, her thumb on the butt steadied her aim as she drove the spine down into the squirming white flesh held fast by her free hand.

"Do you make it a habit to clean the fish while it is still alive?" he asked, closing his eyes against the vapid breeze off the lake.

"There is nothing I have done that you have not done yourself," she replied.

The act, swift and unsentimental, silenced her victim in what could never be confused for a humane gesture.

She considered her hands as she slipped nimble fingers into the trigger mechanism.

"So this is how you'll deliver the punishment?"

She smiled. The injector was made of surgical stainless steel and operated like a trip hammer, with a piston that drove a nail in deep when the mechanism was activated. Enid depressed the plunger several times, liking the sound of each pull.

Click, click. Click, click.

"What a frightening creature you are," he marveled, impressed.

Enid frowned as she loaded a shiny barbed needle into the barrel. Had he any idea what he was putting her through? And what message was God sending her by forcing her to endure this awful test?

"You are the last person to touch me," he whispered.

She forced his head backward, retracting his upper lip to reveal the bony structure of his maxilla.

"How is it that we fell out of touch?" she asked, positioning the barrel just above his right canine. *Click, click's* followed in rapid succession as she pulled the trigger four, five, six times, driving the needle in deep and then repeating the action on his lower jaw.

Heuer shuddered as she wired his mouth shut for good.

She smiled at him. "Did you ever think of me?"

She turned to her instruments and her formaldehyde, her carbolic acid and her trocar—the embalmer's wand—that magically preserved a man's insides by way of many pokes. There were several hanging on the wall, each with its own unique history and owner. Enid reached for the one with the widest diameter. A little over two feet in length and gleaming, this one was hers.

A cloud passed over and the room grew dark.

"Why did you cut your hair?" he murmured.

She did not answer; opting instead to recite out loud his tissue condition, approximate time of death, the date on which he'd been found, the time he'd spent in refrigeration, the date of his funeral service. All these variables figured in how she was supposed to embalm him. She put the trocar down, hoping she'd not need it: he was a "post" and didn't necessarily require one, unless his vascular system was completely shot, and then she'd have to get the fluid into him by poking from the outside.

"I'd forgotten about you," she said suddenly, as she started up the Porti-Boy, a high-pressure injection machine that imitated the pump action of the living heart.

Heuer clutched his throat. He was not ready. There was still so much to do—the files at the office, the pornography under the bed, the holographic will squirreled away in the safety deposit box where no one would find it—all had to be dealt with.

And Enid.

What guarantee did he have that he'd still be here, next to her, after she pumped his body full of chemicals?

"Wait. Please!"

Enid took hold of an Egyptian looking instrument. Hooked at one end, she affixed it to the first suture located at the intersection of the large Y-shaped incision that divided his chest into east and west. Tugging sharply, the stitch gave way.

"No. Don't."

She stopped. "My embalming instructor said there'd be days like this. Mind you, Herr Heuer, he was a guy who embalmed his own cousin—'a final expression of love,' he called it."

Heuer drew back. She was giving him the creeps.

"Why did you stop coming to the house?" she demanded.

Behind her, the Porti-Boy chugged and farted, its candy-colored fluid contents frothing up nicely. Double-checking the clock on the wall, she set the pressure gauge fifteen pounds per square inch, a measure of how fast the fluid would penetrate his tissues if his vessels didn't burst under the pressure.

Her embalming assessment complete, her fluid mixture ready to go, there was nothing left to do than to do it...

Chapter Thirteen

August, 1989

*E*nid stood on the driveway in her silly bridesmaid costume, her back-combed hair askew where the ridiculous baby's breath flowers used to be, before he pulled them out. How sad she was, her lower lip quivering under smudged grease paint. "You've been with someone," he said, not accusatorially. How typical, his lawyer's words—she'd heard them a million times and they no longer impressed her. Of course, when they had, she had threatened to follow him, to go to law school and become like him. What she didn't know was that she'd made the transition already—she was him—and didn't need school to be that way. She took another pull from the scotch bottle she was holding, a damning accessory to go with the royal blue taffeta sweep of her Dior dress. "You poor little bitch," he said. "You have no idea what's been done to you."*

Monday 1:45 P.M.

Enid could not remember the last time they met, and wondered if that was why she never saw him again. Heuer, astonished by her lack of recollection, could not help but be put out by her lack of sentiment. "That's not you at all, *Schön*. You are not remembering properly."

"Sometimes you don't have a choice," she replied.

Her embalming instructor had made that abundantly clear. "When you work in a funeral home, you do your job and you do it bravely." It was like a badge of honor: doing your own. Some funeral directors embalmed their own parents. Enid Krause had a choice and she made hers.

"You'll be amazed by what you can get used to," her teacher said.

Enid finished closing his mouth—the barbs took and the bones held—but her heart was racing. The initial prep was nearly complete and she would have to open him up soon if she was to continue the procedure. She steeled her mind as she closed his eyes and swabbed out his nostrils.

"You've got me now," Heuer said.

Enid shook her head. "No. I don't. You were never mine."

He touched her shoulder. "If that is so, then why do you cry?"

"*Post hoc, ergo propter hoc*,"[21] she sniffled, wiping a prodigious boogie onto her blood spattered sleeve. "And now I go down that road."

He knew it well—the road—a dangerous path where aging rockers often ventured in song, searching for—what? Redemption? Vindication? A reason to party? "I can help you with that, if you like?" he soothed, remembering the last bottle of scotch he'd downed with great fondness. "But there's a caveat, my dear: The past is not a place of comfort, but of disappointment, despicable, full of false memories and delusions. I can take you there, if you promise not to stay too long."

She thought of him, at once wrapping herself in warmth, sympathy and, perhaps, worst of all, *love.*

Shit.

She'd been warned about this at school: The danger of becoming too involved. "Keep your eye on the ball, stay focused, stay clinical, stay professional," her teacher thundered.

She began to sob, sputtering with such vehemence, oaths that ran contrary to her true feelings. "What utter bullshit!"

"No," he said, stepping between her and her patient. "Just unfinished business."

---

[21] Latin. "After this, therefore because of this."

Enid loosened her tie, unaware of the blood on her gloved hand. Unfinished business indeed—the idea was too bizarre—something cherished between her and the dead man on the table was just wrong and she wasn't going to play. She tossed the spring forceps, stiff with the torsion of angry fingers, into the concurrent disinfection bath, where they landed with an undignified *splosh*.

Don't look back, her heart thumped. But she didn't hear it. Against its wild beats, Heuer clasped his hands to her ears. The past *was* a wasteland of wreckage and regret, which was precisely why she had to go there. *"Erinnern Sie sich Schön. Erinnern*—Remember, beautiful. Remember," he urged.

Enid, startled, whirled round. It pressed. It was right behind her.

God help me.

She focused, hard, sifting through dust and faded photographs tucked away in the back of her mind. Images, at first slow, came on faster, spinning, disorienting her, pleading, appealing, making a case for what was: Youth, eyes of indigo, penetrating, distant, in complete opposition to her own made large by the lamplight; her eyes, yellow, coming out of the darkness; at the cottage, undulating bands of purple snaking across the constellations; the late day sun burning large behind the blinds. A dramatic moment, he looked at her, caressing. "You seem like a wolf to me."

Pure lightning followed by an awareness of teeth— her own—their surfaces individual and unique, and very sharp.

You seem like a wolf to me.

He ran his thumb across the surface of her teeth pausing meaningfully at the canines. Mesmerized. What magic is this? He was speaking German to her, winding her long hair tightly around his wrist. "What does the wolf do?" he commanded.

Enid looked at Heuer, blue-black on a festering table. "I'm hysterical. I must not falter."

A weepy funeral director was like a soldier who refused to fight. It was a dereliction of duty plain and simple. And yet, his blood was everywhere—on the table, in the sink—and there had been some splashing when she unshrouded him, so it was on the walls and on her shoes too.

She let out a guttural laugh, its coarseness surprising even her.

"You bastard. You *have* done this on purpose."

Recall happens just like that, and when it does, it's like taking a bullet.

"I think I wanted to marry you. Now I'll push you up the aisle in a box."

She backed away from the table and from the force of him. The survivor inside her screamed—"RUN!"

But not yet.

She was a professional and she refused to bolt from this room like a pimply teenager at a horror show.

She disinfected her instruments, covered his body, and pulled off her blue nitrile surgical gloves with the *clap*, *clap* of man-made material against skin.

"There is unfinished business here," she said, turning her back to him. Alternate arrangements would have to be made. There was no way in hell she'd be able to hold his sternum in her hands.

Chapter Fourteen

ith multiple, intersecting corridors joined by back stairs on different levels, Weibigand's is rather ant farm like. Hidden behind false walls, little worker drones surge trying to get the job done. From outside, business appears poor because of the empty parking lot. Not so. There is a cycle in funeral service that follows logically, much like the cycle of life and death. Beginning with the death call, it progresses to the "getting ready."

The upper floors are silent except when there is visitation or a service in the chapel. Underneath, below the street, there is action. The deceased is brought in through the back door and prepared below stairs in the O.R. just off the staff room, where the workers eat, sleep, wait, in anticipation for the "next thing." Farther down the corridor, past the selection room with its caskets and urns is the galley office where churches are booked, cars are hired, and graves are ordered open. Preachers, soloists, and organists are arranged for here also. Some of these need rides on the day of service and extra staff are called in when necessary...

2:00 P.M.

"Drought's over man," Fat Dougie hollered to Robert, the intern, who picked his way through the back door. Fat Dougie, Weibigand's only funeral director's assistant, was in the staff room inserting incorrect words into Eldon Wheeler's lunchtime crossword puzzle. He did this not out of spite, but out of an inherent need to exercise the imp that struggled beneath his skin. Robert shook his head in dismay. "He's gonna fucking kill you if he catches you." A young man, Robert was keenly aware of Eldon's place in the Weibigand pecking order, and as Robert's preceptor—an elegant word for babysitter or minder—Wheeler held tremendous power over the youngster.

As a candidate for licensure, young Robert was required to complete fifty embalmings by year-end. The "where" and "when" of it all was decided by Eldon Wheeler. As such, the kiddo was at odds over anything that might implicate him and thus threaten his good relationship with the senior embalmer.

"Just a word or two," Dougie said, shrugging it off with ease. "He can't see without his glasses anyway." This was true, for Wheeler's greatest fault was his vanity and he willingly blinded himself in order to preserve his fine looks.

Robert sighed. He'd pulled the dreaded one to nine shift, which, in funeral parlance, actually meant one to three a.m. if they were busy. With five new calls and a rumored sixth on the go, they were getting pretty busy.

"Do you think I'll embalm today?" Robert asked forlornly. He'd had his fill of vacuuming and cleaning out crappers.

"Dunno," Dougie said, nodding in the direction of the O.R. "Krause pulled the first one."

Ziggy and Karl prohibited embalming during visiting hours; the noise and clang of the procedure travelled through the vents and could be made out in the visitation suites by keen, imaginative ears. This meant daytime embalming mostly, except when services took place. And if there was 2-4 and 7-9 visiting, preparation was delayed until *after* that.

This was why taking an intern aboard made so much sense. Senior embalmers went home after five, while a schleppy little newbie looking for a license stayed on, many times through the wee hours, with only the prep room fan and a furtive imagination to keep him company. Robert's imagination was boundless. He believed in ghosts and quite often scared the shit out of himself after dark.

The prep room door slammed big time loud and Enid, unaware of the boys' presence let her guard down. She doubled over in the hallway, clasping her midsection in what appeared to be a case of serious dry heaves. Her head, connecting with the aluminum shelf below the production board, scattered grubby chalk pieces in all directions. The impact hurt her.

Dougie and Robert, startled by the scene—it was a tad melodramatic in their estimation—kept their distance. Krause looked more disheveled than usual; her closely cropped hair stood on end and her yellow cat's eyes, normally exaggerated by Versace bifocals, were cartoonish as they enlarged on their own without aid of pricey specs.

"Need Charlie," she said simply.

"Arranging," Dougie answered, no nonsense. "He has back to backs. Won't see him 'till he takes a piss."

Not helpful.

The prep room, she was fast realizing, had become *Heuer's prep room* and she resented this intrusion. It was by no means the centre of Weibigand's, but it was the nexus of her existence, defining her more completely than the eccentric getup she wore. She tugged at her strangling tie with its black, white, and grey diagonal stripes and ponderous double Windsor knot. He was in there, behind the big metal door with its horizontal slats and peeling paint, commanding her to perform without her consent. At the mere thought of his touch, her skin, made dry by the caustic chemicals she played with, contracted, willing her to disappear.

She reached for the floor chalk and wrote on the board five simple words that summed up her position: "Mr. Heuer—too far gone."

2:15 P.M.

Carla Blue, hitherto lost in thought in the garage,

greeted her friend.

"Hello, Rat."

He bowed elegantly. A dapper fellow, he took care to smooth his shiny black fur before engaging in conversation. "You haven't told him, have you?" His tone was not unkind, merely concerned.

Carla, wishing he'd speak to others as blithely as he did to her, took her time answering offering instead a piece of near day-old doughnut, craftily recovered from the galley office floor where it landed earlier. Rat accepted the morsel gratefully. It was common for her to make these offerings, tiny tokens of friendship others not associated with Weibigand's would never understand. Carla didn't care. Fellowship with one of nature's premier disease carriers wasn't even an issue. He spoke to her and only her, and for that she was ever grateful. Love, in scarce supply, developed on merit, and there was no one as meritorious as Rat; not even Carter.

"There is nothing to tell. I don't even know which man is responsible. And I'm too old to go through with it."

The gastrointestinal problem in Carla's abdomen made a faint-hearted move to which Carla answered with an equally half-hearted pat. "Poor thing doesn't stand a chance," she continued, noting subtle shifts in Rat's whiskers. They rose and fell rapidly with each facial contraction, signaling to her that he was making judgments. Carla's voice rose sharply: "I don't know where it came from."

She fumbled for a cigarette.

"That won't do," he said disapprovingly, wagging his flesh-colored tail in the direction of the offending smoke. Carla looked at the ringed appendage with disdain: it seemed out of step with the rest of him, and that bothered her.

"How 'bout I make you a sock for that thing? Rabbit fur. I could slip it right over."

Rat looked at her uncomprehendingly.

"No, no. I'm not stoned again," she reassured. Danny Blue had seen to that when he let the crop die. "But I have, it seems, a pressing responsibility to attend to." Carla was cutting it close. Two weeks left to make up her mind.

She crushed out the cigarette without lighting it.

Eldon Wheeler kicked open the flower room door which adjoined their garage.

"Look at me," he called out, holding two potted orchids meant for the top floor office. "I'm a hot house flower."

Rat bowed to the great man in appreciation and with that, set off to find something soft to sleep in.

Carla laughed. "Yeah. And I'm a shrinking violet. You going to Charlie's?"

Pride Weekend was mere days away and so too was Charlie's annual bash. This party was legendary for all the characters it attracted. For many old school undertakers that were not "out" and never would be, Charlie Forsythe's rainbow extravaganza was the only time they could put their diamond studs on and rock out.

"Not this year," Eldon answered. "My turn to work. Might hit The Black Eagle after. Don't know." Eldon ran a finely manicured finger across the blade of the band saw he used to make cremation containers. Carla, from her rickety fold away chair paused to appreciate his hands. They were gorgeous. Like the rest of him.

"Guess we won't need your crates. We're using real caskets this week." Carla who had worked with Eldon for almost twenty years had no trouble making small talk with him, unlike Enid and, to some extent, Charlie. For unlike them, she saw through him; the gruff exterior meant to scare the others away merely attracted her more.

"Right you are, dear," he said, smiling his rake's smile. "We got another one while you were mucking around in the suburbs." (Carla was fresh off her second transfer.) "How's Krause making out?" he asked as if to imply that she was not. Enid went into the prep room just after twelve noon, and had not been heard from since. This was unusual, given her annoying habit of singing over the-top-show tunes whenever she embalmed.

Carla, giving little thought to her coworker until now, made up her mind to gossip. "Something happened at the coroner's this morning."

"That so?" Eldon was keenly interested.

"She had a meltdown."

Eldon, helping himself to one of Carla's Virginia Slims paused thoughtfully before lighting.

"Yep," Carla said, nodding for emphasis. "She knows the guy. Pretty good from what I could tell. Know what I'm saying?" She retrieved her cigarette pack from Eldon, deciding, for now, to put all thoughts of old age pregnancy to one side. Lighting up, the garage quickly filled with soft, milky rings that harkened back to pleasanter times, when smoking was okay and abortions were not talked about.

"Didn't think she had a life before that hot little husband of hers," Eldon said, adding smoke rings to the air. He fancied Enid's husband and made no bones about it whenever he found himself in Aaron Krause's proximity.

Carla snickered. "You just like his money."

"No, honey," Eldon corrected, running his hands through her shiny black hair: "I love the dark."

Lost in a mutual reverie, neither one took immediate notice of Robert, who dragging his feet, as usual, pushed his way into their space. The Rube, as they liked to call him behind his back, spoke. "Eldon? Hi! What's on for me today?"

"I'd have you scrub out the old basement if I had my way," Eldon scolded, pointing at the wall clock. Robert was one hour late, again. "But the transfers take priority. You're going to Wauchula."

Carla Blue had a thought. Although not entirely

random in nature, it sprang from an uncommon place entirely independent of her own secret agenda. She smiled. "No he isn't, Eldon. He's needed in the prep room."

2:30 P.M.

From his ceiling top perch, Rat watched with increasing horror. It was past two and without any additional appointments to deflect her, Jocasta lolled in the hallway. The staff in the garage were smoking and gossiping; two behaviors she could not abide. Both dirty and smelly, their effects travelled up the ventilation shafts, permeating the senses, always with disagreeable results. She leaned in. The metal flower room door, with its keyed combination lock, stood ajar just enough for her hear.

Rat cocked his ears. Carla Blue was talking again. Talking, talking, talking—carelessly—without a thought to who might be listening: "If it weren't for my current standing, I'd quit this dump effective—like—now," she complained to a captive Eldon, who encouraged her with an "I should have left years ago" and "this place ain't worth taking a stroke over" and "who would antagonize the bitch if you left?"

Moving closer to better gauge the eavesdropper, Rat noted alternating attitudes in Jocasta's features typified by crooked grins and over-exaggerated whispered hoots to suggest shock and approbation. She recorded every damning comment, he observed, the uptake of information stuffed with enviable speed into a mealy mind, characterized by synaptic flashes behind glassy eyes, signifying raw intelligence of the most malignant kind. She made a sucking noise, not unlike those made by the connection of moist, forced air, and poorly situated dental plates. But on closer inspection—his pale, appraising eyes, screwed down tight to get it right—he determined that she was actually licking the profligate sores that lined her uneven mouth, a result of advancing lupus. The effect wet, and damnably startling, was not unlike the *swish* of an automated carwash, albeit without the efficiency, of course.

In the past, he tried to warn Carla of the beast's near pathological treachery, but to no avail. She was stubborn, insisting that Binns, decaying from the inside out, would never come close to being a worthy adversary.

At sixty-three years of age, Jocasta was ten years older with guaranteed employment for life. A less generous person might have been satisfied on these facts alone, for they were enough to impose one's own superiority over another. But not Jocasta. She hated Carla Blue with her serial marriages, mercurial moods and curious habit of always being in crisis, and after twenty years of suffering her complaints and inane adolescent foolishness, she was done. The old crone made it New Year's Resolution One to be rid of Carla Blue by year's end.

Her whisper campaigns to date had not been entirely successful, although Forsythe, on Ziggy's direction, had cautioned Carla twice about her behavior. The younger woman, as expected, reacted badly, hurtling charges against those who dared conspire against her. Carla was a less than trusting character; new staff for one made her suspicious and rude. She greeted young Robert, for example, with an attitude that was less than kind, leaving only the toughest bodies for him to embalm and convincing Eldon—her acknowledged work spouse—that it was "good for him." Poor Robert's track record to date had been less than stellar, with one embalming failure after another. This caused even the most accepting among them—Krause and Forsythe—to question the kid's place at the college. Such were the machinations of the irascible Carla Blue, whom Rat loved unconditionally.

"And they think I'm a bitch?" Jocasta muttered derisively to the metal door she was listening at. The irony was delicious.

Carla continued to rattle away unchecked in the garage, about her useless husband, her useless job, this useless building they were standing in and the friendship that held her together.

Rat, gripped by the kind of fear brought on by really bad portents, bit down hard on his tail. Tobacco smoked Jocasta out of her second floor office; unguarded chatter gave her an unexpected *raison d'être*. Shifting her considerable heft, she tilted her head toward him. The tiny, almost imperceptible time signature of delicate claws on overhead pipes had roused the gorgon, who held his eyes rapt in a stare that froze him dumb.

"Hic est diabolus, ante me—Here, the devil stands before me."

Jocasta Binns smiled. "Hello, Rat."

Chapter Fifteen

2:15 P.M.

E nid cut right, heading off into the darkness of the north corridor. More sure-footed as she regained her legs, she took pains not to fall all over herself again. Physical failings in her business were bad, but injuries, however minor, were fatal. She touched the sticky sweet blood on her forehead, resisting the urge to taste it.

Most employers paid into a workers' compensation scheme, but not the Weibigand's. They were old school, believing like their forebears, that directors survived through natural selection. It was physical work, plain and simple, and if a man wasn't up to the task, he was out on the street.

Enid laughed under her breath whenever she came up against this. She'd grown chest hair fast enough when she pooh-poohed the little kitty heels management forced on her the first day. Her sciatic nerve gave out right on cue the first week of her internship, and she tossed the cursed footwear into the waste basket with a contempt that was conspicuously reckless. "There's them. And there's me. I am different," was her coda, recited to an audience of none. Learned long ago, quite possibly from a book of philosophy, her *veni, vidi, vici,*[22] had never let her down.

He didn't have to whisper for her to hear: Eldon Wheeler's face said it all that day—"she can't do the job"—and it was incumbent upon her to quash that non-fact before it swept through the passage way up into the owners' stream of consciousness.

And she did. She wore man shoes now— Florsheims—just like the others. And with her wingtips she conquered, going all day without so much as a pain. *This,*

---

[22] Latin. "I came. I saw. I conquered."

she thought, *was how wars were won and nations forged.* By men in flat shoes. The genius of it was breathtaking.

The shoes, along with the right to undress in front of the boys in the common change room were hard won, for theirs was a conservative business resistant to change. While she demolished some old attitudes, she was less able to counter her own.

Enid traversed the long hall with its fluorescent lights and unflattering floor to ceiling mirrors, escaping Heuer, to hide out in The Quiet Room. This, she thought, was entirely apropos. The Quiet Room was, without doubt, the most idiosyncratic spot in the house, and it existed to remind everyone of what was gone. A shrine to time-honored traditions, it was conceived and designed by Karl-Heinz Senior in deference to early classic parlor design. It had not changed since his death, and, as such, was a lasting tribute to the Father's great vision.

At least that was the bunk Enid floated whenever curious civilians wandered into this sanctuary: "Unknown to all concerned back then," she'd intone, "The Quiet Room acknowledges and gives weight to the veracity of Chinese Feng Shui." It faced east and that was "good" in as much as all good things come from the east, and it was red, and that had to be lucky too. It was a marvel of post war design mixing prewar Art Deco with Fifties Scandinavian teak and thick bourgeois corduroy. Heavy velvet curtains framed fake potted palms in conjunction with craft tweetie birds that were wired dead and upright to their elaborate perches. Enid liked this room, often napping in it undetected. It was a place of peaceable reflection best suited to those who derived little comfort from the chapel above, and it saddened her how seldom it was actually used by those for whom it was intended.

She took a deep breath and walked inside.

It was quiet, still, except for the *tinkly* sound of the fishpond.

"Why can't I hear your voice," she called out into the darkness. There were plenty of images coming to her in disjointed waves of thoughts linking her together with him. Twenty-five. Twenty. Fifteen. *Thirteen*...years of age when she knew him. Her mouth tasted cigarettes—Heuer would light them for her when they were in the car after school, and she would pray to God to let the other girls see what she was up to. Every angle of that perfect face, every nuance behind every expression; the touch of his hand—all—returned to her with perfect clarity, but she absolutely could not summon up the sound of his voice.

***

Rat should have seen it coming. He was a rat after all and therefore genetically predisposed to a shorter life. As such, he should have taken better care. But tender concern for his friend obscured his view, and this deprived him of a rodent's perfunctory need to avoid detection.

Mrs. Emmy Shawson-Cooke-With-An-"E" late of The Springs by way of Baycon Hill had died quietly in her bed in her ninety-sixth year. Owing to her advanced age, her family decided that a little-more-than-this-side-of-nothing was required to get her on her way as quickly as possible. To that, arrangements were concluded between Teddy Shawson-Cooke-With-An-"E," her great nephew and heir, and Charles Emerson Forsythe, funeral director extraordinaire.

"I'm very sad to hear of your great aunt's passing," Charlie said somberly, for he liked Emmy very much. A wealthy woman, she was a doyen, a neighborhood fixture, raising funds for world wild life, Christian children and Ethiopian famine relief. But she was more than just money. At the heart of her was a genuinely good human being who said what she meant, and acted on her commitments. In the early years, she was a constant fixture at Weibigand's, resplendent in a magnificent suite of emeralds that Charlie never tired of commenting upon. "I bring in the business,

117

don't I Charlie?" she would say through cherry lips under a pillbox hat. Indeed she did, and Charlie encouraged her familiarity. Both shared a special bond. Even after her (some said) forced relocation to the nursing home in The Springs, she never failed to fire off emails to her Charlie to make sure he was okay. And Charlie always visited her on her birthday and at Christmas.

Emeralds? Rat was barely two years old and so had never met Emmy Shawson-Cooke. But he knew well enough about gemstones and other things too, and so it was to this that he turned his attention as he repositioned himself inside Charlie's monk strap Prada slip on. They were in the front office, Rat's favorite room by far. It faced the street, was pleasantly lit, and with its high coffered ceiling, offered stunning acoustical advantages. Charlie was reminiscing with Teddy about the gemstones: They sparkled blue at their centers, spanning outward only to be confined devilishly in beveled frames of seawater green. Spectacular—like the Bering Strait meeting the Caribbean Sea. Emmy's late husband Cecil joked that they could shame Tsars and tease laughs from stone.

"I beg your pardon," Charlie said noticing Rat beneath him. It was Charlie's habit to remove his shoes in mid-afternoon to promote better circulation, but they were in the way now under the large desk and he took care not to disturb the Weibigand mascot as he moved the shoes off to one side.

Teddy Shawson-Cooke shifted from haunch to haunch, his incredible heft straining the pound for pound capacity of the Faux Toscano Victorian Rococo wing chair he was sitting on. Forsythe, sensing the man's discomfort, did his best to speed up the meeting. Emmy had prearranged her funeral and Teddy was undoing as much of it as he could because, he said, "there was no one left" and "doing her up for nothing was just plain stupid." Truth was, Teddy had the power to add the money saved from a cheapo funeral to his aunt's estate, from which he could pay himself as executor.

Charlie smiled down at Rat who, in an act of implicit trust, dozed off in his shoe.

"Allow me, if you will, to think out loud," Charlie said, in anticipation of what Teddy wanted to serve up next. If the meeting went on much longer, Emmy's casket choice would be undone too and no one at Weibigand's—Charlie most all—could bear to put Emmy into anything less than the mahogany she'd paid for years before. "Your great aunt put her faith in us to carry out her wishes. I understand where you are coming from, but I must insist on the single night of visiting she paid for."

Shawson-Cooke, in saying nothing, red-flagged Charlie, and he picked up speed. "Now the emerald suite. I trust she will be wearing it, as always?" Teddy replied that it was "long gone" save for the ring which, he hoped, "found its way out of the nursing home before someone else got to it."

Down on the floor below, Rat dreamed of Carla and, more particularly, her less than utterly no-good spouse Danny Blue—a musician in a band that had, in the space of two years, eroded the family fortune on protracted road trips through northern Canada. Designed to boost the band's profile and hopefully springboard them into other gigs in Manitoba, the latest tour had bogged down south of Parry Sound and Danny Blue had forgot to come home. The issue at hand was money. Plain and simple. And in dreams, Rat searched for a solution.

3:45 P.M.

Fat Dougie booked it to The Springs and back in record time, delivering Emmy into Robert's trembling hands. Mr. Heuer was giving him a hard time, resisting treatment like no other case he'd ever seen. Worse still, he had lost two blunt dissection needles and a spring forceps—"They're gone man, I swear"—et cetera. Eldon Wheeler, cross over his inability to complete the *Portside Brimstone and Treacle* crossword puzzle, yelled out about "professionalism" and "getting yer head out of yer ass" and "hurrying the hell up."

"Forget the embalming for Chrissakes," he hollered, more vexed than usual. "She's up in three hours. Tintivate and dress. Get going."

4:30 P.M.

Rat padded across the top of Emmy's casket careful not to disturb the pretty, but moderately priced, flower spray that adorned the foot end. It amazed him how quickly a funeral could be cobbled together when family was in a hurry.

Off to one side, taking shelter in his own invisibility, Heuer watched: *Take care my little friend. Take care...*

With all he saw and all he heard, why couldn't he see it coming?

Unfortunate Rat: All he saw was Carla.

Caught in the rapture of his own noble efforts, he took a crack at a sonnet:

"My lady black and blue, for thine my love is true..."

He sang this out as he edged closer to the shiny green bauble, still held in place on Emmy's wedding finger with sticky surgical tape. Fat Dougie, hectored by Wheeler to move faster, hadn't noticed her ring. If he had, he would have removed it before documenting the emerald's existence in the day file. None of this was done. The tape was still there.

Noble Rat sang on as he pulled at the adhesive threads:

"Take this ring and make thee mine, o'er all others 'till the end of time,

"And the Lady Blue will shine a light, for she is free now to take flight..."

The gorgon in the doorway was not moved because she could not hear his pretty verse, nor could she gauge the depth of his feelings. He was a rat, incapable of making love, beauty, or poetry.

"And you will love me, my lady 'tho I'll never see you again."

He was a rat with a ring in his mouth and he was crossing the floor of the Wisteria Room as if he had a right to be there. He didn't.

Jocasta Binns raised her arms above her head with all the passion and sensuality conferred upon her by centuries of Loom ancestors. The pain she experienced when walking from A – B, Heuer noted, had all but vanished; she gripped the shovel with remarkable ease.

"Such a shame," he said, though no one could hear, "that it always comes to this. Is it not the most misunderstood that bear the greatest gifts? And is it not so, that these gifts go unrecognized, because the bearer never has the chance to deliver?"

The shovel came down hard and fast on Rat's erstwhile, erudite head, splattering the loving heart that accompanied it in life clean across the carpet.

Chapter Sixteen

R at's body was found by Enid Krause ninety minutes post mortem in the exact spot where Jocasta Binns had cruelly left him. That she made the discovery was entirely appropriate given the kind of day she was having. She had finished her ministrations in The Quiet Room, resolving to ignore Heuer's death until a more appropriate hour. When she was calm, when she had her work done: Then, and only then, would she call Michael, her brother, and tell him the news.

The funeral home was jumping, operating at full capacity: both transfer vans were out as well as the hearse and she could hear Robert wrestling away in the prep room with his own challenges. The production board told the story: Shawson-Cooke, Shafthausen, Ridley-More, Jacobs, Lubov, Heuer. Six in all and with every staff member engaged in one useful activity or another, Enid searched for something to burn up what time was left in her workday. Shafthausen was an "embalm and hold" pending final arrangements, while Lubov was a direct disposition, free of all fanfare requiring no especial funerary attention. Jacobs was pending—his family was with Charlie that moment arguing over the value of caskets; and Ridley-More wasn't up until Wednesday. Heuer was Heuer and therefore not a concern at the moment, so that left Emmy Shawson-Cooke who was, given the time, undoubtedly in need of a cosmo and curl before her visitation later that evening.

"Bobby," Enid called out, her voice making sparks as it grated caustically through the horizontal slats in the prep room door. "Gimme the cosmetics. I'll do Emmy."

"I'm having a hell of a time in here," came the reply. "He's being a real bitch."

Enid counted the blood spatters on her shoes. "You working on Heuer?"

"Who? Shit! I don't know. It's crazy in here. And I

can't find my stuff. My instruments..."

Enid rolled her eyes. Not knowing who you were working on was not only *verboten* but also a sure sign of hackneyed incompetence. Robert was not conducting viable embalming analyses and without it, was surely using the same fluid strength on everybody placed in his care.

"Take it easy, brother," Enid cautioned. "And take the time to do it right. Heuer has to last. Understand?"

This last statement, while declaratory in tone, struck a chord with the speaker. Enid didn't know if Bobby had heard or not. The rattle and hum of the hydro aspirator cancelled out her sage advice. The machine, used to relieve the pressure in the ventral cavity of a routine case often required as much as one hundred and thirty gallons of water in a single embalming. The machine roared and the water rushed, churning hard and fast down the drain to the sewer under her feet.

No. Bobby wasn't working on Heuer. He couldn't be. Heuer didn't need a hydro aspirator because Heuer was not routine. Enid got weird again, her eyes blurring over as her mind ran the movie for the umpteenth time. Surreally, she was fifteen again, grinning stupidly as he walked to her, backed by vivid blue sky. There was water too, waves rolling up on the rocks at the bottom of the hill. She could smell the swamp, its earthy acrid odors hinting richly at the life being made out there behind the trees. And he was talking, but she could not hear. Enid strained to listen, hoping to pick up these lost words, but they were just sound bites, a word here, a word there.

He was young—twenty-one—and he had a really great car...

Bobby fumbled with the knob on the other side of the door and Enid, appalled by her day dreaming—she looked frantically side to side to ensure no one was looking—banged her sentimental head, hard and on purpose, against the prep room door before he could open it.

I'm not the widow. I wasn't even a girlfriend.

In fact, there was no widow, no girlfriend, no lover. Nobody. Carla Blue quite eagerly passed that information on to her, having pumped Carter and the gossip loving cops at 61 Division for every bit of intel she could gather. Dr. Schaufuss, Carla offered, was the attending coroner, and had joined in on the fun, describing the appearance of his bedroom, the goo on his walls, and his fine wardrobe, all of which seemed to imply all kinds of scintillating things.

Enid closed her eyes to all of this—she didn't want to know—because, deep down, she knew already. In the twenty years since their last meeting, Jürgen Heuer managed to not get caught by anybody. His only legacy, it appeared, was a house full of junk.

On first sight, the attending officers thought that he might have recently moved in, or was getting ready to move out. But opening the blinds put the scene into a completely different frame: it revealed the dust and dirt time deposits and, judging from the amount of it in his rooms; he had been with his boxes for a very long time. His home was modest and his neighbors didn't know him. Though he had many photographs, they appeared old, faded, and disconnected from the present—one could tell by the fashion of the clothes pictured and of the cars with their immense fins and real chrome bumpers.

He died alone, and no one was looking for him.

The idea of it made her sick not just because it was true, but because her colleagues had found out. Spying on him for entertainment, they talked so that she could hear, and she—equally curious—had not removed herself from the case. In so doing, she had become a party to a shameful invasion of privacy.

"Bobby!" she shouted. "Gimme the Crash Box for Chrissakes. I gotta be home in time for swimming." Julia, her daughter, was working on her fourth level badge and wanted her mommy there to see. And Aaron would have news of the new windows that were coming; the ink on the contract was still fresh.

Robert, smoke in mouth, poked his head out, looking bleary. "Here, already. You gonna bitch me out too?" Eldon had been breathing down his neck, insisting that he move faster, that he stop looking over his shoulder, that he stop acting like a first semester Christmas grad who flunks out after mid-terms—all of which was possible because all he had to work with were the decomposed and decomposing.

Enid nodded sympathetically, grabbing the lit cigarette from the kid's mouth. Jamming it into her own, she puffed with a recidivist's conviction. "It's a test, sweetie. We all get tested."

***

The body on the carpet was harmless enough—small, lacking celebrity—and yet, there was something contained in the black diamond whorls flowing across the hide that marked it for comment. Heuer poked at him gently with Robert's eight-inch spring forceps, searching for clues behind the creature's curious beauty.

Rat's fur was lovely, unlike anything he'd ever seen. And he'd seen rats before—in the back streets of India, in the thoroughfares of Zaire. This one was long and sleek like a fine running machine and when he turned it over he saw why. The heart's diameter, made visible through the shattered tissue, was no doubt exaggerated by the force of the impact that stilled it. That said it was an impossibly large organ for a creature this size; quite muscular in fact, much like the rest of him. Broad at the shoulders and haunches, it was oddly compelling, like a woman in mink.

Enid Krause paused in the doorway. Unlike Astilbe, the Wisteria Room was free of pornographic florals and gawd awful ugly faux finishes. Favoring French Provincial decor and blonde wood touches, this room was actually tasteful and Heuer had no difficulty whatsoever in placing her in it.

"Look at me," he commanded. "I'm over here."

Enid walked over to Emmy Shawson-Cooke who, while grand enough in her seven thousand dollar mahogany casket, cried out for a little TLC.

Heuer, keen for closeness, sidled up alongside her, trying to read her thoughts to no avail: she had gone damnably silent.

"Can't you feel me, *Schön?*" he asked, bearing down on her. "Don't you remember how we were?"

She remembered all right. She remembered quite well.

He had been her brother's friend and a welcomed fixture in their parents' home. He dropped by for food and beverage, and, for many years, always seemed to be there, underfoot, and in the way. And he was a peripheral member of the wolf pack; her brother's eclectic—if not eccentric— group of free spirits. Bound by good times and booze, they were in no great hurry to leave. This was how she would remember him, she resolved, dismissing the possibility she was in denial. But then, Heuer's funeral had been arranged by his elderly parents, and while not unusual for a single man without attachments, it saddened her.

She had loved him like a brother—at least that's what she'd say when pressed, because this was an intensely private matter not open for the entertainment of others. And if she remembered anything at all, it would be that. He had taught her to keep silent—insisted upon it as a condition of "friendship"—and she had continued to do so even after they "ended."

Enid *loved* him and the absence of a wife or lover left a huge void, which she found herself filling. This was done under extreme duress. She was married with kids. It was wrong. Still, she mourned.

"I won't tell a soul."

Enid drew out three little paint pots from her box of

tricks—a No. 2, a No. 5, a No. 9—along with a fla-bottomed sable brush. These were needed to transform the dead woman from pebble grey to apricot sky. Next, the hair combed out and then curled with the long iron Dougie had plugged in and then forgot about in the far wall. Heuer disliked him. He found him oafish—a mere smudge—and not worth the bother of a prank.

Enid, working fast, said nothing to the woman, evidently reserving her cruelest cuts for those she knew. She'd been quite stern with Heuer in the prep room, wallowing in self-pity that he had left her cruelly. To that, he had a reply: "I stopped seeing you because you asked me too."

He breathed deeply of her scents of oil, chemical, and tobacco. "And you're smoking again. That's good." He moved in closer, counting the shafts behind her ear. They were sheave-like crazy threads of gold. "*Flustern*—whisper," he mouthed into her ear, compelling the blood to flow faster, calling out to her to hear. "Make the talk for me now. *Bitte.*"

"*Wann habe ich aufgehört, dich zu lieben?*—When did I stop loving you?" she asked.

The iron, hot and unforgiving, scorched her skin, fixing her protein cells like a cooked egg. "*Sie Hure!*—You whore!"

Heuer clapped his hands: she was back!

"That's the third time I've hurt myself today!" she wailed, invoking the old wives' tale. "Now there'll be peace."

"No *Schön*," Heuer soothed. "Now it begins."

Enid wheeled about, searching for the object that injured her, but stopped, held in place by another object just on the outbound side of sight's periphery. It was otherworldly. The little body drawn out obscenely, spread eagled; left to die. Or did he die right away? There'd been violence. And she had found it.

***

Charlie Forsythe wasn't surprised when Enid begged for relief: Love tricked death more often than people cared to believe.

"It's getting too weird in here, Charlie," she said, apologizing for backing out of her duties, while others, maxed out, carried on. Wheeler, for example, had thrown Bobby out of the prep room after an unfortunate trocar accident. This device, when used inexpertly, often bunged up with blood clots and "chicken fat," causing the hydro aspirator to reverse the draw and send the contents meant for the sewer out onto the ceiling. Carla had to employ the big squeegee to undo Robert's damage and Fat Dougie, no less mischievous now than earlier in the day, suggested that a large steaming pile of dog poo in front of the building needed attention. Charlie, fresh off a taxing arrangement, quaffed back two large ibuprofen gel caps. He had a sonofabitch of a headache and downed them whole without aid of water.

"Didn't want a casket," Charlie clucked, shaking his head as if customer stinginess was a new thing. "'What do we need a casket for if we're cremating?' Can you imagine? People asking that?"

Enid shifted uncomfortably from hoof to hoof. Her feet hurt, along with her soul, and she had to go. She gripped the cosmetic case tightly, securing the precious contents. Rat's body weighed only a few ounces, but the responsibility of getting him out of the building undetected was crushing. *Rat's dead.* She cried inwardly. Strangled words, said in German, forced to the back of the throat so that no one else in the building could hear.

Though Rat's body was shattered and a bit dried out, she would preserve him. She'd worked on worse. But Heuer, relentless in his refusal to "pink up" even after three gallons of embalming fluid—was another matter. He had done it to her again; showed up without warning, expecting her full attention. She'd be damned if she gave it to him. He would never mess her up again.

"He was like a brother to me," she lied to Charlie. "And he had a really great car." If Eldon could pick up where Robert left off, she'd be happy to work on the other funerals.

Carla, taking it in off side offered a "Get your head seen to." For a moment, Enid thought she was referring to her mental state, but on touching the scabby gash growing comfortable over her right eye, she caught her gist.

Enid blew them a kiss, fake laughing her exit in an effort to sugar coat the crappiest day of her life. Heuer, fast behind, watched as she gathered her things, not stopping to change out of her morning suit. This disappointed him: he'd hoped to see more of her.

In the calm of the garage, she wound Rat up into a durable plastic cocoon fashioned from the white non-descript sheeting spooled up on a large roll suspended on the back wall; the same kind of sheeting used on Heuer at the coroner's office. Next, she grabbed two pink fluid bottles from the cabinet behind her, stuffing them, along with her package, into a bright orange oversized handbag which reflected beautifully the amber gradients in her big yellow eyes.

"What are you playing at?" Heuer asked, taken with the wry comedy of the situation. "You have a dead rat in your purse."

She clutched Rat close to her heart.

"Heuer was my brother's friend," she said, repeating the lie to make it true, "but a mere sideshow to my own life." She smiled, looking through him. "Weren't you?"

"Look for me," he urged. "You are my legacy."

Fueled by a new resolve, Enid walked past him heading for the back door and its three steps that tripped her earlier that day; these marked the line between Heuer's world and hers.

"I don't even have a picture of you," she cried out, choked.

"You don't need one. You know me."

She took great care, taking each step slowly, deliberately, looking down at her feet like she used to do when they slow danced. Then she walked through, slamming the door behind her.

Softly, imperceptibly, he traced his elegant fingers along the ancient beveled glass set deep into the heavy door, its mottled surface reminding him of lurid time and its weary effects on unprotected surfaces. How he wanted to follow. How decidedly he could not. He tried the door once and then again, as if to confirm the one single undisputed fact at hand: he was anchored to this place and try as he might, no single amount of effort would allow him to cross the divide.

Chapter Seventeen

U nder the hard top of her vehicle, with its reliable four-inch sidewalls and fuel-efficient four cylinders, she was free to let go and she did. It felt amazing. Dry sobs, stifled beneath false pride and petty regrets, turned manifest to water, oozing out of every pore. Cleansing water, lazy at first, took its time, as if working against gravity until—at last—reaching her feet, it thickened, binding her to the pedals of her rusted out Honda. She threw it hard into reverse.

He died alone and no one looked for him.

She was on the main thoroughfare, having somehow managed, through repeating waves of snot, to make it out of the parking lot. She didn't remember making the turn, only the troubling picture of a dead man covered in blow flies, festering in a dirty house—Christ, he couldn't even die properly—and then, heading north, managing to negotiate the phalanx of pedestrians, baby carriages, and battery charged motor scooters for the physically impaired that bisected the street. On the other side was the highway and home. They called this intersection 'The Gauntlet,' for it offered so many perils at so many times of the day. Getting through it was an achievement. It was, to Enid, a miracle that more people weren't killed here.

Driving above acceptable speeds, she scattered the sleepwalkers in mid tweet at the second crosswalk. Cyclists, bobbing in and out around faltering electric buses, returned the favor of her less than courteous driving technique with colorful hand gestures that accompanied vigorous vocal admonishments. If she made the freeway in time, she'd be home well before Julia and Evan, giving her the time she'd need to retrieve what she sought. Stopped at another red light, she revved her engine. She was seventeen hundred pounds of determined metal alloy on four wheels, while the well-intentioned, environmentally conscious, bicyclists on two were mere flesh. An idiot in three-toned Lycra mouthed oaths at her, while she, in no mood to be bested, responded with a colorful hand gesture of her own.

"Screw bike lanes. Screw pedestrians. Screw carpools. And screw you Heuer for coming back after all these years."

***

"Would you like a cigarette?" he asked, from across the Chevelle's bench seat. Enid sucked in her breath. The Chevy, a modified 1968 4-barrel beauty with Turbo Jet carburetor, housed 454 cubic inches of undisputed power under a high gloss pin-striped tapered hood. She'd never been in a car like this, much less known a man that owned one.

"No thank you. I don't smoke." She was fourteen, perspiring copiously into her cap sleeved tee. With an Indian bindi dot of a zit forming between her eyebrows, she second-guessed the Cheetos she'd hoovered back after metal shop, praying they'd cleared the gaps between her middle and front teeth.

"Ah, but you should," Heuer said, his English clipped, precise and ever formal. Enid held her breath. The Pontiac, her mother's car, had given out in the driveway just half an hour before she was to pick her up and he offered to go instead. It was raining, he said, and the walk was too far for a princess to make without the protection of an umbrella.

From her side of the car, she shifted uneasily. Some found his tone arrogant, even offensive; others, like her, found it curious and alluring. Perhaps it took them back to a less certain time when people like him presumed to rule the earth. Most of the Krauts she came across were older, like her parents, or downright ancient like her Oma and Opa. But Heuer was young and not that much older than she was. Not by a long shot. He was Mike's friend and so, by her calculation, just six years ahead of her. Not much older at all.

Enid liberated a generous sized portion of inner cheek tissue caught between the metal bands of her braces. Dr. Engelhart, her pedodontist, promised they'd be gone soon, and then maybe she could get on with her life.

Heuer laughed, his blue eyes an impenetrable indigo against the late day sky. The lighter popped in the dash and he lit his Marlboro cigarette expertly.

"Open," he said simply, and she complied closing her lips around the brown filter tip.

"Breathe."

***

Enid jammed on the breaks averting a rear end collision with the four-wheel drive hybrid in front of her.

Damn. That was close.

She pulled into the scarcely used car pool lane and accelerated.

"I'm fourteen and I don't smoke." She laughed, lighting one of Robert's purloined cigarettes. Her son was adamantly opposed to smoking. The school had done an excellent job of getting the message across, and she made a note to eat a garlic clove once she got home.

What happened to you?

His voice, unlike her memories, took its time reassembling. At first teasing, it hinted subtly at what might have been, obliterating conjecture and the inane desire to reinvent what never was. The voice and scenes that accompanied it rolled in on waves that were hot and cold; grainy and garishly colored, like the eight mm movies her dad would take with the old camera. They'd watch them in the living room in the old house on Friday nights; the old projector beaming up life stories on the fabric screen perched on a hokey tripod. She'd forgotten that until now. The synapses in her brain fired faster and faster, and she cried behind the wheel of her aging chariot with its crappy four-speed transmission. What a shit box. It could barely handle the slippery surface it had to negotiate for it had started to rain. Enid cried harder.

A hurting song would have come in handy right about now, but the classic rock radio station she favored played more commercial advertisements than tunes, so she contented herself with a banged up CD—one of her favorites—that skipped and stuck just like the old LPs she grew up with. Between gulps of smoky air, she managed a smile as the familiar chords played to her. Cold Play, Hip Hop, and jazz fusion all had their place, but not today. She needed the Rolling Stones to get her home.

With Rat in tow, Enid crossed the threshold of the house she shared with Aaron and Evan and Julia, her family. Their home was pleasant, a sprawling pile of soccer balls and dirty socks. It would be called *gemuttlich* in German—comfy and safe. The Krause home was lived in with gauged walls and dried boogies embedded in its paper surfaces; trophies to the children's development. Society held that she should cry in anticipation of the day they'd leave her because it was normal and proper that they do so. And it was, by turns, normal and acceptable that she'd feel low down and raw when they did. But what would society say about Heuer and his funeral director?

Time was at a premium and, eyeing the liquor cabinet, Enid made note to raid it later after everyone was safely tucked away in bed. She'd need a stiff toot after the kind of day she'd had. It was strange, combative, difficult, and dirty.

Down below, in the cobweb-infested crawl space, she searched for him: His hair, his eyes, his teeth; every line, every pore. And then the voice came, with its inflections, accent, squeak, and buzz.

He was a little guy and his voice was a bit high on the scale—he squeaked when he got excited. But he could modulate it when he wanted to. He'd whisper to her softly, slowly, deliberately, inaudibly. He was white noise and he was intoxicating.

She hadn't thought about him in years; drag racing near the overpass after dark: the thrill of going beyond mere law and getting away with it.

Searching. Searching. She tore through the boxes with amazing speed. Objects, papers, books she had not seen in two decades, but had retained for their aesthetic importance—symbols of the old life—were carelessly discarded because she was looking for one thing only—a little blue photo album that held twelve or possibly fifteen snapshots. These snaps had been taken over a ten-year period and they were very important to her now.

"Where are you?" she demanded aloud and with mounting anger. The more she tried to grab hold of what she'd lost, the more she found it being taken away. The little blue photo album was their album. It contained the "proof" of their existence.

Young Enid had craftily assembled their book one stolen moment at a time. He was paranoid about discovery, so it was always very difficult to get close to him in public. Yet, she had managed to do just that one precious shot at a time. She did this under the auspices of the group shot: the Christmas parties, the cottage sojourns, backyard BBQs, house parties and even Mike's wedding. She saw every picture as clear as if they were in front of her now. In all cases, she managed to maneuver herself beside him just long enough for friends to capture on film.

When she was young, she would pore over it for hours looking for traces of the heat that existed between them. She wanted to show her mother this book every time she got on her ass for not marrying and moving on. Many times, Enid had wanted to say, "I've got somebody. I've had him for years, so leave it already!" But she had not. If she had exposed him, he would have left her.

Enid treasured this book because it was the only physical evidence she had that they'd existed as a couple, and now she cursed herself because she was afraid she had lost it. The last box was next to her on the floor, opened and emptied out, and he wasn't there.

Chapter Eighteen

6:30 P.M.

Was it irony that brought him here, or a sick sense of humor? Jürgen Heuer could not decide. One minute he was trying a doorknob, next he was out. Leaning up against a ridiculous Doric column inside Legacy Funeral Home, he mulled the question. When last they met, he told Enid that *she* was his legacy, whatever that meant—she was stuffing a dead rat into her purse along with some pretty heavy-duty chemicals, and his emotions, strained by his confinement, no doubt, prompted the Shakespearian outburst. What legacy could she possibly offer?

"Look to those that deny you, for they will open the doors," the lamp said.

He looked at the names of the dead, posted neatly on a shiny magnetic board in the main lobby and shook his head. No. The circumstances of his being here had nothing to do with Enid or legacy; Panos, his dead neighbor, was Greek and Legacy was where all the Greeks went.

"Panos Vasily Drakoulias, b. 1957 in the Village of Croquillion, Visitation, Monday 7-9, Funeral Service, Tuesday 1 p.m., St. Nicholas, Bond Street, Lansing."

Heuer, frowning, pulled an errant hair jutting out from his left nostril. Panos never denied him— they got on quite well—so what was his new best friend and oracle on about?

Those that deny you, open the doors.

Sure. Whatever.

He took in his surroundings, wondering if this new cage would let him leave after his work was done. The building, as long as it was wide and a tad moldy, sported grand vestibules and overstuffed furniture, reminiscent of a fantastical age like those romanticized in the books his mother read aloud to him when he was young. Pausing before a large oil on panel portrait accompanied by a huge explanatory plaque, he half expected Henry James and a boring dissertation on *Portrait of a Lady*. Instead, he found the company patriarch and a brief history of Legacy.

Constructed in 1867 from temperate limestone hauled in on barges from the St. Lawrence River, the Legacy Chapel began as a simple family dwelling occupied by undertaker Lorne Hickenlooper and his brood of six. As a student of Holmes—the father of modern embalming—he excelled in his craft, refining techniques alongside his mentor on the battlefield where union army regulars fell. Word of his heroic deeds under fire—he'd dodged canon to pull dead and dying to safety under the protection of Old Glory—spread, and after the war, his funeral parlor became *the* place for Portside's elite.

Heuer read on, transfixed. Three generations of Hickenlooper's oversaw the business as it went from a quiet establishment that offered up its front parlor to families with quarters too small to have a casket at home, up to the 1970s, when the family expanded the business for the third time. Acquiring adjacent lots, they grew the space from three slumber rooms with a one hundred-seat chapel, to five, with a seating capacity for over two hundred.

Heuer smiled. "No wonder it's called 'Legacy'."

"I was dead by then," the lamp offered, over a lengthy conversation in the Weibigand basement, earlier, "but news of the Hickenlooper's and their last ditch effort to knock us out along with Seltenheit's, made it through the wires."

Heuer, reclining then on a dirty enamel embalming table not used since the dark ages, propped himself up on an elbow searching for wires.

The lamp flickered, clearly pleased by his rapture. "But they overextended, underestimating our combined resiliency." She crackled, giddy with the telling.

Did lamps chortle?

"The bank called their loan," she continued, "and the Greeks picked the place up for a song."

The Pangaea Odyssey Consortium moved swiftly. Capitalizing on the public's fascination with all things Aristotle Onassis, it redesigned the building, co-opting Doric columns with statuary reminiscent of the temple of Aphrodite at the Acropolis adjacent the Parthenon.

Again, the lamp shook recalling the birth of the new Legacy. "It was so over the top in appearance that people bought into it. Even the Anglos, but that probably had more to do with Jackie than anything else."

Heuer moved from room to room, thinking of Jackie O. Her style, her class, commixed with Ari's gaudiness. Clearly, Legacy had toned down since that time. Gone were the white and blue motifs reminiscent of romantic ocean ports that summoned up grand vistas navigated by Aeneas and Odysseus.

"Louche," the lamp sniffed, depriving him of any private joy inside his now incredibly cluttered mind. Her ability to jump inside his head, quite unlike their jovial face to face's, was irritating, the invasion of privacy as offensive to him in death as it was in life.

"Peace," he commanded.

He ran a smooth, unblemished hand along the length of cool white plaster anchored by heavy oak wainscoting stained mahogany to accent marble fireplaces, Waterford chandeliers and faux antiques that copied an age that went down with the Titanic.

Outside the "library"—a room with real books—he noted another oil portrait hanging over an elaborate scrolled mantle. Lord Admiral Nelson, scourge of Napoleon and British hero of the Nile, loomed tall and proud; his presence, a strange nod to the seafaring romantic buried in every man. He sighed: Better Nelson than Captain Hook, although the fantastical nature of the place could easily accommodate a Disney character or two.

"Why am I here again, oh mighty Burning Bush?"

"Don't call me that!" the lamp snapped. "You know I hate that moniker."

Yes, he knew. She said it smacked of blasphemy with a touch of the puerile.

"You know why you're here," she reminded him. "You must make peace with these people."

"Why?"

"Because they actually had the audacity to care about you."

"Even Alfons? I doubt that. He hated me."

"Press on and see for yourself."

Heuer pushed aside his disdain for the assignment. Panos fell to his death while checking on his well-being. And while he was moved by the man's sacrifice, he failed to see what more could be accomplished spooking around the Drakoulias funeral visitation. What would he say if he ran into him?

A goofy looking chap approached from a side hall. Decked out in head to toe black, he perspired heavily from the top of his bald head to the tips of his hairy fingers.

"Are you ready?"

Heuer drew back. Only the lamp could "see" him.

"Yes, Mr. Creighton, and thank you for all you've done."

Stavroula Drakoulias, accompanied by her daughters Olympia and Pelagia, and sons Panayiotis and Stavro advanced past him, unaware that he'd come to pay respects.

"You fix his neck?" the widow asked.

"Yes," the mortician assured in hushed tones.

"And the icona?"

"The Christ and the Panaea are here."

"And the candle box for church?"

"Ma, he's got it covered," Panos II snapped, clearly not looking forward to what lay at the end of the hall.

"Make that two of us, brother," Heuer chimed in. He

hadn't been to a funeral since Cousin Christophe's at Weibigand's, which compared poorly to the luxe ostentation of Legacy. "At least your dad's in a cool place. I'm stuck in a dump."

"Mind your manners!" the lamp commanded, her tone defensive.

"My apologies. Perhaps you can fill me in later on how things got as bad as they did when we get back to the ranch?"

The small group moved down a long corridor with a high ceiling and perpendicular halls vivisecting their passage. At the intersection of each hall, stood a three-legged ornately tooled Firenze Plastoni table, the same kind that decorated the foyers and anterooms at TRAVAT Ion. *Coincidence?*

Heuer shrugged, reminded of Poe's *House of Usher* with its vertical family tree that went nowhere. Christ, he hated funeral homes.

"Your friend, Alfons Vermiglia, waits for you in the coffee lounge," the bald undertaker said, effecting solemnity.

Heuer fixed steely eyes on the man. There was something false about him.

"No!" Stavroula said sharply, her carefully coiffed and glued helmet head not giving up a single strand. She checked herself, crossing her heart three times by way of apology. "That is to say, Mr. Creighton, Alfons does not need to wait. He was with us when Panayiotis died. We were on Mr. Heuer's lawn—"

"Easy, ma," Olympia, a comely young thing of twenty, soothed. "You don't have to relive everything now."

"I do! I do!" she responded, voice rising. "I was more worried about Mr. Heuer than my baby mou..."

The funeral director produced a box of tissues out of thin air. "Would you like a moment?" he asked, gently.

"No," she said. "I want to see him—now!"

***

"I was there the whole time," Alfons fog horned to a captive audience in Legacy's upper coffee lounge.

"Sonofabitch," Heuer cursed, hiding the large biscotti plate provided by the Vermiglia family behind a potted palm. "And show offs too," he harrumphed. Funerals were muted affairs punctuated by the occasional outburst from the YiaYia's that mourned at the casket. They weren't designed to enhance one's self-importance like Alfons was doing with his stupid cookies.

Alfons leaned in for emphasis: "If anyone's to blame, it's that bloody hermit."

The reference, a clear dig at the late Mr. Heuer, resonated with the group assembled around the speaker. Friends, neighbors, they all had a stake in Panayiotis Drakoulias. Now Alfons was sullying the affair with a little mean spirited gossip, the *Schwein Hund.*[23]

"You saw the inside?" Quan from across the street piped.

"You bet your ass I did," Alfons puffed. "I had to turn sideways to get to the stair with all the boxes and shit he had packed in there."

Heuer bit down hard on his right fist, an act more characteristic of Alfons than a quiet German guy who preferred to be left alone. He had no right to invade his privacy. No right to mock him, especially at Panos' funeral. Tacky.

Justice is blind and the scales always tilt presumably on the side of the righteous. The lamp couldn't stress enough the need to keep calm, to see reason—this was the way out. Yet Heuer could not see his way to perfect grace.

"Wouldn't be surprised if they found a head or two in the basement," Alfons continued, picking up speed before a

---

[23] Pig dog.

crowd in thrall. "Not even a week, and his old man has a dumpster out front."

"To cover up what's inside," Gia Vermiglia, Alfons' wife, confided.

"Steele yourself," The lamp cautioned. "You will not advance your position if you do harm."

But Heuer wasn't listening. Before she could finish her sentence, he was half way across town, positioned squarely in his backyard. Alfons had been right about the dumpster, which was cordoned off behind yellow police sticky tape.

He looked at the acacia tree, which swayed gently in the cool of the evening breeze. Breathing deeply of its scent, he remembered his initiation into the Masonic lodge, the chaplain's words, referencing the importance of the acacia in relation to the Great Architect of the Universe. He dismissed it as a lot of bunk at the time, joining only to advance business connections. Now he felt the meaning. Heuer raised his arms.

"If you hear me; if you are real; give me justice and I will give you whatever you want."

Chapter Nineteen

8:00 P.M.

Enid sat on the plank steps leading from the door of her house into the garage, where an oversized enamel cauldron waited for her. Typically used for bratwurst making, something her father did every fall in keeping with old country traditions, the cauldron was critical for what needed to be done next. Focusing hard, she tried to summon the correct calculation that would enable her to embalm Rat by immersion.

"What the hell are you doing?" Aaron asked, coming up behind her.

"How'd you mean, buddy?" she replied, exhaling a huge plume of cigarette smoke.

Circling around her, Aaron Krause took his place on a rusty old kitchen stool liberated from the neighbor's garbage.

Enid sighed: retrieving old crap was a thing he liked to do, his beliefs in restoration as strong as hers. "As you see," she continued. The last time she uttered those words, he'd caught her red handed at three o'clock in the morning with a freshly opened bottle of warm champagne. Its contents dripping from the kitchen ceiling like freaked out stalactites in crystal and quartz, the champagne debacle paled next to a squashed rat in a sausage pot.

Aaron's pale green eyes tightened, judging. She hated this more than his garbage collecting. "I had a very curious day," she offered, "the kind that might require a little Neil Diamond."

Aaron pointed to the wound above her eyebrow. Enid remained mute.

"We can't do the Neil two days in a row *bubbala*. Fat Larry will call the cops."

He had a point. Larry, a perpetually retired

schoolteacher on long term disability had nothing better to do than drink beer, burp, and spy on their activities like some angry old hillbilly.

"Fine. No Neil."

"And the smokes?"

Enid crushed Robert's tobacco out under her pink flip flop, a shame given that the kid had saved her ass and needed the smokes even more than she did. "Mr. Heuer," he complained before she left the building, was a real pain in the ass. The viscera bag, used to contain the autopsied organs, placed in the ventral cavity by the coroner's assistant, malfunctioned—split at the seams—and wriggled out of Robert's grasp, tumbling Heuer's brain, heart, lungs—everything—out all over the prep room floor. The delay, brought on by the clean-up, drove Eldon wild, the range of epithets shouted facilitating a cease and desist call from Ziggy three floors above.

Aaron shook his head. "Twenty years and you fall off the wagon?"

She pushed off from the wooden steps, advancing heavily to the cauldron that, on closer inspection, needed a good cleaning. "I could use a hand with this," she gestured, ignoring his comments about smoking.

He grimaced. "I'd rather not touch the hog pot, if you don't mind."

Enid laughed for real, something she hadn't done since the morning. Aaron was Jewish, sort of, a lapsed soul that ate bacon and celebrated Christmas. "Don't hide behind swine. You're just lazy."

She widened her eyes at him.

Aaron assumed a defensive pose, raising both hands to cover his eyes. "Don't flash those things at me."

"Then don't make me howl."

The door opened, interrupting their cozy idyll. "Ma, phone." Evan, at six foot one, looked more like an elongated green vegetable than a boy. Just how he even managed to hear the phone under his Dr. Dre Beats was open to speculation.

"Yeah," Enid said, taking the hand held and shooing her men away.

"Nice freakin' greetin' beyotch," came the *tinkly* reply.

"You high?"

"Nope," replied Dale Somerset Exeter Wembley Crewe, her oldest friend. A writer, Dale was both recognized and celebrated as a leading purveyor of ninety-nine cent horror smut. "But I should be."

Enid reached for the crumpled pack of smokes on the garage floor. Righting one of the less damaged examples, she lit it expertly with a single stroke of a Weibigand match.

"You have writer's block," Enid accused. She saw through Dale every time. It was the only time her quirky friend called her.

"That's not fair. But…yes."

Sometimes Dale would caustically troll the remains of Enid's workday in search of something she could turn dirty fast. Her first e-book, *Magic Mushroom*, was based on a wine-soaked plea from a cashed up trophy widow. Dwelling endlessly on the "gifts" of her beloved, she beseeched his return to her by night so that she could ride again. The tale went gold, earning Dale a place on the international registry of journeymen smut writers. She was especially popular in Germany.

"Wo sind Sie mien Herr?"[24]

"*Magischer Pilz*! I'm delighted you remember."

"*Magic Mushroom* was your breakthrough, although I wish you'd stuck with the mainstream a little…longer?" Enid replied, taking care to soften it with a question. Dale was still prickly over her protest when her friend decided to

---

[24] "Where are you, my lord?"

go deep down and dirty. It smacked of something unseemly.

Silence.

"I'm sorry," Enid said quickly, exhaling more smoke. "Something happened today."

"You're smoking!" Dale exclaimed, the volume rattling the receiver in Enid's hand. "I knew you'd go back."

Not a supportive response, Enid thought, but a true one. She loved smoking, always had. "I won't answer that."

Dale chuckled through her own cigarette smoke, the short, sharp *ssssss* of drawn air clearly audible through the handset. "Wasn't a question."

Dale and Enid shared an extensive history going back thirty years. As such, she assumed certain rights where Enid was concerned, rights that extended beyond the purview of Aaron Krause. She knew *Enid Engler*. She also knew Heuer.

"Heuer's dead," Enid said, her voice dropping several octaves. "He's at the parlor."

Dale didn't stop to pause, or, by the sound of things, exhale her smoke. "Holy shit!" she choked. "Your parlor?" The last bit was coughed out.

"You can't write about this."

"How's Mike taking it?" she asked, ignoring the comment.

Enid froze. She hadn't called him yet and she didn't know why. Mike was the kind of brother who took big brothering to an extreme level. When they were young, he made it abundantly clear to the wolf pack that his sister was off limits. Talking about Heuer would betray her true feelings, and she couldn't have that. She'd promised Heuer never to speak of it and she hadn't. She was only thirteen. "I haven't talked to him yet."

Now there was a pause. "If you could see me, you'd know that I'm rolling my eyes and pouring another glass of

Chablis."

Enid chuckled. She needed Dale now.

"What's it like?"

"Ma said I'd be a rich widow if things had gone right."

Dale laughed her unrestrained laugh. Honest and rich, the alchemy of it turned tragedy into comedy. "That sounds like Oma. She's right, you know—about the widow thing and all."

"I know."

"You had the hots for him, honey. But if I recall correctly—and correct me, please, if I'm wrong—it's been twenty years and twenty vintages—" The sound of Dale gulping back some more Chablis made Enid drool for a beverage of her own "— but I'm pretty sure that dog didn't hunt."

Enid cringed. It had been twenty years with a lot of booze and a lot of mistakes in between. How it was, how it should have been, and how it would be remembered from now on was wide open.

"Yes," Enid lied. "It's true. He never put a finger on me."

Chapter Twenty

10:00 P.M.

It was bad enough she pulled double shift, but it didn't compare to the feeling of an empty house. Carla Blue, pushing past the pile of "floor" bills that had accumulated over many weeks, allowed herself to speculate on the amounts outstanding. She screwed her face down tight. If she was even half close, she'd be out on the street in a week. Rat had been right: Danny was a bum and completely unworthy of her love. But so was Carter Bilsson.

"An epic mistake," she said aloud to the potted Dieffenbachia, one of the few things her husband gave her that hadn't gone to shit. "Young men and me...don't work."

She kicked off her man shoes. Stupid men notwithstanding, what she really needed was a bath and a nap, but she bargained that joy away when she invited her friend and former work colleague Scooter Creighton over for a little wine and a pity party.

"What are you wearing," a deep male voice yelled through her closed and heavily locked front door.

Another one wants to know. Great, Carla thought.

"And don't say 'a meat cleaver.' That's my joke, honey."

Carla threw open the door, scattering the niggling floor bills several feet. Dramatically, she fell into his arms.

"Whoa, baby. Am I getting lucky tonight?"

"Screw you," she cried, suppressing the water that gathered behind her eyes. "You're a pain in the ass. I'm so glad you're here."

Scooter gathered her up with expert arms well-honed from years of moving the dead. Stiffening against his touch, she made the job easier.

He crossed the room, searching for a viable place to

land. "Christ, your place is a mess. You on the sauce?"

"No," Carla said, tightening her abdominal muscles. "Booze is the last thing I need right now."

He frowned, dropping himself and his package on her cheap Swedish futon, the only free spot available. "But I thought I was invited for wine?" He wrinkled his pointy nose. "I was expecting wine, Dingy."

Carla gripped her abdomen, which shrank against her touch. The motion, involuntary, was wholly independent of the rest of her body, as if she were a host occupied by some malignant parasite. She thought of her morgue attendant boyfriend, Carter, and suppressed a dry heave.

"Hey! Hello?" Scooter called out petulantly. "It's all about me today. Remember?"

Dear, dear, Scoot, she thought. Could his day be any worse than hers? The Shawson-Cooke visitation had been a fiasco with the fat nephew bitching about the lighting, the quality of the coffee, and the state of her uniform, which he found "mannish" and "unsettling." *Cíoch*.[25] The man was an imbecile, tricked by Charlie into having a visit he didn't want. Then to his complete surprise, the people he claimed would not show up on account they were all dead, suddenly did, and not because of a séance, but because they were actually healthy, active, viable seniors with years of contributions ahead of them.

"It's worse this time, isn't it?" Scooter interrupted her thoughts.

"Huh? This jerk accused me of stealing his mother's ring."

Scooter rolled his eyes. "I meant Danny."

Danny crossed the border weeks ago, heading north to a place called Nipissing. He could be dead for all she knew, though she doubted she'd be that lucky.

"Danny's past tense," she replied, the finality in her

---

[25] Gaelic curse meaning "tit."

voice as temporary as her current address.

"Well," he said easily, "I had an interesting evening if you're up for a rant." He rolled her off his lap into a pile of spent frozen dinner trays, the aluminum rectangles crunching under the weight of Carla plus one.

She cleared her throat. "I think I'm knocked up."

The pronouncement was a lofty one and it stole his thunder, at least for a moment or two. "You're too old."

"I'm fifty-two and it's been known to happen."

"It's gas."

She looked around her cramped apartment with its Art Deco alcove and beautifully crafted cornices. Danny said it was the perfect room to make love in and they did so, quite often, in the early days. Her face darkened with the thought. Her husband, whether physical or in the abstract, could raise her up on a whim as if by magic. She hated that power he had.

"Okay. It's menopause," he pressed, not leaving it alone and quitting himself of the saggy futon to fire up her vintage Marantz turntable with its platinum needle. Sister Sledge filled the room. "I remember my mom at your age. Nuttier than a—"

"Fruitcake?"

"No. Not so clichéd." He tapped the side of his head with a hairy finger, like he always did when caught in a deep brain search. "Nuttier than—a rat on cyanide."

"Huh?"

He looked disappointed, but then he did better in chemistry than she did, and so should not have been surprised by her lack of scientific acuity. "Cyanide smells like bitter almonds. Right?" he gestured. "Almonds are nuts. Cyanide is a poison. Poison kills rats."

Carla laughed. "Okay, man. Whatever you say."

"My day was the shits," Scooter continued. "Wonky

family and a crazy *concetta*[26] who accused me of stealing the biscotti. "'Where are the biscotti? Where are the biscotti? You people took them for yourself.'" He threw his head back, pleased by his imitation of the penultimate busy body.

"Pretty fucking good biscotti?" Carla asked, swaying to and fro to Sister Sledge.

"Yeah. I had a few before I put them out. Where they went after, I didn't know until...much later." He cocked an eyebrow to create a sense of mystery.

"So it was an Italian family?"

"No," he said, rooting through her refrigerator for beverages. "Greek. But the neighbor was Italian. Tried to hijack the visitation, like he was immediate family or something. Had lots to say—building's too hot, not enough shit paper in the crappers, the candy dish is empty, where are the tissues? Stavroula needs more tissues..."

"I hate that. We got seven in the house. And the only family that's behaving is Kraut."

"Really?" he cocked his head in surprise as he raised his right hand in a Hitlerian gesture. "Lucky for you...I guess." He withdrew his hand, as if self-conscious by the rude gesture. "I found the biscotti in a flower pot."

"Weird."

"Yeah. But you know what was even weirder?" he asked, returning to the pinot noir in her fridge and pouring out generous rounds into large, balloon shaped cognac snifters, wedding gifts from Danny's parents.

Carla beamed, accepting her glass. "The neighbor?"

He clasped his big hands together, pleased at her mind reading, signifying their enduring simpatico. "Yep. I left him alone for a moment. Next time I saw him, he was white."

---

[26] Colloquial stereotype – mourning woman of Italian origin: usually elderly.

The two friends resumed their places on the messy futon, sipping comfortably from their pinot snifters.

"He saw something," Carla said, affecting a thoughtful gaze.

Scooter shrugged. "I guess so."

She took another sip. "They're always seeing ghosts, aren't they?"

Chapter Twenty-One

11:59 P.M.

Just how the lamp found its way into the old Weibigand basement was a subject of intense interest to Jürgen Heuer. People died; people waked. But not everybody got away. Whoever was in charge wasn't letting her off the hook and if her time on earth was any indication—she'd been dead for decades—he might have a long wait too. That said, he congratulated himself on the evening's accomplishments. While he could not open the Weibigand back door on his own momentum, he had succeeded in leaving if only for a short time. That was progress.

Back at the funeral home, he was driven by an epic desire to tell his new friend everything. This feeling intensified as he sought her out in the dark.

"Wo bis du, mein Schon?[27]" he called out softly. "There is much I need to tell you."

The sound of Alfons' pressure treated yellow southern pine fence giving way, for example, was well worth a revisit; the fence having been forced upon Heuer by an uncompromising Alfons, who declared the rusted chain link a safety threat to his bratty children. The cost of the new fence, combined with the reasons given, irked Heuer tremendously. Succumbing to the demands of a man he could not stand in the name of small children had placed him in an awkward position. He protected innocents at the expense of his pocketbook, but he'd also ceded his position to an enemy and that made him weak.

Heuer grinned: not more than a minute passed between his emotional appeal to the Great Architect and the yawling snap of the acacia's trunk, which, upon falling,

---

[27]Where are you, my beautiful?

threshed the fence boards like so many husks in a cornfield. "Yes! Yes!" he shouted. "There is a god!" The above ground swimming pool, a buttress-free confection of galvanized steel sides and tensile top rails moaned like a wounded whale harpooned as the tree's weight bore down on it. The satisfaction obtained outweighed the consequences the mean spirited act might garner. Years of angst over dirty pool water was made moot in a single blow, and it was worth it, even if it went against the lamp's do gooder ethos.

Heuer narrowed his eyes. He'd been at Weibigand's for less than a day, and as such, had failed to decipher the building's internal geography. Boxes filled the basement, stuffed flush with newspaper wrapped treasures. These blocked his way, and every effort made at reorganizing his cell structure so that he could pass failed. If only he could see better. The night had been moonlit, but none of its glib silvery beams found their way to where he was now.

He sighed, wrapping his arms around himself to make sure he was still real. The characters in Dante's *Inferno* fared less than he, yet the idea of being swept away without a trace had begun to take hold. Life as an ottoman or abandoned beach ball was better than being nothing at all.

His face connected with something crunchy. Disgusted, he pressed on.

How did lamp get to this place, and how long had she been here? He dared not ask without further intel to back the query. Lawyers never ask questions they do not know the answers to. And the lamp did most of the talking anyway.

Heuer's toe hit something hard and he kicked it as if to get a response. The object complied, collapsing with a *sis sis* and a rush of sand. Somehow, he'd made his way into the bric a brac room he explored earlier that contained among many things, unclaimed urns of human ash. "Euw." He shook off his pant leg and the air around him filled with

155

grit.

He felt his way, searching for an out, until, at last, his hands came to rest on something smooth and reassuring. Lamp was much taller than he remembered, with a broad solid brass base supported by four phoenix paws that gripped the floor with a decisive permanence. Solemnly, he placed his hand on his chest:

"You told me to go to Legacy tonight, and I did. I listened, learned, and reacted, as per your instruction. It's my intention to make a full report now."

The lamp remained silent.

"Hello?" he said, feeling awkward. *"Bist du da?"*[28]

She neither flickered nor shook.

Heuer tightened. He did not appreciate being ignored. Adjusting his footing, he continued. "It was with the truest of intentions that I sought out Panos' family with hopes of letting them know how much I appreciated them." This was a lie; he didn't want to go, didn't know why he was there. He had to keep asking her, and even with the unhelpful "you know why" he still didn't know what he was chasing after.

He cleared his throat, a habit picked up in second year law that—he was told—hinted at enough vulnerability to soften juries and disarm opponents.

"Panos and Stavroula are, without question, the only friends I ever had on that street, and for that friendship, I used them badly. Any kindnesses offered me were repelled with suspicion, and I want to say again how sorry I am for the death of their cat."

Heuer shifted again, self-conscious at the admission. He hadn't any use for goddamn cats—hated them in fact—but his disdain for raccoons was even greater.

"I do not, however, repent for the raccoon that I caught up with tonight, or that I drowned it without

---

[28] Are you here?

remorse (in Alfons' broken excuse for a pool). The opportunity was a gift, and I took it without reservation."

A heady rush of emotion overtook him, such that his guts began to reel. "If you are looking for contrition, do not look for it here. I've had a few regrets, quite a few—" He lowered his voice. "All of them, worth a mention..."

He reached out to touch her, something he'd not done before. Cool hands running along her sturdy shaft, he tightened his grip at the midsection, which curved sensuously like tree bowl hips on mother earth. "This," he said, "is the surest way to catch a familiar sensation." Lamp was his only connection to this new life; "a conduit" she said between two worlds, offering tremendous benefits to him as long as he did exactly as he was told. Why not? Tagging along never hurt, so long as one got what one needed. He stroked her again: Delectable steel, sublime and unbending, stirring his mind to awaken his body. Giving in to her, he let go, not really caring what happened next.

Chapter Twenty-Two

Tuesday, 9:00 A.M.

■ ■ "Where's the rat?"

It was a simple enough question that deserved an answer. Enid's throat closed. "What do you mean?" she croaked, thinking about her late night near miss with Aaron, who would have given man-birth if he'd caught her smoking again.

Carla, rumpled in the summer heat, leaned up against the far wall in the lower office, her left hand sticky with a goopy day old doughnut, her right balancing an extra-long menthol cigarette. Like her, Carla looked lost and in the weeds, but her worn out state wasn't enough to give Enid the courage to confide the whole truth. She gestured at Carla's smoke. "Feeling defiant?"

Where Enid lacked in the courage department, she gained in the deceptive arts. This she blamed on Heuer. Deflecting the conversation always bought time, he insisted, and she embraced his ethos as if it were her own.

Carla took a deep cowboy draw, exhaling slowly like one of those trench coats in a porno. "I don't care. I don't care if that silly bitch kicks me out the front door."

Jocasta had been on a tear all morning and it was only Day Two of what Charlie now called Resurrection Week, his idea of what the overall theme should be, World Pride notwithstanding. With nine funerals on the go, Happy Hour Friday was guaranteed: all they had to do was make it to the finish line with minds intact.

Happy Hour Friday was a feature of older days, when drinking in the office was okay. In the Sixties, Weibigand directors stocked a full bar at the brothers' insistence. Of course, it was the responsibility of a senior undertaker to pilot them home, as neither Ziggy nor Karl-Heinz were ever fit enough to be entrusted with the Cadillac.

Discontinued in the early Nineties, happy hour only re-emerged on signature birthdays and high holidays. Bringing it back for Heuer seemed apropos and wrong in equal amounts.

Enid relieved Carla of the goopy doughnut. "Take a seat, Kitten. There's something I have to tell you."

Carla eased in next to where Enid had been sitting and began flipping random pieces of paper over and over on the desktop. She hated the lower office with its bunker like accoutrements and accompanying mentality; she had said it aloud often enough.

Enid took the adjacent swivel chair with difficulty. She'd had a rotten night. Awakened by a thud or *screetch* of car tires—she couldn't tell on account of the sedative she took along with a generous shot of Campari—she made out distinct shapes at the foot of her bed. Swirling, horned-like things that scared the snot out of her, rose and fell between floor and ceiling, canting off to one side as another muttered: *'Immer mit der Ruhe. Ich bins. Wir treffen Sie uns an der üblichen Stelle.'* "What?" she yelled back, jostling Aaron from his own dreams, "I don't understand you." The beasts seemed to laugh, mocking her in her naiveté. "Take it easy," said the big one. "It's me. Meet me in the usual place…"

Enid gripped Carla's hand, something she didn't routinely do. "You look like you took a brick to the head, and I'd love to hear about it. But right now, it's got to be about me." She released her hand and grabbed hold of the communal pack of office smokes, remembering how many she'd sucked down the night before when mixing up Rat's formalin-borax mixture.

Carla smiled, getting it. "That's pretty much what Scooter said. You go first, but then it's my turn."

Enid lit up a smoke. Confidences were frowned upon in the house she grew up in. They were secrets already lodged in the past. What business was it of hers to crack everything open now and what did she hope to gain?

"I don't wanna have a queen attack or anything, but this Heuer thing is really messing me up." The cigarette, long and lovely, sent delicate plumes up into the vent, ambient smoke signals bound to send the Jocastrator their way before too long.

"You banged the guy, didn't you?" Carla's tone took on a strange tang; no doubt because of her no good husband, whose indiscretions were intruding on Enid's own.

"Not entirely. It was thirty years ago."

Carla rose from her chair. "Thirty years? You can remember that far back?"

"Thirty years. Then twenty, and then—maybe—fifteen...?"

"How long you been married?"

Enid sat up tall in her chair; the effect, ostrich like, made her feel ridiculous. "Aaron and I are going on twenty years, and I'm not talking about physical love making. I'm talking cerebral seduction—a comprehensive takeover of the mind."

Carla flopped back into her creaky chair, incredulity shadowing her features. She was not given to higher concepts: only the absolute in front of your face counted.

"If you want to get out of doing the funeral..." She stopped, alerted to footfalls on the floor above them: "...then just say so. I got Robert to do the embalming for you..."

That was another thing that struck Enid. Carla wasn't big on favors, unless she wanted something in return. "What do you want?"

There wasn't time to discuss it. With doughnuts, smokes and a half drained coffee cup gathered up in her arms, Carla gestured frantically to Enid that they should make good their escape. "Spray some Windex, and turn on the big fan."

Safe in the back parking lot, they took refuge, feigning busy with a soap bucket and a couple of shammies which they applied to the big old hearse with over abundant zealousness.

"I'm not saying we weren't physical, years back," Enid continued amidst suds and scrubby bubbles, "but it went beyond that." She pointed to her skull. "He was in my head for years, and now he's back. Last night, I dug out my Heuer Boots."

Carla frowned. "Boots? What boots?"

Enid was miles above the parking lot, drifting lugubriously across time to her parents' annual Fourth of July BBQ party.

"I have been waiting for you," he whispered, having not seen her for two years.

"No, I think not," came her reply, as curt and affected in tone as if she was the foreigner instead of he.

His lips curved into a knowing smile against her ear and she hated it, because he was playing her again and she didn't mind. "I saw the most excellent pair of English riding boots in a window the other day. I believe you must have them."

She looked at Carla who, poised on the edge of her seat, conveyed suspense. Enid felt foolish. "He told me to get them, so I did. And when I put them on the other day, I was home."

Carla's response, like all of her responses, was succinct and cuttingly accurate: "This ain't Oz, Dorothy, and you might be giving too much power to the Wizard."

Enid wiped her nose on the black sleeve of her morning coat, leaving long, fibrous snail tracks for her coworker to see. The silly water attempting to spill out of her tear ducts, however, would have to wait, as she fought them back into their place. Composed she said, "Maybe so.

But every time I clicked my heels, he was there."

Chapter Twenty-Three

10:30 A.M.

Jocasta took an uncomfortably long amount time to walk from one end of the long hall to the other, pausing like a worshipper in a cathedral every three feet or so as if to pay homage to the station crosses.

What now? Charlie moaned, sandwiched between the casket orders and a stack of messages that littered his desk. He fingered the pink slips of paper, a throw over to older days when they had a receptionist to record every missed call. Not one to adapt easily, he fought unsuccessfully against the woman's dismissal, poo pooed the buzzy phone devices offered him, and almost took a stroke when forced to take a word processing course, culminating in the presentation of his own laptop. With all the trees out there, he saw no reasonable need to trade paper for silly metal and plastic devices that probably emitted cancer-causing rays anyway.

"Something back here smells, Forsythe," Jocasta barked. Charlie pretended not to hear, counting off the one, two, three…seven messages from the Imam at the mosque. He shook his head. An affable fellow, the cleric had a tendency to overdo it where death calls were concerned. 'Have you picked up the body? Have you picked up the body?' was all he'd say over and over through a torrent of repeat phone calls, in spite of Charlie's reassurances that the body would not disappear before they had a chance to get it.

"Did you get the Muslim?" Jocasta yelled, butting into his business. What had got into her? It wasn't like she was in charge or anything, yet she was hastened on, much like the rest of them, inspired by the flurry of activity that overtook the place. Charlie answered her if only to shut her up. "Shawson-Cooke has to go to the crematorium first.

163

Then, maybe, we go get Mr. al-Nadir."

Jocasta squared her squat frame. At a distance, she looked more distorted than in close quarters, her neck disappearing into the core of her body. In repose, she would look foreshortened and malformed, and it was at that moment that Charlie realized she had never revealed her funeral plans to him. He laughed inwardly: it was not uncharacteristic of funeral service personnel to believe they could live forever. Or maybe she counted on outliving her brothers and ascending the throne? Perish the thought.

Jocasta continued her unspecified review, running stumpy fingers along the chair rails, pointing out the fog on the mirrors and taking offense at the cobweb infused tube lights that cast a pall to exaggerate her already greenish features.

"Who's decomposing in there?" she demanded, pointing to the prep room door. "It smells like a latrine."

Charlie pushed off from the Thinking Chair, aggravated on the one hand by her persistent carping, relieved on the other that he did not have to respond to Imam al-Mahdi, who would have to cool his heels for another hour at least. Halfway down the hall, he understood what she was getting at; the smell of methane was strong with this one, and if they didn't start spraying ammonia soon, the odor would dominate the floor and window treatments. He looked at the production board—seven deceased in all—and more on the way. A smile crossed his lips. "The man you smell, my dear Jocasta, is Jürgen Heuer. He was a hummer found dead in a hermit house."

Jocasta wrinkled her nose, the bulbous end disappearing like a turtlehead beneath folds of pock-marked skin. It was hard sometimes to believe that she'd ever been pretty.

"I don't care if he died at Mt. Sinai. Get him out to the garage before he takes over the whole building."

Charlie held up a hand to silence her, a move that no

one would ever dare attempt lest they lose an arm. "He is German Jocasta. A big funeral. Five figures on the high side, at least."

No stranger to the superstitions that governed them all, she cracked open the prep room door to see for herself. "He's had an impact on our numbers," Charlie offered. "Our Enid calls it 'The Heuer Effect.'"

Jocasta sighed, knowing it to be true. In death as in life, it is more than possible for one individual to change the course of everything around him. Everybody knew that.

She surveyed the room with keen eyes. There were three in there, but there could be no mistaking Heuer. Still "open" to allow Robert's phenol-soaked sheets a chance to dry out his soggy ventral cavity, he looked like marine life after the propeller. "Any photos?" she asked suddenly, an unusual question given that she rarely took an interest in the dead anymore. They inched into the room, taking care not to trip over the buckets of hardening compound that housed Heuer's viscera like canopic urns in ancient Egypt.

"No," Charlie said. "The family hasn't brought any."

"Because he'll be closed," Jocasta said evenly, staring down at the ruined face. "I'll bet he was good looking once." She cocked a penciled eyebrow at the dead man, lapsing into silence for several seconds.

Charlie wondered who or what took over her thoughts at that precise moment and dared to hope that she would not make his arthritic old body drag the embalming table and its occupant out to the garage.

"Never mind what I said," Jocasta murmured, volunteering an ungloved hand to stroke the man's hair. "Your leg's gone gammy and I need you fit this week."

Charlie exhaled unaware he'd been holding his breath for the length of her pause. Not even experienced morticians got used to the smell.

Jocasta brightened "I'll get Krause to move him."

Chapter Twenty-Four

Few were surprised when Enid Engler announced, at the ethereal age of sixteen, that she wanted to be an undertaker. Tall, gangly, and slow to bud up topside, she possessed a child-like curiosity for all things forbidden. That Heuer took advantage of these qualities could be understood if one took into account his diminutiveness and fondness for the fantastic. Looking younger than his twenty-one years, they almost looked like contemporaries when they stood side by side. So when he began taking her hand in crowded rooms where no one could possibly see, it became as natural to her as it was to the one initiating the contact.

"Mächen, Mächen," he'd purr in her ear, "You are too young to be drinking." At this, she would smile, her large eyes widening over her beer stein, as if to dare more. "There will be more," he promised after the first time, "so long as you keep this to yourself." In the back seat of the Chevelle, supine and satisfied, she confirmed with her eyes an obedient assent.

Upstairs in the prep room, Enid smiled, remembering. It was their little pact, played out every time—she on her knees in front of him, lips glossed, teeth slightly parted, releasing tiny gasps as she groped for air. "I will be a lawyer like you," she said, pushing aside her dreams. How sweet that she wanted to mimic him; how naive that she thought she could follow.

"You are an artist," he countered, playing with her hair. "The law will choke the life out of you."

Heuer shifted in his seat; the creaky old leather office chair reminding him of the one he left back at home. He looked around the Weibigand basement, marking time, making calculations as to the time of day. What to do now?

He had taken the opportunity to go through some of the boxes, many of which contained old books on embalming procedure. Theoretically, not much had changed since Cleopatra. *Tintivation and the Art of the Cosmetic* was far less engrossing, Heuer correctly predicting that his body was too far gone for theatrical pancake. One book did catch his eye, and this one kept him entertained for hours. *The Incredible History of Embalming* not only catalogued and explained the methods of Dr. Thomas Holmes, a wacked out civil war undertaker who kept heads on his coffee table, but provided peels of unintentional laughter when it soberly called him the Father of Modern Embalming.

"My dear, little Hun," he said aloud. "How is it that you became such a ghoul?"

Upstairs, Enid dropped her instruments, necessitating a thorough cleansing before proceeding on a rank old fellow killed in a car accident. This was done furtively, in quick tweetie-bird-like motions, so as not to disturb the body tightly shrouded behind her. She could not look at him; yet she thought of him constantly.

***

Heuer laughed. That was good enough.

Next up were some moldy old photo albums, tucked away in a far corner. Flipping the pages, Heuer chafed at the happy faces posing in front of an old Chev in one frame and then a huge all wood inboard motor boat in another. He threw the book down, bored with the exertion. The lamp promised he could leave the basement again as soon as she returned from the wherever-it-was she went when she switched off. That had been a little under ten hours ago, and he longed for some kind of diversion beyond this prison.

What mischief could he get up to? There weren't any flies to startle or miscreant neighbors to scare. And the lamp kept drawling on about the "route to salvation," and the pressing need to right some wrongs in order to get the mourning started. Affronted by this suggestion, he cited all the wrongs done to him. His father, for example, backhanded him for "softness" when he was little, while his mother cooed much too much over his looks, insisting he take up piano and embrace an arts future. That, of course, could never happen—Werner kept the faded sepia photograph prominently on display in the front parlor. In uniform, his dad was beyond real; the peaked cap, skull and cross bones insignia, and matching lightning bolts on the lapels, made him bigger than he actually was. And it made him terribly scary too. Werner's son played with guns, not pianos. Full stop.

Heuer looked at his smooth hands—a musician's hands—with their perfectly tapered fingers filled with music that went unplayed. Peace? There was no peace to be made with Werner.

The door at the top of the stair rattled, followed by hesitant steps illuminated by the soft glow of a torch. Don't these people ever turn the lights on? Evidently not. He craned his neck, listening for Enid's unique stride, a half skip that seemed elfin if there was such a thing.

"*Schön?*" he called out, and for a moment, he almost felt the lurch of his stilled heart. How pretty she was at thirteen, with her buttermilk hair to go with the peculiar eyes—yellow at their centers enclosed in a thin band of slate finished with a thick indigo border: A stunning look, made more pronounced by firelight, when they were alone at the lake, or by the Christmas tree, set aglow in her parents' basement long after her brother passed out from too much booze.

"*Have some.*" *He pushed a strong drink into her tiny hands and she gulped greedily peering over the edge of the cup; her freak's eyes boring into to him, her child hand on his knee.*

The footsteps came nearer and with it an accelerated excitement, pyroclastic—flowing—around his bones and hollow organs. Although he had not thought of her for many years, the intimacy they shared now made him want her more.

"Come," he said in German, offering his hand. She hesitated, but only for a moment. It was so cold outside, and the Chevelle was warm...

Footsteps came out of the dark and with it the face, framed by a Coleman lamp. Base, shoddy, pedestrian, not his *Schön*, but a vicious old hag brought to him to taunt instead of please.

Do it. Do it. The voice in his head clanged. He clasped his hands to his ears to shut out the drone. *Do it. Do it. What kind of a pussy are you?*

Heuer rose to his full height, squelching out the light cast by the ugly visitor and her preposterous little lamp. "I am not a pussy," he shouted, taking hold of her lapels. "Do you hear me?"

"Oh, I believe she does," the lamp trilled from her place in the corner. "The last time she ran that fast, I capped her with the back of my hand."

He looked down at the light, broken on impact after Jocasta let go. "Who was that?" he asked. "And what did I just do?"

"You revealed yourself," the lamp said with unrestrained glee, "and for that you have my thanks. She is the one who placed me here, and you are going to help me salve an old wound."

Heuer stared at her quizzically. He knew sooner or later that a devil's bargain would have to be struck—no one gets their freedom for nothing. But what price would freedom command?

"You have been a very bad boy, *mein Schlecht*," she went on, reading his thoughts. "And I am no daemon, certainly; just a misunderstood old floor lamp trying to get her body back."

Heuer caught himself; losing his body—this body—

terrified him.

"You won't." She violated his head space for a second time. "But you won't get out of here as long as you're ghosting around like the *Blithe Spirit*." She chuckled at her weak attempt at humor. Heuer, of course, was well aware of the works of Noel Coward, another favorite of dear mother, who filled her bookshelves with the works of many esteemed homosexuals.

"You appeared to your neighbor at the Drakoulias funeral and you gave him a terrible start."

"I did no such thing—" Heuer moved in defense. "He assaulted my reputation and I merely tried to stop him. Only—merely." He grinned.

"The man needed nitroglycerin, *mein Kind*. You cannot move along by killing people, *Verstehen Sie?*"

Ja. He got it. But the joy at seeing Alfons go down to angina was inestimable. He held out his hands to her in abject surrender. "All right. *Mea culpa*. When do I get out of here again? At least let me out of this room."

The lamp crackled and popped, her old white luminescent bulb struggling beneath the weight of what had to be some pretty formidable energy. "The girl," she purred. "You want to see the girl."

"It is preferable to going through some old trout's photographs."

The lamp stilled. He had said something wrong.

Heuer understood. The stern looking old broad in the photos with the braids and ass as wide as an axe handle had to be her. He looked down at the floor, contrition and shame washing over him.

"You want to know my story?" Her voice strangled, rising an octave. "I will tell you." The lamp raged on for what seemed like an hour about the pain and misery that dominated old women. Her husband was a rat, bedding over many years flat chested, pale skinned, strumpets—*unter Mensch*—their weakness as appealing to him as his wife's strength was not. "I endured it." She affected a saintly tone. "But at a cost. This business was as much mine as his, and I wasn't about to give it up to him, his bitch, or the little mole rat she gave birth to."

"You're Irmtraut Weibigand."

"I am, forced into this shape by a bastard."

"Your husband fathered a bastard?"

"Worse—a she bastard. A bitch. Plain and simple."

Heuer sat silent—his experience with ranting women deeming it the best course.

"After my funeral, she cleaned house. She put me here."

"The mistress?"

"No. The mongrel bitch. She worked here. Still works here. Was just here now, remember?"

Heuer thought back to the epic fights his parents had when they were still together. Werner was a tool and die maker who somehow convinced Hannelore that he needed to travel. Disappearing for days or sometimes weeks at a time, he would reappear at their home cursing, in poor health and, inevitably, broke.

"To my knowledge, I am the only bastard in my family," Heuer offered.

Irmtraut flashed three times in assent—it was her way of displaying profound agreement and displeasure.

"A bastard born; a bastard's life lived. You have much to answer for, and thus far you have failed."

Heuer grinned. "I went to Legacy. I paid my respects..."

"You revealed yourself to the neighbor," she repeated, "and you destroyed the man's property."

"No." His eyes twinkled. "I didn't destroy a thing. Our master did."

Chapter Twenty-Five

11:00 A.M.

Pound for pound, the older of the two had the weight advantage, but for sheer electricity, Enid had the edge. Standing in the main foyer, her fists knotted balls spiked by a pair of *bon voyant* cocktail rings, she appeared "this close" to knocking the shit out of the old witch.

"He stinks," Jocasta hammered, "and he has to go. If you won't move him, Dougie will." She turned on her fat ankles and lurched off, a daytime monster mumbling about "families" that she needed to see.

Enid pressed her hands to her temples, which raged and flared with an increased flush of blood. There she remained, oblivious to the comings and goings of her coworkers, who ran willy nilly in every direction. Some carried flowers, another a feather duster while still another, bringing up the rear, pushed a clunky Hoover vacuum cleaner.

Heuer remained fixed in his spot outside the chapel doors, resisting with great difficulty, a desire to comfort her. He really didn't have the right.

"There you are," a porcine little man no taller than he puffed, relieved at finding her in her place. "The Shawson-Cooke asshole is on the phone with Charlie insisting Emmy had a ring."

Enid shrugged. "I wasn't on that call Doug. I don't know anything about it. What does Carla say?"

He wiped his sleeve across his shiny forehead, the July heat outside, impossible. "She doesn't know if there was one or not—won't commit either way. She's busy looking for Rat. He's still missing you know."

She passed him a crumpled piece of paper towel from her left breast pocket, which he used in place of his sleeve.

"The Jocastrator is going to ask you something and I want you to ignore it." She drew in closer, such that Heuer had to move for a better listen. "She's gonna ask you to move Heuer, and you can't do it. Tell Robert to close him and double up on the phenol. I'll take care of the rest."

"But what about the ring? What about Rat?"

Enid shook her head vigorously. "Doug! One rat at a time. Okay?" She shooed him away.

Heuer savored the moment: Being alone was always a production.

"Hello?" she said, turning to him, her eyes soft with the unmistakable look of recognition. The look, greatly welcomed, made a fitting bookend to their last chapter. Twenty years had passed, but it didn't erase the force of her flat hand against his face. He opened his arms wide to take her in.

"What are you doing?" Her features creased at the center, depriving her of the youth locked away in her sentimental heart. Struck to the core, he wanted to run from her, as past and present crushed together. Perhaps the old songs were right: you can't go back.

She walked past him, crossing the foyer in three formidable strides to the cloakroom underneath the grand stair. Once there, she reached out in front of her, carefully, as if retrieving something made of fine paper or silk cloth. The article to be extracted warbled pigeon-like and he resisted the urge to move forward to see for himself what it was she sought. Funeral parlors were, indeed, very odd places; even stranger than the many legal establishments he'd endured over the years.

"Don't be afraid," she whispered, taking hold of soft, rose water skin. "Where is your husband?"

***

Shame or contrition had nothing to do with Heuer's decision to leave Enid back in '89. And for those that needed to believe that the move was unselfish or borne out of a desire to ultimately do right, there could only be disappointment. The truth of it was that Heuer didn't think about Enid after their last contretemps. Why would he? There were no rules in law compelling him to do so. If anything, there was romantic literature of the kind his mother relied upon to drive the message home that he had some kind of responsibility to her, but even these failed to impress him.

Enid wouldn't play with him anymore and so what was the point of continuing the connection?

Heuer bolted, exiting Weibigand's in favor of higher ground. The choices of just where to land were few.

When he was young, flight was easy. First, cutting ties with the impediments that dared to hold him back, he always remade himself with god-like zeal, emerging phoenix-like at a new destination. Immersed in foreign languages, schooled in the life and times of Richard Nixon, and slavishly devoted to the *doctrine scandaleuse* of Rand, he was shiny, slick, hard to pin down, and—incredibly— highly sought after. What he never advertised was the gargantuan amount of effort he applied to the consumption of Hitler documentaries provided courtesy of History Channel. Had they known, observers might have concluded that he was searching for his identity, but that was not the case. He knew very well what he was, and as sure as his father's portrait stood on the mantle to remind him, so too did the bad blood that ran through him without interruption. The films were a tonic that underscored his heritage. After '89, he made a conscious decision to rock the dark side.

Being educated and proud of it, he did not do harm for harm's sake. He could very easily have shorted out the machine that pumped goo into his corpse; tipped water on to the fool that tried to embalm him; lock the sexy coroner in the freezer; or take Enid by night, when she was sleeping. But he did not. He had his standards.

Standing in front of the chrome, steel, and glass

monstrosity that housed TRAVAT Ion's north central corporate office, he felt rejuvenated, as if he were back at Harvard Law, itself a silly place of privilege and aimless cloying. He watched, bemused, as the suits and IT wonks in shorts and sandals scurried past him in the suffocating heat, to make meetings or meet lovers. The women, he noted, did the same thing, yammering into cell phones about very important things, their limp hair dangling past their shoulders with that "I don't give a damn air" he found so incredibly unattractive. How he missed the Eighties—and Harvard—where aristocratic affectations took him farther than a scholarship. Ingratiating himself into some very fine homes, he received an endorsement to join one of those "social clubs" that owned its own island as well as the ass of each member that signed on in blood. This invitation, he refused, politely, in favor of the Masonic Order, which he did not buy into until he had sufficient coin to do so. TRAVAT was the last stop after strange stints at an Anglo law firm followed by a French one that specialized in open pit mining on the African continent.

Heuer did not know what to expect on entering the building, but he counted on the same kind of prurient gossip that dominated every water cooler in every office.

"Did you hear?" Redmond the Queer from corporate assets burbled to the assembled gathered around the fifth floor health and wellness bar. "Texas Bob has been recalled to Houston."

A hush fell over the group. Bob was popular.

"It's so over for him," clucked Samantha, ever the smoky morsel well worth getting busy over. Heuer watched, longing, as she parked her generous cheeks on the corner console that dispensed seven different kinds of organic fruit juice. "I can't say I'm surprised."

"Oh please," snarked Redmond as he looked down his aquiline nose. "There's no way you could know that, unless information is conferred by osmosis...and no amount of cum, my dear, can inform the brain. I don't care how many people you boink."

Heuer laughed, for as much as he sometimes judged the gay sex, he had plenty of time for Redmond—he was clever.

"I must concur with Miss Samantha," said Guillaine, Heuer's sexy French speaking secretary from Ivory Coast. "Mr. Heuer worked day and night on the bio spill before he passed away. They're still taking boxes out of his office..."

Boxes? What boxes? His flesh froze, such that any sudden movement would shatter him. He looked at Guillaine, a gift given him by his previous employer, who dismissed her capabilities with a crass comment "nice bit of chocolate." In addition to speaking several languages, she possessed enough knowledge of environmental and employment law in central and West Africa to ably take his place. He studied her, as if seeing her for the first time: A long neck capped by a squared jaw, pronounced cheekbones, and short cut hair defining an intelligent, elongated skull that reminded him of an Egyptian queen. Why had his Ebony Beautiful not followed protocol? TRAVAT was not the Nixon Whitehouse, but he'd made it abundantly clear to her on several occasions about what had to be sent up the smoke stack if he were to suddenly disappear.

A thick-trunked horror of a winged beast entered from the side door adjoining the juice bar. "A word, Guillaine," it said, gesturing to the east corridor where HR lived.

Heuer scowled. Why did women turn into men after their menses shut off?

Dear Guillaine followed obediently. There was no point in challenging the HR head, although he had tried on many occasions, succeeding each time. Not since his mother had Heuer met a person more duplicitous than himself. Watching the director sludge around her enclosure, he acknowledged that the torch had indeed been passed.

"Take a seat," the director said on arriving in her office.

"Don't mind if I do," Heuer said, parking a top her fake antique coffee table with its ugly green faux Lalique glass insert.

"This interview will be short and it will not be taped. Do you want representation?"

Guillaine settled into her seat, radiating the confidence typical of a warrior princess. "That depends on what you are looking for Ms. Grissom."

"It is a delicate matter. Something that doesn't bear examination post mortem, I suppose. But I've had an informal report, and if it is true, then the complainant is entitled to a share of his estate."

Guillaine, statuesque and still, betrayed nothing of what she was thinking and this relieved him considerably.

"You are referring to whom?" Guillaine asked, her features blank, but her mind whirring.

"Good girl," Heuer muttered. He didn't like going outside his tastes, he preferred the vulgar office manager with the big tits, but he went out of his way to make Guillaine comfortable, particularly when they were alone together. Not once had it occurred to him that he ever made her uneasy.

"Mr. Heuer," of course, replied Ms. Grissom, who tapped her pen like a metronome at a piano exam.

Guillaine's heart beat faster.

"It's no secret Guillaine that Mr. Heuer had a few run ins at his previous place of employ."

"I know nothing of the sort." She pushed flattering images of him out of her mind.

"And that he was slow to get off the ground here."

Silence.

"And that you were extremely fond of him."

"This is a breach of privacy." She moved to leave.

"Agreed. Which is why this is off the record. Not only are Mr. Heuer's files under review, but there is word of a sexual impropriety that, if corroborated, might lead to a generous award."

Rising to his feet, Heuer joined Guillaine, who, stopped at the door, listened closely.

"I'm not a lawyer, but, certainly, it would be a sensational case if the DNA matched—post mortem paternity—of course, why not? The mother has promised a finder's fee..." Ms. Grissom shifted her heft from one side of her chair to the other. "A hair brush, Guillaine. A comb? It's all she needs. And you picked up his dry cleaning."

"The damn shrew," Heuer muttered, not sure who to be angry at first—the cow in the boxy suit, or the fake baby mama going after his dough.

"This interview is over," Guillaine fumed.

"Think on it," she called out, as Guillaine exited her office. "This is America. If the child is his, the plaintiff has promised generous recompense to anyone that assists."

Chapter Twenty-Six

Hannelore Heuer, stuck in the Weibigand coat closet, was a mystery Enid struggled to unravel.

"Here's some water," Carla Blue said, offering an eight ounce crystal tumbler, one of Weibigand's finest. She lingered, scanning Enid's face for clues. Enid replied with a shrug. She suspected Frau Heuer of not being in complete command of her wits at their first meeting, but now her suspicions were confirmed. "Thanks Carla, I have it."

"You are very kind, *mein Kind*," the old woman said, switching to German.

"I can speak German if you prefer?" Enid offered. "Although mine is a dialect and horribly affected."

"That is all right," the old lady said, brightening. "I am Austrian. There isn't a Berliner anywhere that could make sense of me."

"What brings you here, Frau Heuer and where is Werner?" It was not Enid's custom to use first names with families unless first given permission. By rights, she should have been able to use their names at the outset, but Heuer kept her secret when they were young and she never benefitted from a meeting with the old folks like a real girlfriend would.

Hannelore tugged at her blouse as if looking for something beneath—a locket, perhaps, or maybe a cross and chain. "I brought clothes for him," she said, ignoring the second question. "I brought a blue tie to match his eyes."

Enid swallowed hard, suppressing all thoughts of dressing him.

"I put them in the closet," Hannelore said, her hands gaining speed beneath her clothes.

Enid's concern over Heuer's care dissipated. "Frau? Is there something I can help you with?" She rose from her chair in the pretty front office, circling round the big oak desk to take a seat next to the old lady.

Hannelore drew back as if to dodge an anticipated physical attack. Enid lowered her voice, effecting calm, a tactic taught her at mortuary school by a smart alecky professor who called it "Old Lady Wrangling."

"Don't be afraid. I want you to trust me as if I were your own."

The old lady's hands shook a dozen little tremors and Enid wondered if she had Parkinsons. "You *are* mine," she said. "I recognized you immediately."

Scratch that; Alzheimers.

"Shall we go look for his clothes?"

Hannelore, gentled, reached inside her blouse, retrieving a pendant on a delicate filigreed chain. "In a little while," she said. "Tell me about my son."

Enid froze, her eyes locked in place on the old woman's child-like face.

"I know it's you, my dear. I would never forget eyes like yours."

Enid, intrigued, ventured out on a limb; stories abounded about second sight and of the disturbed having a unique relationship with things unseen. "Tell me how you know me, Frau Heuer."

Hannelore released the pendant to take Enid's hand. "My son was a great artist, as you know. He never tired of taking your photograph." She paused, smiling at some private thought. "In this regard, he was very much like his father."

Enid didn't know where to begin: should she ask about the pictures first, or the improbable link between art and the formidable obstinence that was Werner Heuer?

"I loved him very much you know. But I could not keep him. I lost him, just like you lost my son."

Enid touched her cheek with her free hand.

"Don't cry," Hannelore said, lowering her voice. "He will always be with you, just like his father is with me."

"I don't understand," Enid burbled, letting go of any pretense to professional conduct. Hannelore reached for the pendant—not a cross—but a Star of David. Enid still did not understand.

"His father was a musician and a survivor of the camps. To be with him was a way of forgiving myself for the war and for all the terrible things we did."

There were so many questions to ask, but the circumstances denied Enid the satisfaction of probing further. Entering the office, Charlie Forsythe blundered into an amazing mystery that included Heuer's parentage and his penchant for portrait photography. Enid dried her eyes on her sleeve. "Mr. Forsythe, I was just talking to Frau Heuer about Herr Heuer's clothes."

Charlie smiled. "Forgive me, ladies, but after all these years, I still don't speak German."

"Forgive me," Enid flushed, covering her mouth with her hands. "I completely forgot myself."

"Not at all," Hannelore jumped in. "I was reacquainting her with her true self."

Ironic, Enid thought, given that Heuer wasn't a Heuer after all.

3:00 P.M.

Night fell fast on the funeral home as thick inky clouds laced their way across the late day sky. Down below, in the Weibigand prep room, staff toiled under the shrewd eye of Eldon Wheeler, who could tell before Robert even tried that they would not be able to close Mr. Heuer. The tissue flaps were firm and dry—like they should be—but the hide had tanned to leather. Deprived of elasticity, there was no way the two and a half foot incision would meet over a viscera bag stuffed underneath.

"Turn the lights on," he barked, frowning over the creeping dark that eclipsed the glass blocks and the natural light they held within.

Dougie, rushing to oblige, tipped a pot of cosmetic powder onto the uneven tile floor, sending plumes of lilac scented dust into their noses and lungs. To this, the senior embalmer, armed with a too wide necktie destined for the car accident victim, blew a blood vessel, ordering every incompetent sonofabitch out of his goddamned prep room before he strangled them all.

"And that includes you," he glared, as Carla waltzed in to see what the matter was.

"I can help if you let me," she replied, ignoring his rage. He was getting on in years—almost sixty—and his ability to handle three funerals in a day was diminishing. Only no one dared tell him. He knew anyway, of course, but wasn't going to let it get in the way. Weibigand's was more than a place of work; it was his home, though he could not admit it. He loathed an empty house, loathed going home to one every night. At least here, there were people to harangue and love in equal amounts, Dougie and Robert included.

"His guts won't fit," he snorted, bobbing his closely cropped thatch of steel grey hair in the direction of Jürgen Heuer. "Even if we remove all of the hardening compound, they'll never go back into him."

Carla popped the lid on the barrel that contained Heuer's organs and inclined her head in agreement.

"He had an enlarged heart by the look of things..."

"And liver," Eldon added. "Thing's huge. Must have been an epic boozer."

Carla placed a hand over her midsection. "People do all kinds of crazy things when they're hammered."

Eldon grunted, retying the car accident's tie for the third time.

"I might need to take some time off," Carla said suddenly. "I know we're busy, but it's for health reasons."

The old man snorted again, before shooting an

impressive wad of spit across the room to land squarely in the biohazard waste container. Looking over his steel-rimmed glasses, he weighed his answer, because he had no real power when it came to leave takes. Carla was a hard worker and loyal apostle; in all her years of service, she had never let him or the firm down. Even with Jocasta riding on her harder than usual, she reported for work, kept her temper, and refrained from killing the old bitch. If she was ailing, she deserved time off, regardless of what he thought.

"I always thought it was Krause who'd go into rehab first," he sniffed. "Not you. But then you married a fag, and then you married an idiot, so I guess anything is possible." Dr. Salinger, Carla's first husband, had a fondness for the fellas—a predilection Carla wished he'd shared with her before putting a ring on it. And then there was the idiot Danny Blue, a boy baby who couldn't stop playing with toys.

Carla would not be cowed. "Be serious, darling. I have a cyst. I need it out—sooner, rather than later."

Eldon, finished with the car accident, pushed the cosmetic powder out of his path with the big broom kept inside the room in violation of funeral board regulations. The inspectors were due in early next week, he thought, sniffing the air. That was more than enough time to get Mr. Heuer's stink out of his beloved prep room.

"Help me with him," he commanded, pointing to Heuer. "Go over him again with the hypo-trocar; I'm seeing tissue gas."

"Aye, captain," she said, running gloved hands over the raised tissue that reminded everyone of bubble wrap.

"And the viscera?" she asked, eyeing the biohazard box with disdain.

"Absolutely not!" he said, and then paused, wanting to be very clear about their difficult patient. "Everyone leaves with what they came with. Those..." he pointed to the pail "...those will go in the casket where they belong."

At the other end of the hall, Charlie Forsythe lowered himself into The Thinking Chair. Worrying compulsively over Emmy's lost ring and the damage Teddy Shawson-Cooke could do if he really wanted to, he nearly missed the phone that buzzed for an indeterminate length of time at his right elbow.

"Hell—ohhhh," he said, praying for a salesperson and not a new death call.

A clear, spirited trill of a woman's voice sang through the other end: "Is this Weebiggins?"

Charlie stifled a laugh. Not only had he answered the phone incorrectly—he should have named the establishment and announced himself—but he knew the caller too. "Dale Somerset Whatever Your Name Is."

"Exeter Wembley Crewe, and don't be daft, darling. You've met all my husbands."

"I buried a few."

More laughter. "And I wrote about them."

"I don't read your filth. How goes the smut business?" He looked up at the cross of Jesus hanging on his wall and shook his head.

"Pretty dry, actually. I was writing about lesbians for a time…"

"Surely not!" Charlie couldn't abide lesbians. Every time a decent club opened in Portside, they invaded with the intent of taking over. Equality was a good thing, but it had its proper place and *his* club was not it.

"Surely yes. And don't be such a snob. Anyway, I got bored really fast."

"The conventional way is better."

"Absolutely. I'm sticking to what I know." After a pause: "Listen Charlie, I want to know what's going on with Heuer."

Charlie frowned. As a two-time widow and loyal customer, Dale Sommerset Whatever Her Name Was, knew the rules about privacy. "My darling, you are not next of kin—"

"I don't want details, silly. I want to make sure Iddy's okay."

Charlie's mind wandered back twenty years, when Dale's husband—"he was my fiancé," she corrected—was stretched out in the Chapel. "I wasn't aware that Enid was off. You threw her out of your boyfriend's visitation, remember?"

"How could I forget?" she replied, exhaling what had to be cigarette smoke. "I mean, she banged him before I did. But then she shows up at the funeral acting like the widow and, I mean…well, it's just tacky. Right?"

Dale threw Enid out the front door onto the concrete. It was an outrageous display, though nothing he hadn't seen before. Misplaced grief, at its very worst, is selfish, trampling on anyone that gets in its way: sisters usurping the wives for volume of tears, ex-wives sitting in the front row with elderly kids while wife number two sits stewing four pews back. People taking ownership of the deceased when they had no right to do so were stupid. Stupid beyond the pale.

"I'm afraid she's behaving like that again, Charlie, and we want to nip that before she makes an ass of herself."

Charlie scratched his head, searching for hints of this strange behavior Dale was insisting upon. Her hasty departure yesterday aside, Enid had conducted herself properly. She disclosed to him her relationship to the dead man—they were lovers as far as he could tell—with a plea to be excused; directors were excused for far less.

"That's just it, Charlie. She swans around pretending after a great love affair…but it never happened. She's manufactured it."

Now that was complicated.

"And—geez—I don't want her to get skinned for this…you must handle this sensitively, but you know she took chemicals from the shelves to embalm a rat in her garage."

Charlie noticed the day old doughnut on the console: Rat's daily supplement, untouched.

"She has our rat?" He smoothed his eyebrows back into position, having become stuck somewhere just south of the hairline.

"If that's what you think. Sure. Why not? But you must agree, her behavior is off."

"It's bizarre."

Dale wrestled with something on the other end of the phone. "Give me a second will you. My Chablis glass is empty."

After a respectable amount of time passed, she returned to the phone with a cryptic: "You met Heuer, you know."

"Did I?" Charlie couldn't place the face, which was sliding off in the prep room.

"At Jimmy's funeral. You were drooling all over him," she chuckled, "which would have been painful to watch if it was anybody but Heuer."

Charlie laughed. Was Mr. Heuer that extraordinary?

"Hair the color of corn silk and blue eyes like you've never seen. The most Germanic looking man I have ever encountered."

Charlie wondered why she didn't go after him herself if he was so damned fantastic.

"Well, you see, darling, that's the whole thing: I wasn't his type and neither was she."

Charlie scratched out a doodle on a rainbow colored scribble pad that also contained detailed notes for the party this coming weekend. He had never invited Dale to any of his Pride soirees before, and he hesitated to do so now, for while he appreciated her concern for Enid's well-being, he was troubled by her fallacious declaration that Heuer was gay.

"Now, darling, just because he got away doesn't mean he was part of the Sisterhood."

"Well, we'll never know now, will we?"

Charlie covered the handset after a hasty "hold on a second."

"Jocasta!" he yelled out, spying her leaden figure heading for the back door. "Jocasta! A word, please."

"I hate her," Dale's voice piped through the muted earpiece.

"Jocasta. I was wondering if you know anything about our rat?"

Chapter Twenty-Seven

8:45 P.M.

Heuer stood outside Enid Engler's house, looking into the front window for any signs that she might come out. Nothing yet. "What are you doing here?" Irmtraut demanded. "You have no business with this woman inside her home!"

"Yes!" Heuer yelled back, his disdain for two-way paranormal communication at its apex. "And as you see…" he looked around, wondering if he'd find her lamp body behind him "or, perhaps you don't…I am not inside. I am waiting outside."

"You are not in a court of law," she chided, "so don't play the semantics game with me. And her name is Krause—not Engler. You must acknowledge that."

Heuer struggled with that one. Although he threw her away without a word, he never imagined Enid with another man.

"Her brother was relieved that she didn't convert to Judaism," Irmtraut offered. "I suppose your arrogance will assign that decision to some perverse allegiance she still held for you."

Heuer grinned. This was where he held an advantage over Irmtraut Weibigand, whom, he suspected, was never decently mourned. "She loves me still. Did you see how she cried over me?"

"Women cry over a lot of things," Irmtraut conceded. "My husband made me cry all the time."

"Really?" He was intrigued. "I can't imagine you ever crying."

"I had a body once and a heart to go with it. My husband was a serial philanderer. I fully expect he's keeping company with his flat-chested whore in hell right now."

Ouch!

"Only one whore?" Heuer couldn't resist the dig.

"He had his favorites. But the one that pushed out his little bastard was his favorite of all."

And so here it was. "Frau Binns?"

"Binns was her husband's name, god rest his soul for taking her on. Jocasta Loom was born of the chapel organist, who divided her time between the Hammond and my husband's legs."

Heuer shook his head. The heavy rains that brought on premature darkness earlier had receded to let in bright sunshine. With the sun slipping under the horizon, his hope that Enid might appear slipped too. His disappointment, coupled with the clutter of Irmtraut's bitterness inside his head, began to overwhelm.

"She had a big mouth," Irmtraut continued. "Helme Loom, the organist. Of course, I did not. There are some things one should never put in one's mouth."

Enid's garage door opened just enough to reveal a crack of yellow light. Her domain soft and inviting, he drew nearer, taking care not to cross the line. "She must not see me," he said, sequestering Irmtraut's rambling monologue to a distal place in his brain.

Inside the garage, Enid got busy, first checking on a strange brew in a large bratwurst kettle, the same one her father used every autumn. Heuer smiled, warming to thoughts of the good times spent in the Engler family home when they were young and he had a place there. *"Spiel mit Mir,"* he'd whisper to her, from their hiding place behind the furnace, a private heaven that was their own.

"I'll be back late," she called out to someone inside the house. "It's an autopsy."

Heuer frowned. Was she heading back to that awful place?

The answer was "no," ringing out loud and clear as she screeched rubber on the road, crossing town in under half an hour so that she could park three streets over from his house.

"I don't understand," he said, pulling up alongside her. "What are you doing here?"

Panic gripped him. She had never seen the inside of his home, despite her urgent pleas, years ago, after she'd grown up and wanted to live with him.

Enid moved ninja style in silent leaps, quite unlike the elfin waif he'd longed for but refused to love. "Love, my love—," his mother would say over her tea cup in the little kitchen they once shared, "and desire—*Sensucht*—longing. These are the things that make the history, the things upon which great legends are built. Without these, you have dust in your mouth." He didn't know what she was driving at when she said it. Watching Enid Krause break into his house, it became all too clear.

"I knew it was bad," Enid said, surveying his filthy basement with the aid of a large flash light, "but this, Heuer, asks more questions than it answers." Boxes piled floor to ceiling, choked the rec room that had once been his bedroom when his parents were still together and living upstairs. After their split, and his mother's descent into dementia, he moved back into his boyhood room. Once Hannelore relocated to the nursing home, he was free to surround himself with all the things he loved.

"Don't go there, please," he begged.

Enid opened the first box containing his stuffed animals—Jogi, Boo Boo, Bulwinkle the Moose—and his very first GI Joes. At these she smiled, as thoughts of her younger self playing with her brothers over took her. "You kept your toys," her voice wavered.

Heuer cringed. He kept everything, including things not meant to be seen by others. He wanted to stop her, wanted to preserve some vestige of his old self in her memory. She wanted to marry him and when he refused her, she offered herself as a mistress. She wanted to live with him, and when he refused, she contented herself with his body, which, she knew, was not exclusively hers to indulge. She wondered about his sexuality, never betraying her doubts, and when he started to hit her, she pretended it was love.

Enid flipped through his marvel comic books, and then his pornography: No children; no animals; no men. She breathed a sigh of relief. If he switched sides in moments of weakness, he didn't leave any evidence to suggest it. She smiled as she allowed herself to love him again.

Guns, of course, were never a problem—she loved them as much as he did, or at least she pretended to. And as she happened upon his firearms collection, illegally stored without trigger locks, and within reach of crates of ammunition, also unlocked, she shook her head, clucking softly like a disapproving mother hen. "Shame, shame."

When she ascended the stairs into what should have been a kitchen, she found piles and piles of dirty clothing, unwashed because his laundry room was inaccessible, choked over with newspapers and empty tin cans. Enid clasped her hands over her breasts by way of exclamation. Newspapers and tin cans were a constant in every hermit house she had ever seen. That he repeated this pattern made her sullen and she stopped loving him again.

"No. No," he protested. "I was never a hermit. I went to work. I had friends."

"But not all of them were real, were they?" Irmtraut demanded, fighting her way back into his consciousness. "You pretended to be a sailor, so you bought hundreds of chinos."

"I went on a yacht once," he protested.

"You pretended to be a car guy, but you left yours to rot on the driveway."

"I had every intention of restoring her after I retired."

"You told everyone who'd listen that you bought a

condo on Lake Placid, but you maxed out your credit cards. You have nothing."

Irmtraut went too far, and he was about to tell her so when he noticed that Enid was gone.

"Where are you? Where are you?" Heuer drifted from room to room searching for her thoughts, for while he could see easily enough in the pale grey dark, he could not perceive her physical body through the mountains of garbage he'd hauled from every office job he'd ever had, a practice Guillaine found peculiar since their work neither threatened national security nor endangered the lives of anyone outside of Africa.

Familiar footfalls from above alerted him to her location and fearing she'd react to what she found in the same way the coroner had, he flew to her. What bothered her more? The preponderance of flat screens in his boudoir, the telescope he used to spy on the neighbors with, or the wall of boxes containing rat poison that he used to kill errant wildlife?

She couldn't decide. Enid stood in the centre of the bedroom, the chalk outline of his body, dramatically drawn out by hasty cops intent on proving he'd been murdered, clearly visible in the waxing moonlight. The ambient light suited her, he decided, because it stripped the years away. Back at the lake, she'd emerge from the water, silvery naked, young, washed clean, her bruises hiding from him. He'd enfolded her in his arms, made promises, and broke every one of them.

Her eyes, intent, scanned the photographs that littered the floor; smiling faces, friends and foes, some clipped from magazines, others downloaded from the internet. They amused him for hours; faces and places—some of them had names—others were made up and assigned, lovingly, by Heuer himself. And then the photographs she did know, all taken by the Pentax: Christmas parties, cottage getaways, the young Republican convention. Her joy quickly faded as she moved through the stacks: she was looking for herself, but she wasn't there.

What was that stuff on the wall? Enid looked closer, but did not touch. Did she recognize the essence, deposited over many years? Heuer chuckled. The woman in HR actually believed that he fathered a child, perhaps by force. That simply wasn't possible. The only person Heuer had sex with was standing right there in the room behind Enid Engler Krause.

Chapter Twenty-Eight

Wednesday, 6:30 A.M.

Gale force winds combined with sheeting rain slowed Enid's progress, as she looped through the back streets leading to Weibigand's. Sleepless, she got up ratty, bitching at Aaron about his snoring and of how it kept her awake. This, of course, was a lie, another in a series of many unspooled to the guileless people that loved her.

"What a piece of shit I am," she said to the steering wheel of her equally shitty old Honda. Not only had she allowed Heuer back into her mind, but he'd thoroughly violated her heart for the second time. How could this be? Not once had he offered his love, let alone pay for a meal. He never bought her a gift either—the closest he came to that was the riding boots, which she bought herself though she could ill afford them. "You are thinking with your pussy," Dale accused, when she still believed her friend was in a real relationship. That was a lie too, wasn't it?

Enid leaned on the horn, impatient to get to her destination. The local weirdo, an incorrigible old hag on an apple red scooter, crossed in front of the car, flipping the bird as if to taunt Enid to run her over. "I could do just that," Enid shouted, "and make you go away so that no one could ever find you."

She performed a quick calculation, sizing up the woman's body fat to muscle ratio. Four gallons of embalming solution was needed for sure, along with some MetaBlu for extra firming. Enid congratulated herself. After all these years, she still performed a pre embalming analysis, providing each and every body in her care a unique chemical solution. She thought about Heuer, resting with his equally quiet companions in the prep room. Had Robert done what she asked? In cases of advanced decomposition, where desquamation—the sheering off of the top layers of skin—was a constant challenge, the embalmer applied searing gels and top sheets soaked in phenol to dry the skin and stop the weeping. If Robert did as he was told, Heuer would be nice and dry and well able to hold a stitch without tearing.

A rich baritone horn sounded behind her, reminding her that she was not alone in the race to get to work. Spying a large Ford Fairlane in her rearview, she waved to the driver, a local merchant too scared to drop in for coffee, owing to his belief in lost souls and the spirits that guide them. She chuckled, forgetting for a moment the influx of tumbling thoughts that hounded her.

How could she love a man who kept children's toys in a box next to his pornography? And what about the garbage in the living room? Enid didn't know the first thing about mental illness, but she'd heard plenty enough about it from Carter and cop friends at 61 Division.

In the time it took her to negotiate the last three blocks, she went through the key stages of grief for the dozenth time—the sadness, the anger, the pain, the regret, the longing, the lying, the wishing things were different. The only thing missing was the "letting go."

"I don't want to," she said, answering her own questions. "Not yet. Not yet."

***

Charged with purpose, Heuer searched the boxes in his filthy basement, knowing exactly what to look for. A private man, he should have felt violated by Enid's peculiar invasion, but he didn't. Time had not changed her, not really: she had preconceived notions of how things should be and remembered them accordingly. Time solved everything, obliterating the unpleasant in favor of the benign. When this fragile deception was skewered, it produced chaos. He could not stand back and watch her buckle.

Sounds from the backyard interrupted his search. His

195

father's voice, measured and controlled, thanked another that persisted in offering help. Heuer moved to the mud-splattered little window that provided the only source of real light.

"It's no trouble, really. I have a brother in the business."

Business of what? Heuer craned his neck to see who Werner was speaking to, but failed to identify the other male through the rain that sluiced the windowpane.

"Come inside," Werner said at last, "before we are flooded out a second time."

Heuer's eyes widened. The only flooding that happened lately was in his own backyard and the only person who shared in that mishap was the pesky neighbor.

Werner and Alfons entered the house via the back door, which had been re keyed to enable his father's access. "I apologize for the state of things," he said, stiffly. "My son was a mystery, as you see." He gestured with his large hands to the pile of dirty clothes on the floor. "It appears he bought new instead of washing like a normal person."

Alfons shook his head, a look of genuine concern traversing his features. "I never really knew him, Mr. Heuer, aside from neighborly disagreements over the fence line and the tree."

Werner held up his hand. "My son's estate will take care of the cleanup, a fence and pool, of course, will be included."

Heuer bristled: even in death, he was denied victory.

"I appreciate that," Alfons said. "And I'll have my brother contact you. The dumpster out front won't be enough. You're going to need five, at least."

Werner smiled, his little eyes disappearing into a fat, piggy face. "Thank you. I see little value in going through any of this. He can take all of it."

"You'll sell?"

"The house? Of course. I have no need for this old

place."

Heuer sank to the floor just paces from where the men stood. If all Enid Engler had to show for the past was false memory, what did he have if all of this—his life's work—was thrown away without an afterthought? He loosened his tie, as if to relieve pressure on his throat. Dead people didn't breathe, nor did they experience accelerating pulse rates. What they did feel was density; a heaviness that weighed them down when saddened, effectively blocking their ability to move from place to place. Inert at his father's feet, he felt exposed, fearful and small.

"You can't take my things," he cried, associating his "treasures" with his physical being. "You will not erase me."

"Of course," Werner continued to Alfons, his new friend, "we are still looking for the will. Fortunately, he left life insurance to his mother and I, and this will help expedite matters in due course."

Liar! Heuer, twisting on the spot summoned up rage sufficient to speed his molecules and free him. He had made provision for his mother, but not his father.

"How is your wife?" Alfons inquired. "I never had the privilege of meeting her."

"Why would you?" Heuer balked. "They're separated. Has everyone gone insane?"

"My wife is fine. We are moving into a new house."

"The hell you are!" Heuer countered, wondering how the old bastard finessed Hannelore out of the nursing home without a power of attorney.

"What was that?" Alfons cried. "Someone is in the basement."

Heuer moved quickly as feet shuffled and something clanked against the floor above him.

"Call 911," Alfons commanded. "Don't go down there!"

Heuer grinned as he extracted that one precious

object he sought before the interlopers arrived to rudely interrupt him. The object, gripped tight to the chest, was his armor against approaching evil. Irmtraut promised him release if he did two things: make good on past injustices, and separate the past from what she called the 'now and forward.' The object was a slam dunk and a ticket home.

Werner Heuer entered the room, cursing. Arrogant to the end, he moved through Heuer's possessions, knocking them over like cardboard cutouts of past transgressions.

He moved in behind his father. Irmtraut, the all-seeing and all-knowing, would be disappointed when she found out, but she was just a circuit court between him and the high judge. He'd have plenty of time to reason out an argument and make his case when the time came.

"Show yourself," the old man hollered.

"I will. Don't you worry," Heuer said, standing over top the crates of ammunition he'd been stowing for no reason other than they were on sale and really cool to have. He didn't know what he needed them for—until now. "I love old things," he said, pulling a box of Weibigand sulphur matches from his pocket. "Without them, there is only ash."

Chapter Twenty-Nine

Carla Blue sat at the workstation nearest the back door. Deep in conversation, she white knuckled the phone, oblivious to Enid's presence. Sweaty, in spite of the strong air conditioning Jocasta insisted upon, she conveyed an attitude both resolute and desperate. Danny Blue, surfacing after three months, had announced that he was in love and would not be coming home. Could she send his things along prepaid? He was a little short of cash.

Enid, noting with rancor that the flower room was no less empty than the previous day, wondered if Robert and Fat Dougie had goofed off in hopes that she would pick up the slack. Fat fucking chance. She was still in a miserable mood, the wretched cur piloting the scooter moments earlier stoking her.

She looked at the production board. It was going to be a monster of a day with a cathedral service for Ridley-More at 10 a.m., Salat al-Janazah at the mosque for al-Nadir at noon, and back-to-back arrangements for two new families called in overnight.

Also, there was Heuer, whose tissue condition remained a mystery, albeit a controlled one. Robert had done as he was told; the fact that the building didn't reek was proof of this. But was Heuer ready for viewing?

He assured her that he was when he visited her in a complicated dream. The setting, a luxurious penthouse of many floors in aluminum alloy and aquamarine glass; a tall, skinny balding man in livery with a tray of Scottish short breads and arugula; a large room done up in mushroom monochrome accented with base metals and rich amber inlays with Lalique glass thrown in just for fun. Mistress Biscuit, the host, was preoccupied at the moment; perhaps she'd like a swim before the fried chicken? Enid supposed she would, knowing full well that Heuer was there too, waiting for her.

Line two flashed and Enid ran to it, sending water droplets to and fro via the ratty squall jacket she'd grabbed from the hook in her hallway at home. "Weibigand Brothers—"

"Frau Krause?" the caller interrupted, his voice rasping and papery thin.

"Karl-Heinz?" she replied, flabbergasted. Not seeing the owner for several months had convinced her that he was dead.

"You must send someone over. I have fallen in the bedroom."

This was too much, and she regretted betraying the feeling with a frayed sigh into the receiver. The man was not well—close to dropping dead any minute—but work was exploding with activity just as her life was coming apart. (Aaron had caught her red handed crying in her sleep.)

"Frau Krause?"

'Shut up, man,' she wanted to say. 'Can't you see I'm struggling?'

Aaron hadn't said much about her peculiar behavior other than to inquire after work and the rat in the garage. But just as Heuer got to her in dreams, Aaron deduced her through her eyes. Heuer was all over her, she reeked of him.

"I will call 9-1-1, Karl-Heinz, immediately," she said, affecting formality. KH was a Kraut—he expected that. But in matters of personal care, there were few he could trust, his brother Zigsmond, being a shit of the highest order, not even a consideration. Not surprisingly, he rebuffed 9-1-1.

"Noooo. You will find Frau Binns and send her to me."

She did exactly that, ringing the old hag out of bed amidst protests and slurs that included the 'B' and 'C' words in that order. Enid, hanging at the other end of the

200

receiver, wondered if Binns boozed too. She had the look of it—yellow skin and spider veins on the back of her hands—ready signs of stage four cirrhosis. And she was a constant bitch too. But on hearing the source of the trouble, her demeanor changed. "Is he all right?"

"I don't know," Enid said, suddenly worried. "He refused 9-1-1. He wants only you."

They rang off leaving Enid at 6:45 am still in her jacket; still at the back door.

Carla rose to her feet, her voice, pitched and loud, picking up velocity. "I'm not saying it's yours, Carter. But I have a pretty good idea that it's not my husband's."

Enid gritted her teeth, her fingers playing with the five button combination lock on the prep room door. The purpose of coming in early was to be alone with Heuer. Carla was screwing this up.

"Yeah, well I'm sorry if I'm buggering your day, but too much has happened, and I'm making a clean break." Carla swiveled on her man shoes to meet Enid full on; for a moment she seemed vulnerable. Enid swallowed hard; the generous pail-sized grandee coffee mug in her left paw quavering. Carla was throwing the switch on her relationship and that would make her today, and quite probably for a few days thereafter, about as useful as a box of matches in the rain.

"You heard me. You were lotsa fun but we're done, *capisce*?" Carla hung up the phone. "Can you believe that fucking guy?"

There wasn't a whole lot Enid wanted to believe. "No I can't, but then again, I have lengthy talks on the astral plane with a dead guy so—"

She threw off her soggy squall jacket, depositing it in the staff room where newspapers, bagged up in pretty pink plastic to protect them from the rain, waited, untouched. There'd be no time for crosswords today.

***

Jürgen Heuer did many things in his lifetime, but murdering another human being was not among them. Of course he considered it at times—having Fuhrer blood in his veins practically demanded it—but logic always trumped emotion and that was what kept him from breaking the law this time. Standing over enough explosives to level a half block, he replaced the matches in the pocket of his pimp suit, leaving Werner to curse and mutter at the 61 Division cops who had better things to do than visit the hermit house a second time.

Irmtraut, understandably, was not impressed when he appeared before her to explain. "Since our first meeting, you have forced an angina attack on your neighbor, preyed on the wits of the only person who loves you, and wreaked havoc at the office juice bar."

"That, I can explain—" he interjected, relishing, somewhat guiltily, all the drama he'd created. "I merely sought to dispatch any papers incriminating to me. Instead, I found a bunch of tawdry shits besmirching my name." He flapped his arms chicken-like. "They decided I was peculiar and with all these rainbow flags going up over town, they were making allegations." He was not gay. He was nothing at all. Why did everybody insist on assigning labels? He was dead. It didn't matter. And he hadn't meant to set all the juice-o machines to malfunction in tandem, nor had he intended for Miss Samantha to go ass over heel and break an arm.

Irmtraut laughed at his childish protests, suggesting that he busy himself with the World Cup soccer scores. "Germany is leading, and the betting octopus is expected to weigh against the Spaniards."

He scoffed at the suggestion; a German victory was a foregone conclusion. "Why waste time on a sure thing?"

"Indeed?" Irmtraut said. "Let's look at something unsure then—your peccadillos, for example."

"My what?" He was not familiar with the term

'peccadillos.'

Irmtraut wiggled her ponderous mid-section to an unheard smoky beat.

"Oh, that," he recalled, cringing over his play at self-release.

"Yes," she said. "When you thought I was sleeping, only I wasn't."

He would gladly discuss the arsenal in the basement, the strange paste covering his bedroom walls, or his intriguing disdain for the prodigal father. What was not up for examination was his wandering hands and the miracles they accomplished.

"You will not do that again," she commanded.

"I am a busy man—I *was* a busy man—I do not—did not have time for—people."

"And you were too stingy to pay for them?"

Heuer took offense. Sometimes he wondered if Irmtraut only pretended to know what he was all about. But when he said as much and she threatened to switch off, he readily shut up, a nod to a growing, grudging respect.

"You have one last chance to move forward," she said, "but before you do, you must do me a favor..."

Moments later, Heuer stood in the Krause family garage marveling at how unlike it was from his own. Neat to a fault, Mr. Krause kept everything in pricey rubber made storage containers, neatly labeled, and stacked, using movable shelves triple deep, like those found in hospital records offices. The engineering behind the system that moved the shelves back and forth by means of wheels and pulleys captivated him, and it was at that moment that Heuer decided to like Aaron Krause.

Picking his way through the space he indulged in a little careful snooping. Bicycles trussed up in the ceiling; fishing rods; an assortment of machetes like the ones they used to clear the brush at the cottage; the old gun racks they used before the laws forced them to lock everything away...

Enid. How he longed to go back to the cottage with her. He touched his chest, the nagging heaviness beneath his sternum returning. He picked up an empty bottle of formaldehyde and examined it. "Metaglow, for natural results." The heaviness eased, and he smiled, making the connection that while he might derive adequate satisfaction from spying inside her mind, there was something about actual objects that made his links to her real. He patted his breast pocket. The thing inside was still there—now if only he could get it to her.

Pitter patters of tiny feet rattled behind him, and he turned expecting the paranormal elegant Mr. Rat. But, no: nothing of the sort. Behind him, on her worktable, dry and freshly stitched, was the glossy black body of the little rodent that so captivated the women at the funeral home.

"Hello, my friend," he said, poking at the dried corpse on the dish rack. "You are as shiny and fine as when I first I found you." The body, inert, did not respond. He picked it up, remarking aloud that it was so much more than a rat, more a trophy and a warning. Could embalming be an act of love? Or was it a harsh reminder that the real thing was gone?

"Take the body back to Weibigand's and leave it where you found it," Irmtraut whispered. "That should knock a thing or two loose."

11:00 A.M.

Standing at the back of the hearse with Carla and Eldon, Enid fired up a smoke in spite of Charlie's death stare. He hated that she started again—made it quite clear.

"What's his problem?" Carla whispered over loudly so that Charlie could hear. "We're on schedule and we're making money." Not only were they going to make payroll and have Friday afternoon cocktails like the old days, but they were getting attention from the competition, which had taken to calling in, faking bereavement, to get a handle on how busy they actually were.

Enid checked her watch. Father Ciarán Clough, presiding over the funeral mass inside, was pissed to the gills, adding unwanted extra time to their day. Fat Dougie was back at the parlor, cosmetizing Jacobs for the two p.m. visitation, while Robert, under threat of castration, moved the Heuer flowers up to the visitation suite sparing staff the trouble. She looked at Charlie, rocking his worried look. What *was* his problem?

"He's fretting over Karl-Heinz," Eldon said, taking her hand. "KH is the better brother, which is why he'll probably die first."

Enid squeezed his hand right back in agreement. With Karl-Heinz gone, decisions would fall to Ziggy, who'd probably strip mine the assets and shutter the place until he could sell it to a steak house chain.

"Are you ready to see Heuer?" Eldon said, suddenly.

Enid threw her cigarette to the ground, nodding to Carla. "She tells me you closed him last night. Thank you for that."

Carla smiled at them, her thoughts unspoken.

Eldon was a master at closing troublesome autopsy cases; especially the decomposed. "I used the right amount of cavity fluid and searing gel," he shrugged. "He took the stitch and he held."

Enid imagined Heuer at the cottage years ago, watching her gut fish at the butcher's block; an act, he claimed, that thrilled him. She knitted her brows together. "How does he look?"

Eldon understood her squeamishness; he'd experienced a similar loss many years before. "He'll never measure up to your expectations; but you'll be glad to have something to say good-bye to."

Charlie signaled them to get into position: Enid on hearse to receive the casket; Eldon and Carla on church doors to ease the way, Charlie and the limo driver—a personal friend of the deceased's—steering the box down the aisle to its rightful destination.

Enid secured the locking device, anchoring the casket into place. It was a short ride from the cathedral to the cemetery, then lunch, final tweaks and polishes to Jacobs in the Wisteria Room and then, at long last, Heuer. Tomorrow was Thursday, and he'd be set up in Begonia—her least favorite room—for two days of visiting. This would be followed by a small service in the chapel on Saturday, followed by interment at Pleasant View Gardens Cemetery.

Somewhere in all of it, she would make the time to be alone with him.

"Darling," Charlie whispered into her ear. "Darling, I have news." She closed the back door on the hearse with a satisfying *thunk*, a rich sound the result of good old solid American engineering. At Weibigand's, the dead always went out in a Cadillac.

"Darling," Charlie repeated, his cell phone buzzing in his left hand. "Listen to me. There's been a change."

She knew what it was before he even said it. Late day changes in funeral plans were common. Sometimes an updated will was unearthed stating clearly, decedent funeral wishes. Other times, family just had a change of heart. Heuer's family fought Charlie every step of the way through arrangements, at first rebuffing the notion that funerals were for friends *as well as* family. Mourners took all shapes, and to exclude friends was cruel.

Werner didn't place a lot of value on Heuer's supposed friendships, insisting his son was private, kept to himself, and didn't know a soul.

Eldon, in the passenger seat next to Enid, commiserated.

"You're not the first woman to love a fag."

She didn't think Heuer was, although the number of messages, increasing each day, came only from men.

What she and the dead man had could not be defined.
Heuer said as much in the dream at Mistress Biscuit's
house. Lying on a massage table wearing only a white robe,
he beckoned her over. Wearing the same, she slid in,
embracing him with arms as warm as he was cold. "Do not
second guess me," he said, accepting her. "I will never
leave you again."

"It doesn't matter what he was or wasn't, Eldon," she
said, her throat closing. "What matters is that he came back
to me, and now, through no fault of his own, he's forced to
leave again."

"Dear, dear," Eldon tutted. "You really are getting
screwed here, aren't you?"

Yeah, she thought bitterly. Werner Heuer called in
after they'd left for the cathedral, wanting to cancel the
arrangements. Unlike his son who kept everything, Werner
Heuer left no trace. The past was a burden to be swept
away, coolly, efficiently. Heuer wasn't going to be buried
at Pleasant View Gardens after all; he was going up the
chimney stack.

"I'm to contact the German consulate and get the
appropriate paperwork together." Heuer was going back to
Germany where he'd be greeted by an old war buddy of
Werner's, who'd agreed to scatter the ashes thousands of
miles away from her.

Chapter Thirty

2:00 P.M.

Fat Dougie fumed as he went about his duties in the Begonia Room. Not only had he been commanded to set up the Heuer flowers *tout suite*—which made no sense because the Jacobs visit was up first—but it had been implied that he was lazy when in fact he was not. Robert, working alongside him, harbored similar feelings, exacting revenge on an oversized floral with hideous gladioli in menstrual red.

"Why do we put up with this shit?" Robert demanded, also pissed at the notion that not attending Mr. Forsythe's Pride party would be career suicide. He had better things to do: Friday was opening ceremonies, followed by days of bar crawls with friends before his shift began anew Monday morning.

"It's not that bad," Dougie said, snapping the head off of one of the ugly glads, "just an hour or two out of your day, and Mr. Forsythe has the best buffet lunch in Portside."

Pride was a big deal at Weibigand's because so many of its employees over the years were either gay, or gay-friendly, owing to the unique nature of the business. "Gay men," Charlie opined once to Robert over too much scotch, "possess the unique qualities of physical strength and attention to detail. We are good listeners, adept at bitch control and, on those occasions when a queen attack is warranted, capable of dispatching all nastiness without a trace of blood and all for the greater good."

Dougie, himself an unconscionable cooze hound that favored large busts and wide rears, concurred with Charlie's observations with one addition: "and they don't marry."

"They do too," Robert protested, grievously affronted

all of a sudden by the stereotyping. "In Canada and those Scandinavian countries."

"Sure," Dougie said, not arguing. "But in the old days—no. 'Bachelors' were sought out because they lived in-house and had no one other than the funeral directors they served. Charlie's from a different age—that age— that's what he was on about."

Oh, that made sense. All those gorgeous well groomed and incredibly courteous men Robert took note of and admired when his parents dragged him to family visitations were 'bachelors' play acting to widows for the greater good. Thank God things had changed.

"Fine," Robert conceded, "I'll go to the party. But I won't take another bitch slap from Krause."

***

Dougie left the Begonia to check on odds 'n' sods in Wisteria. Close on his heels, Heuer followed, awaiting the perfect opportunity to deposit his package. His time on earth was coming to an end, and it was imperative that he stay on task. In seventy-two hours, he had shown mercy, sparing a devil the flames; magnanimity, helping a friend he could not warm to; and, beneficence, conferring love through dreams. Pushing hubris aside, he had shooed Guillaine in the right direction of a file that would absolve Texas Bob and TRAVAT of any wrong doing and he'd muttered a few words to the Great Architect that included 'praises' and 'thanks.' Superciliousness of thought persisted, however, though he no longer hated Alfons with the old persistency. He'd even played around with the notion of visiting Roger the Idiot, but with motives still sketchy, this was not permitted him: the back door remained closed.

"When do I meet the Poobah?" he asked, when Irmtraut dropped in on his consciousness.

"When you commit a random act of kindness without thought to yourself, your things, your universe, even..."

Random act of kindness? Hadn't he heard that in a movie?

"Skittishness and a lack of resolve are the defects that keep you here," Irmtraut assured. "Here's a clue: Hurt the one that hurt me, and I go free. Set me free, and you will follow. *Verstehen Sie?*"

Sure, he guessed—anything to get out of here—but hurting went against the rules, didn't it?

Irmtraut laughed. "I could have phrased it better. Jocasta's hautiness is *her* flaw. Calling her out on the rat is her ablution. We'll be doing her a favor."

The fat guy in the lumpy suit continued his rounds, fussing over some biddy in a casket. Her mouth and left eye had fallen open, the result of too much gravity and not enough epoxy, and he mucked about with a tube of crazy glue to fix the problem.

Heuer checked the wall clock: 12:30 p.m. Enid would be back soon, but what about the target?

"Jocasta will be back too," Irmtraut said. "She'll hunt down Zigsmond and give him proper druthers for neglecting Karl-Heinz. Make sure everyone is in the building when you drop the rat."

From his position on all fours in front of a large chinz couch, the fat man yelled for Robert. "Come see this!" Correcting his position, he planted both cheeks on the floor, grinning like a drooling idiot at Christmas. "Look, look!" he shouted to the younger man, who entered the room flushed and vexed. "Like a miracle or something."

"Whatcha got there?"

Dougie beamed. "An emerald ring. Emmy Shawson's emerald ring!"

The sonofabitch fell out of the casket clean onto the floor, where it evaded vacuum cleaners and Jocasta's keen eyes.

"But there was no ring," Robert said, scratching his greasy hair. "We checked the file; there was no report."

The two men fell silent, staring dumfounded as the implications associated with the ring's retrieval took hold: turning it in made them liars, complicit in a fake report; not turning it in made them thieves.

'For cryin' out loud' Heuer fumed, having no time for rings and fatuous dopes looking for an easy answer to a nasty ethical problem. That said, just how did the ring travel from the old lady's finger to the dark recesses of the old chinz couch? He thought of the rat, resting comfortably in his left breast pocket. Had he taken the shiny thing to add to his nest, or was he giving it to someone more deserving?

He withdrew the little blue photo album secreted in his right breast pocket. Retrieved from his nest of treasures, and at great risk, for he'd nearly revealed himself to Werner in the process, it suddenly meant more to him now than it might have twenty years before. Its surface cover cracked, and the once clear filmy pages now yellowed with age, the book contained pictures of a life that had been real, but got lost. He looked at Enid in black and white, in repose, her long hair loose and spread across the back seat of the Chevelle, looking up at him, expressionless, behind eyes that promised everything and more. Next page: at a party wearing a silly straw hat; Next page: scarfing back a yard of beer at the fish fry; Next page: sitting astride a black horse, boots on, grinning; Last page: miles of bed sheets, coiled around her, the dirty cottage window with the lacey curtains prominent behind her gauzy silhouette.

He smiled. He was sure. Returning the book to her would be the greater act of kindness over what Irmtraut proposed.

Irmtraut Weibigand would have none of it. "Do not second guess me, *Schlecht*. Do as I say."

Alarms rang in his head. "What good comes from turning these people against each other?"

"The kind of good, my dear, that comes from

realizing that we are not alone in the room; that something else—something unseen is in there with us—and like the smallish, frightened, insignificant little bug she is, Jocasta will take flight and, God willing, fall down the goddamned stairs all on her own."

Heuer replaced the album in his pocket, as yin and yang continued to argue over the ring and what to do with it. He dismissed Irmtraut out of hand: he would not harm another human being—living or dead—not for his own sake, even if he believed Irmtraut's claim that she was the promised land. He would take the rat back to Enid and let her do with him whatever it was she intended.

"We must report this to Mr. Forsythe," Dougie said, grabbing hold of a threadbare arm on the old chesterfield to lever himself up and into a standing position. "It is the right thing to do."

Heuer smiled, for all at once he knew. The woman they called Carla was beside herself over her pet's disappearance. That, taken together with her cash problems, could only mean that the little fellow intended the ring to go to her, only the poor bastard failed and it had cost him his life.

Heuer took up a position next to Robert, such that he could smell his pomade. "Finders keepers" he said, not materializing, but making the most of a shift in air currents that clearly recommended his presence. He couldn't tell what astonished them more: the sharp gust of wind that shook Mrs. Jacobs casket from side to side or the specter of Emmy Shawson's emerald ring flying on its own across the room, where it rebounded against the wall and then traveled down the hall like Oswald's magic bullet in Dallas.

Once lost, once found, only to be lost again, the shiny bauble continued its improbable journey down the stairs to the lower office, where it came to rest at Jocasta Binn's knobby feet.

Chapter Thirty-One

1:45 P.M.

Over the course of many days, Heuer went from a forlorn shade condemned to wander, to an ebullient being busting with a desire to do good. But how long could this last? Could he deny his true nature?

He did not leave Rat in Wisteria as instructed, nor did he involve himself directly in the mendacious affairs of others. Casting jewelry about in the hopes it would be found by the right person was up to heaven now; he had merely tossed it out into the realm of the possible. If Irmtraut didn't like it, she could go to hell: she had her chance to grind axes when she lived. That opportunity had passed. Jocasta Binns, Enid Krause, Carla Blue—hell, even the little queer who dropped his guts on the floor—would find their place in the world whether he assisted or not.

Profound relief settled over him. Maybe one had to die in order to be truly free? He hated to think that was so; life on earth hadn't exactly been the shits. Spiro, his old benefactor and mentor, was convinced he'd become an asshole because of law school and he had; but he'd also acquired the knowledge needed to make balanced decisions like he was doing now.

Weibigand's: what an unlikely place of learning, with its peeling wallpaper, seedy floor lamps and old lady smell that permeated the fabric of every room. He patted Mrs. Jacobs on the head with a hand that, curiously, began to wave again like a faltering satellite signal on a grainy television monitor. "Sorry darling for rocking your ship, but I had to get those two idiots out of our room." In repose, she was dignified and truly at peace. He tugged at his ear to stave off a burning sensation, something new that began with his involuntary materialization in front of Alfons. Life after death didn't come with a book of instructions, but he had a clearer idea about how things rolled. Those with bodies had the benefit of movement, but with limitations. Those, like Irmtraut Weibigand, consigned to an inanimate object, had a harder time. They were not free to move physically, nor should they (too shocking), but they had the benefit of foresight and telepathy. He scratched his head. He had both.

Suddenly, the hall lights went on, along with some tacky spa music piped over the sound system to announce that visitation was about to begin. This frightened him because he was losing control of his body just as he was gaining insight into his spirit. Since Alfons, he had phased in and out of the living world, like a time traveler in a transporter device that cannot land. He fizzled and cracked like an old transistor radio with a faltering battery, and the stiffness underneath his ribcage grew. As time passed, he sensed his spirit's need to flee, while the body, protesting, fought hard to stay behind. These forces, opposite and fractious, had to be squared before he blew apart all over again.

Leaving Mrs. Jacobs, he crossed the hall, passing Begonia where his visitation would take place, and then Rose where some old pacifist was stretched out amongst marijuana fronds, arriving at the pickled pine office with the ugly Finn Juhl chesterfield. The door to the old basement, hanging ajar, alerted him to the possibility that a staff member was down there, but he doubted it. Only Jocasta paid him visits; the others, too busy with their work, never bothered.

It was supposed to be a museum—that basement— with its old treasures, lovingly curated by the people who put the stuff there. Only they died off and the treasures became junk and a burden for those who could not see the value.

So Werner was going to sell his house after tipping everything he cared about into dumpsters?

He'd see about that. But first, he had to sort things with Irmtraut.

The words came into range, at first soft and ethereal. Heuer paused at the bottom of the stair, honing in on its music, a voice, sweet and reassuring.

"I love you, only you, right now and in this moment; like all moments before and for all the others to come...your time has been struggle; and that is no more, for you have returned my son to me, and in return, you shall have peace."

That voice, masculine, familiar: he had heard it before. Heuer closed his eyes against the images forming around him: blue hills, water song, and a violin crying softly from the old phonograph; his mother's voice cooing dove-like that he would be a musician, and the air tasting of rain.

***

"*Mutter! Mutter!*—please!" Heuer took Hannelore's hands; she not in the least bit surprised by his visit.

"I was hoping you would come," she said brightly, her arms extended in greeting from her place on a ratty sofa in Werner's cheap art deco bachelor. "As much as I knew you'd go to your father, I wasn't quite ready to let you go."

Heuer, taking a seat next to her, noted the indentation he made in the saggy cushions. In his mother's presence, he was reassuming his old form and the density that came with it; curious though not surprising, given the old wives tales that linked lunacy with supernatural ability. Dear mother. Looking at her lined face, he saw, not a woman ruined by years of ill use and dementia, but a heroine that lived her life boldly and unapologetically.

"*Mutter*," he began, lighting her cigarette, which she waved in his face like a diva from old Hollywood. "*Mutter*, I've come to ask about father...he is, I think, looking for me."

The sky outside, darkened by heavy cloud, seemed to

answer before she could. A cool breeze, gusting through a dirty screened window, rustled frayed curtains, stained by years of tobacco smoke, to tickle their surroundings. He laughed. Werner would sell his home and move up with the proceeds, leaving Hannelore here with a sketchy caregiver. He would not let any of that happen.

Her eyes vacuous and deep, Hannelore drifted off into a reverie, humming Schubert over the wind's gentle interruption, making Heuer sentimental for home.

"Let's talk about Germany for a moment, mother. You met my father in Germany?"

"No *mein Kind*, in Austria before the *Anschluss*."

Heuer remembered their stories, told often over many beers—torchlights, marching, Kristallnacht and the camps...

"I don't mean Werner, mum," Heuer pressed, relighting her cigarette, which had gone out.

The wind outside picked up speed to feed the room, oxygen-deprived in the gathering darkness. Hannelore grew pale. "That's *exactly* who I'm talking about. Werner sent his family to the camp. But your father got away, and after the war he found me." She smiled. "You were born in '59, the same year Castro took Cuba."

He never wanted to believe it. The man with the violin who stopped playing because he didn't come along. Another man, waiting for him at home after another school yard thrashing, who turned his fists on him because he was cowardly, womanish, and loved music. That was Werner.

"Werner married me when we got off the plane. He demanded to see my papers because he could not believe I was thirty."

She was slight in stature, blonde, lovely, with an excellent singing voice, and she pretended to love Germany as much as Werner did.

"What happened to my father?" Heuer demanded, his shade flickering in the diminishing light. "What did you do with him?"

Hannelore sighed as if taking Werner's side. This withered him. Her sigh and the way she used it was one of the few things that actually diminished Jürgen Heuer. Whereas Werner's fists and insults served to strengthen his resolve, Hannelore's downcast looks eviscerated him like so many spears to the body.

"I want to go to the ocean," she said suddenly. "I am supposed to meet him there." Him—Heuer's dad—the man she pretended to adore had abandoned her without a thought. In her madness, she was sanctifying him.

"No," she protested. "Never that. He was a real man with flaws. And it was you he didn't want, not me."

She paused, allowing him time to process. "He made such music with that violin, you know. Played in one of the orchestras. Naturally, I told him about you, but he'd collaborated during the war, and you were a Jew. It was too painful for him."

Chapter Thirty-Two

2:30 P.M.

C harlie arrived back at the funeral home loaded for bear. Pleasant View Gardens Cemetery made a mess of the Ridley-More interment, forgetting the liner that was supposed to hold up the grave walls in heavy rain. This resulted in a cave-in causing insults and threats from the already stingy family that wanted a fees reduction.

"I expressly outlined the need, given the forecast. Don't you goddamned people listen anymore?" he fumed into his cell phone. The Pleasant View staffer on the other end could not have cared less. Camaraderie between family run operations like Weibigand's and grave diggers like Pleasant View had eroded steadily since a change in law allowing cemeteries to act like funeral homes. Instead of complimentary service providers completing two halves of a whole, they were competitors, with Pleasant View routinely screwing up the minutiae.

"They're throwing us under the bus," he hollered as Enid and Carla pushed their way into the lower office. "They're saying I forgot to place the order."

"That's bullshit," Carla sputtered. "I double checked the order sheet myself." She pushed the Ridley-More service file on to the floor, her mind somewhere else. "Money," she complained to Scooter over a boozy late night phone call, "is the only thing between me and a half decent existence. Without it, the best I can hope for is poverty and a shit room with a hotplate."

"How is old Scooter?" Charlie asked between fists of herbal remedies washed down with cold coffee.

"He's invited me to come and share his cardboard box under the bridge, but that, I had to decline."

Whether Scoot lived in a box or not was debatable— they joked about it—but he never disclosed where he lived.

The only thing he admitted to was a part-time job at a grimy gym owned by a friend. "I hand out towels and balance the cash drawer. That's all."

Could she hide out at the gym for a couple of days until she found a place?

"'Of course,' he says—and he was quite giddy about it too—as long as you're not still pregnant.'"

If Carla wanted silence from her audience, she got it.

"We suspected, dear," Charlie stammered, "but we didn't want to intrude."

"I don't know why it would be a problem," she continued, searching the floor beneath for her missing friend. "I was never knocked up in the first place."

Enid glared at her, her look uneasy and weird.

"It was gas. Just like Scoot said. Gas. Nothing more."

Charlie choked on his coffee just as Jocasta Binns' frame sullied the doorway. Was it his imagination, or had she doubled in size over night? Her skin florid and with a slight yellow tinge to the eyes, she looked like something mythical culled from the ancient histories.

He barely had a chance to inquire after Karl-Heinz's health and whether Zigsmond was even aware of his condition before the drop kick was delivered. Like the Theban Queen out of Sophocles, Jocasta was dramatic, effecting history without even knowing it.

"Tell me, Mr. Forsythe, have we had any further word from Teddy Shawson-Cooke in respect of the ring?"

No, he had not. In fact, he assigned Cooke's aggressiveness over the non-existent emerald to a terrible misunderstanding that happened years ago.

Jocasta sucked on her bridgework. "And so there is no ring?"

Eldon, barging in for a mid-afternoon coffee stopped mid-pour, his back straightening. Charlie was walking into a trap, and he was powerless to stop it.

"What's this then?" she said, proffering the bauble, which appeared larger than Teddy's description. "I found it," she lied, "secreted away to be recovered at a later date..."

She paused. Like Irmtraut Weibigand, she had little use for lady undertakers, only, in her case, because she had practiced without a license until that was stopped by the Weibigand matriarch.

"Hidden," she repeated, like a character out of a mystery novel, "by the one person in this place that needed money most." She cast a hoary eye at Carla Moretto Salinger Blue.

Carla rose from her place behind the office monitor, its screen open to a fetching Chevy up for auction on Barrett's.

"You are making a wrong turn, Jocasta dear," Charlie drawled, recognizing the ring instantly. "That is a child's paste ring; and if you found it under a chesterfield or chair (which he doubted because her knees did not bend), it could be anybody's..."

Jocasta licked her cracked lips. "This is Emmy Shawson's ring as sure as those bracelets she gave you..."

That was years ago, the genesis behind Emmy's gift to Charlie a mystery. Charlie shrugged at the inference; that was for another book.

Enid Krause, boiling over for close to seventy-two hours, had had enough, and she rose in defense of her friend. Carla Blue had treated her cruelly when she first arrived at Weibigand's, but her vulnerability had made itself as clear to Enid as Enid's own weaknesses had to Carla. It was time to push back.

"Your time would be spent better if you stuck to things you knew about, instead of speculating. Why not put your rocks down, and tell us about Rat?"

She had never challenged the Jocastrator directly, knowing that her protector and brother, Karl-Heinz, could have dismissed her with cause. His life was ebbing now, and that gave Enid courage.

Jocasta grinned, pleased that someone had finally called her out.

"Rats are rats—but they aren't men..." she looked directly at Carla. "That is to say, they are not substitutes, not even for a bad one. You traipse around her like something out of *Oedipus*, emoting—for what?"

Carla tried to answer, but didn't have a chance. It was like her batteries had been ripped out of her back. Jocasta owned the moment:

"You think that you are so clever—all of you—with your cigarette smoke and your conceit. I hear you, I hear everything. You aren't the only ones eavesdropping through the air ducts."

She pointed to the hole in the wall overhead, its opening lined with dreck and fur accumulated through years of forced air.

"And your misdeeds—" she looked at Charlie, "—and your graft and your dirty little rodent. I could wish it all away with a phone call, but I don't. All I needed was a shovel and a lucky strike."

She pushed the emerald, too small for any of her digits, onto Carla's ring finger. "Take it. It's yours. Just knowing that *you* know I did it is all the satisfaction I need."

Black rolled over, sweet and sticky, like free molasses under a hot sun, to cradle her and slow her fall. Her breath shallow, her feet miserably cold, Carla warmed before losing consciousness to the words Charlie uttered, words she hadn't time to say herself:

"Oh! You awful, awful bitch."

Chapter Thirty-Three

3:00 P.M.

Irmtraut, the floor lamp, flashed blue-white-hot in pulsing bands that looped across the walls and under doors to grab hold of everything and somehow make it special. The effect, startling and beautiful, blinded him. Was she leaving without him?

"I've instructed him to leave the body out in plain sight," she said, "which I know he won't do. When he disobeys me; that is when you will take him."

"Yes," the voice, disembodied but close, replied. "Give me something true and unsullied, and in exchange you shall have your freedom; undeserving of it, though you surely are."

Heuer grinned. Irmtraut the feral, the deceptive, and the fraudulent had brokered a deal based on faulty assumptions. Didn't she know he never did as he was told?

Jocasta Binns certainly did, albeit unconsciously. Heuer actually found a comforting sympatico with her. "I know you're here," she said, inching down the stairs looking for him, irrespective of the great light that seemed not to touch her.

The first time she saw him, she dropped her torch. She was afraid. This time, she wasn't.

"What it is it, dear one? Can you not see the light?"

Relieved? Or was she elated?—she did not say. Instead, she saw only him, sheltering behind a divan. Watching, hedging her bets like a child uncertain, she did not approach, although she needed too rather badly.

"What have you done?" he asked, frowning, as images of blood and shovels overtook him. She had done awful things. He studied her intently. At a distance, she was small and quite frail—not the picture painted by the perennially angry Irmtraut. Heuer wanted to ask her about

222

her brother, Karl-Heinz Jr., who dominated her thoughts. They were close, but distant, owing to the laws of god and man. 'I love you,' she said, the words buried deep in the far reaches of her brain, where sensuality and care for one's fellow hides. In Jocasta, it was buried deep, but it was there. He understood—completely.

"I am a creature," she said, sadly. "I can only act the way my heart forces me to."

"As you should," he said, motioning her to go with a hand gesture.

She paused, as if wanting to stay below with him, but this he couldn't have: she had options; she could fix things, and he was in the middle of something.

"Go, before it's too late."

Her features calmed, indicating that she got his meaning. He was benevolence without ego. He was simply being kind.

He waited, until she departed safely, before confronting his savior and nemesis.

"Where is he?" Heuer demanded, interrupting Irmtraut's strange reverie.

"It is for the best," she soothed, abandoning all pretense that she was looking out for his interests and that he was going to a better place. "There is nothing worthwhile in the life you leave; nothing worthwhile for you in the nether either. You will take my place here among the ashes with our minder to keep you company."

Heuer thought of the Chevelle beneath the tarp in his driveway, a rusted, molting statement of scotched dreams. Werner would tow her to the crusher and cash in on the sale of his house. It wasn't right. He had to stay. But not here. He would not stay here.

He reached for her in violation of her earlier fiat, shaking her with enough force to squelch her lights. These, recessing, disappeared into the walls, only to be replaced by a mid-level buzzing that intensified. He dropped her.

The cicada's song, a hateful thing he associated with hydroelectric towers and home, stole his resolve to finish what he started.

"The cicada gets you every time," she noted wryly.

Heuer hung his head. "They only come out every five years or so. Back home, I heard them. I must have been around three at the time."

"You lived in the city," Irmtraut corrected. "The cottage you remember was only a vacation spot your mother took you to, to be with *him*. He was a terrible man—turned in his own people to stay alive. Yet your mother loved him; loved him enough to wear his star."

"I always thought she did that to annoy Werner. I can't believe Werner is not my father."

"You will," Irmtraut chuckled. "I guarantee it. He has cancelled your funeral. He's sending you to the fire."

Heuer covered his ears.

"*Your* last name is Jakob. Your life is a lie."

"Enough!" he shouted.

"No one wanted you. No one looked for you when you died."

He thought of Enid.

"No. Not even her. She pretends to mourn you."

"She doesn't know what she's about. She never did."

"And you will help her, I suppose?" The tone mocked. "It is too late for that, *mein Herr*. There is no release for her. And you are promised elsewhere. He is here for you. Right now."

The voice she'd been speaking with—whether his actual father or something worse—based its claim upon Heuer's desire to finally come clean. It no longer required Irmtraut's puerile company, preferring a sinner-turned-saint to a soul that was neither. But she miscalculated again. Whether in ego, eros, agape, or contempt, unworthiness was always his badge, and Heuer the dreamer, Heuer the liar, Heuer the beater, Heuer the lover, could not, would not, embrace the truth.

"My name is Jürgen Manfred Heuer, son of Werner, and I denounce your lies and deny your daemon. You want out? I'll show you out. It is a wonder to me that you never thought of it before…"

Did she know what hit her? Maybe so. Release of any kind was better than an eternity of bitterness. So, Irmtraut said nothing when Heuer took hold of her once again; this time, to smash the life out of her on the concrete floor.

Thursday, 10:00 A.M.

Werner Heuer tucked the Pentax beneath his arm, ready to toss it into the dumpster. He remembered it well; a gift to his wife's son from Cousin Christophe on the occasion of his twelfth birthday. Small, sickly, pale, he was nothing like Christophe, a tall, chiseled, and accomplished athlete.

He looked at the Chevelle in the driveway; a woman he'd never seen before had offered him a thousand dollars and when he declined she tripled her offer, insisting that it would complete the clone she'd been working on for years. A woman working on cars: how absurd. He waved her away, thinking her a kook.

"I think that is the lot," he called out to Alfons, who dithered in the basement trying on a pair of Heuer's old cowboy boots. He didn't hear. Heuer, abandoning all pretense at concealment stood before him maladroit and ready to do harm.

"You have fucked with the wrong guy again," he said, lifting an awestruck Alfons to his feet. "But the boots look good on you, so I'll let you keep them, if you please."

"I don't understand," Alfons stammered. "You're dead, man."

"No."

"But I saw you, blown up like a navy raft and

covered in flies..."

"You saw him," Heuer said, pointing to the rotting corpse on the floor. "A mere body. Not me—"

Alfons, too petrified to fight, pissed his pants instead.

"That is just an image culled from that perverted mind of yours. You thought I kept heads down here, and you are half-right. If you don't clear out, I will take yours."

He chuckled at the theatrics of it—knew he'd have a lot of explaining to do when and if he made it to the high court.

"I'm still here," he shouted to the ludicrous man in wet pants fleeing the scene in his favorite cow boots. "So I must be doing something right."

He pulled the box of Weibigand matches out of his suit jacket. If there was ever a time for cliché, it was now.

Chapter Thirty-Four

2:00 P.M.

E nid crossed the threshold separating her world from Heuer's. Still covered in sheeting, he gave her the time she needed to prepare herself. He recognized the suit bag—Savile Row, London—and he smiled, glad that Hannelore found the best one in his closet. Enid placed the bag on top of the new intake, ensuring that his neighbor's shroud was free of blood and would not spoil his new suit, then unzipped it, placing each article of clothing on a makeshift clothes tree of exposed wires hanging from the prep room ceiling.

"It's a beautiful day, my darling," she whispered softly as she drew back the sheet to look at him.

Heuer frowned. If this was embalming, he was not in favor of it. He looked terrible, wrapped from the neck down mummy-like in wide plastic strips to hold dry chemicals in place so that he didn't leak.

"You are going today," she continued, "and you will go in your best."

He watched as she scissored long cuts into the back of his shirt, vest, and jacket, which she draped over him, and then cinched tight with needle and thread to give him a fitted look. She did not do the same to the pants. For some reason unknown to both of them, he was thinner, sleeker, like when he was young. That was how she remembered him and how he wanted her to keep on remembering him.

"Let me help you," he said, placing the expensive silk tie that had slipped off its hanger onto the table behind her.

She turned and smiled.

"Oh, Manny. If you're behind me like they say at mortuary school, then I want you to listen. If I thought you wounded me all those years ago, it was only because you didn't need me. And if I poured it on thick when you arrived, carried on like I was your widow, it was only because I needed to. I wanted to keep something alive. And so did you. I saw your junk—no! I'm sorry—your treasures, and I think I understand. We all need proof that we exist, and we need to keep that proof after we're gone. I'm sorry that I didn't understand. But now I do."

The cops at 61 were only too happy to tell her about the loaded firearms in the house and the cum covered walls; she couldn't tell them that she'd seen it herself with her own eyes.

"You didn't want me, because you couldn't want me. At least, that's what I've decided."

She paused to wipe her nose with the back of her gloved hand.

"And besides, where on earth would you have put me?"

Carla appeared at the door with Eldon close behind. "Whenever you're ready."

Heuer had taught her many things, chief among them, to protect their secret.

Enid placed her hands on his chest. She would never tell.

"We're ready."

The cremation container, already in position on one of Weibigand's better church trucks[29] waited, its lid unscrewed. She noted with approval that Eldon had lined it with an old duvet in an effort to jazz up the plain presswood interior. Carla, her emerald ring prominently featured on her left hand, produced a poofy pillow left over from the old cotton wood precision cut casket, water damaged when the sewers backed up.

"Thanks, guys," Enid said. "It means a lot."

"She's keeping the ring," Eldon chimed, his face creased with a curious mix of levity and grief. "Let's put

---

[29] The wheeled device used to push caskets back and forth.

your man to bed."

It took three of them to move him, Enid not wanting to strap him into the body lifter. "Manny's been through enough."

"Manny?" Carla hadn't heard that name before.

"My name for him when we were alone." She thought of her parent's cottage, blue skies and the lake behind him. Smiling, he waved her over, but she did not go.

"*Schön*," Heuer whispered. "Don't do this to yourself."

But she already had. Tears again. He hated tears. Hated it when she cried.

Now in the casket, there was little time. She straightened his tie and minding the others, switched to German so they could not hear:

"You leave me nothing but hope that one day I will see you again in the good place."

"I have something for you," Carla said, after an appropriate amount of time had passed. "Something you need to have."

Enid stepped back from him, motioning Eldon to close the lid.

"And I have something for you," she replied, the color from her cheeks draining away with the memory of something forgotten. Running over to the cabinet where their embalming chemicals were stored, she called out to Eldon to 'stop' with the screwdriver. "There's one more thing to go in."

The little bundle, no bigger than a 20 week fetus, could have been anything really except that it was Rat, and therefore as precious as her man in the casket. "I took care of him for you. Just as you looked after Heuer for me."

Carla fingered the package tenderly, her multifaceted emerald refracting light from the fluorescent tube bulbs glinting overhead. It really was a beautiful ring.

"I found this in the basement," Carla said, "next to

the broken lamp. I don't know how—I didn't pry—not when I saw what it was."

Enid took a seat next to the big garbage can, while Carla placed Rat carefully at Heuer's feet. It wasn't apropos that they should go together, it was just plain right. For beauty and elegance is not always spotted or even appreciated even when it's right in front of your face.

She turned each page, looking carefully for traces of the heat that existed between them and found, to her amazement, that it was still there. The little blue photo album was Heuer's testament to what was, what could have been, and of how things would be remembered. For that, he was a true artist.

***

Heuer paused, looking longingly at the back door, which hung open.

"It is a strange world I live in and it is, perhaps, to an even stranger world I go."

But peculiarity was something he'd embraced his entire life and so he was not afraid. With great certainty, he mounted the three steps leading out and beyond. He did not fall.

The End

Jürgen Heuer and Enid Krause will return in The Heuer Effect.

Epilogue

■ ■ "Who is that?" thirteen year old Enid Engler whistled through the metal braces in her teeth, as the shiny red car pulled into her parent's driveway. She remembered being super excited when it slowed in front of the picture window she lolled in and then made the turn. A visitor! They didn't get many of those anymore not since her brother Mike had gone away to university. Before that, her home was overrun with big boys who made her place theirs, playing card games and drinking beer late into the night. When her brother left, they did too, and Enid, thirsting for excitement buried herself in forbidden books that fueled colorful dreams.

"Your brother," her mother called out absently from the kitchen, where heady smells of gulash and roulaten wafted.

Her heart lurched; the only other words that set her mind to rock in a similar fashion were "David Bowie" and "The Rolling Stones;" both off limits to her because she was young and her Eastern European parents disapproved of boys who wore makeup.

"I don't know this car," Enid called back, dazzled. It had hood scoops, black pin striping, and side badges that hinted at something monstrous under the hood. Whoever owned a car like that, knew how to drive, and probably knew a whole lot more about other things too. She thought of the Judy Blume book her friend stole from an older sister and the hours they spent under the apple tree reading and then re-reading the dirty bits.

She smiled: funny what came back in times of great stress, and with all the things on her mind—a rat to embalm, a husband to be nicer to, a couple of scores to settle—she did not look under the tarp on Heuer's driveway. Could that have been Shelley?

"It's a '68," the young man with the thick blond hair

and pretty blue eyes said. "Do you know about Chevelle?"

Enid nodded, lying. She didn't know anything about cars other than that they were pretty and that she should only buy North American.

"It's very special," he said, enjoying her zeal. "It was made in Oshawa, Canada and began as a straight six."

Enid canvassed her memory banks. Her friend Helena had a brother with a muscle car; sometimes they'd hang out in the garage, eavesdropping on the car guys who gathered there. "Not anymore," Enid replied, craftily pointing to the badging. "You have a 454 under there."

"Yes," he replied, knitting his brows together. "I modified it."

Enid grew flush, the heat in her cheeks flaring up. She tried to look away from him so that he would not see, but it was too late.

"It's okay," he said. "One day, I'll take you for a ride."

About the Author:

A.B. Funkhauser is a funeral director, fiction writer and wildlife enthusiast living in Ontario, Canada. Like most funeral directors, she is governed by a strong sense of altruism fueled by the belief that life chooses us and we not it.

"Were it not for the calling, I would have just as likely remained an office assistant shuffling files around, and would have been happy doing so."

Life had another plan. After a long day at the funeral home in the waning months of winter 2010, she looked down the long hall joining the director's office to the back door leading three steps up and out into the parking lot. At that moment a thought occurred: What if a slightly life-challenged mortician tripped over her man shoes and landed squarely on her posterior, only to learn that someone she once knew and cared about had died, and that she was next on the staff roster to care for his remains?

Like funeral directing, the writing called, and four years and several drafts later, *Heuer Lost and Found* was born.
What's a Heuer? Beyond a word rhyming with "lawyer," Heuer the lawyer is a man conflicted. Complex, layered, and very dead, he counts on the ministrations of the funeral director to set him free. A labor of love and a quintessential muse, *Heuer* has gone on to inspire four other full length works and over a dozen short stories.

"To my husband John and my children Adam and Melina, I owe thanks for the encouragement, the support, and the belief that what I was doing was as important as anything I've tackled before at work or in art."

Funkhauser is currently working on a new manuscript begun in November during NaNoWriMo 2014.

Acknowledgements:

More than one futurist has said that there will be jobs abundant in fifty years that have yet to be defined in the here and now. That makes a lot of sense. The guy driving the horse cart never thought about the helicopter, even if Leonardo did. It's the same with people: many of us don't know what we really are until life cues us.

At various times, I've worked as a shoe clerk, bank teller, lobby receptionist, legislative assistant in an august house of parliament, executive assistant to an auto lobbyist and, finally, funeral director in a family run establishment operating, at the time, for close to seventy years. This last position, my vocation, my calling, was to be my last—I thought. Little did I know that two people—sadly no longer with us—would inspire a few words in pencil (remember cursive?) in a loose leaf notebook. These words sounded nice, and shyly, I shared them with a writer friend who declared them "fiction" and something to "run with."

I like to think that a cool HBO show running from 2000 to 2005 inspired the funeral director in me. In fact, it awakened a long dormant fascination that began with my first trip to a funeral parlor in 1976 when I was eleven. My grandmother had passed away after years of illness, and my parents, both of Eastern European descent, thought nothing of taking the kids. My brother at five years old was even younger. What kind of kid admires furniture and fixtures and cross questions the guys in morning suits about their jobs and how they got them? Me. But I had to wait. Life intervened as it always does, and set me on a very different path. HBO brought me back. And with the generous support of my dear spouse John, I began a new career at forty-one. John made the funeral director; my late friends made the writer.

Working with death and bereaved persons on a daily basis was bound to inform the written word. But losing people I know brought it home. I so wish I could name them, for inspiring me, for driving this compulsion to write down what I was thinking; but they're not here to ask, so I will only say that a day hasn't gone by these last five years that I haven't thought of them, and in the language of our forebears I want to say: *Du lässt mir nichts außer der Hoffnung, dass ich dich eines Tages an diesem guten Ort wiedersehen werde.*

Enter the B7 and the Writer People

I blame my sister Cryssa Bazos for pulling me out of my comfortable existence. The year before all of this started, she began her own journey into the 17th Century, culminating in a fabulous manuscript THAT SOMEONE NEEDS TO BUY. Through her, I joined the Writer's Community of Durham Region (WCDR) which opened the door to mentors, teachers, muses, and open mic reading, which I really enjoy. Of that group, I single out Ruth Walker and Gwynn Scheltema, for calling my voice "strong and unusual." I also thank the good people who put on those short story contests for providing amazing feedback like "superb imagery." It was a major clue that I should keep going.

Then there is the Brooklin 7, the writer's group to which I belong. Once described by yours truly as an eclectic group of guerilla writers that know no boundaries, I wish to add that they are indispensible to me and more than friends, they're family. In alphabetical order, they are: Marissa

Campbell, Susan Croft, Connie Di Pietro-Sparacino, Ann Dulhanty, Yvonne Hess, and Rachael Stapleton. They made the writer too.

The Beta's and the Cheerleaders

Every artist needs a cheering section. Why else make art? To the crew at Metro and the Wine Rack: Rosa E. Gauthier, Kate Korgemagi, Jan Weitmann, Elena Novakovic, Gina Clements, and Craig Belanger; the car guys at Canadian Poncho, especially Carl C2 "The Preacher" Hicks; the Florida Crew: Suzanne DeCesare, Pat Head; the undertakers: Scott C. Hughes, M. Wayne Hamilton, Thomas Joseph Pearce, and Fatima Newbigging; and, my oldest, most endearing stalwart friends: Gilda Heinrich Rousseau and Suzanne Stacey, THANK YOU.

My Publisher, Summer Solstice

Summer Solstice is a mid-size Missouri-based publisher that has been growing steadily since its founding back in 2008. From Editor In Chief K.C. Sprayberry, C.E.O. Melissa Miller, and editor Judi Mobley, I got the validation every first time writer seeks. Their "yes" will keep me going for years.

And Finally

My family: John, Adam, Melina; and the mom's: Eleanor and Despina—I did it!

Social Media Sites:

Website: www.abfunkhauser.com

Twitter: https://twitter.com/iamfunkhauser

Facebook: www.facebook.com/heuerlostandfound

Made in the USA
Charleston, SC
07 May 2015